MYTH MANAGEMENT

ALEX MUSSON

*To Thomas and Harry, who will
be old enough to read this one day.*

BECOME AN INSIDER

Sign up and receive **FREE UNCANNY KINGDOM BOOKS**. Also, be the **FIRST** to hear about **NEW RELEASES** and **SPECIAL OFFERS** in the **UNCANNY KINGDOM** universe. Just visit:

WWW.UNCANNYKINGDOM.COM

MYTH MANAGEMENT

ONE

YOU KNOW THE FEELING. THAT SUDDEN DREAD, DEEP IN YOUR gut. The one that tells you, with chilling certainty, that something, somewhere has gone terribly wrong.

Is it animal instinct, a fight or flight message from the lizard brain? The tingling of some supernatural sixth sense? Or perhaps it's divine intervention, a warning whispered in your ear from a guardian angel.

Whatever it is, I was feeling it now. A sudden jolt of panic had woken me in my bed, my heart beating nineteen to the dozen. Then came the slowly dawning horror as I gazed at the terrifying sight in front of me. It seemed so impossible that my first instinct was to reject the evidence of my own eyes. But as I stared into its lifeless, jet-black face, I could not deny the truth.

It was dead.

My phone was dead.

My alarm had not gone off, and – this morning of all mornings – I had overslept, and was late for the most important appointment of my life.

But how late?

I bolted upright and quickly took in the evidence from my

room. The light seeping in from behind the bedroom curtains was weak as dishwater, which meant it was still early, thank God.

Why hadn't my alarm gone off? I'd checked, double-checked, even triple-checked it before I'd gone to bed. The timer was set, the battery was on charge. So why had it betrayed me? I flicked the switch on my bedside lamp, but it refused to light. That solved that little mystery; we'd had another bloody power cut.

I jumped out of bed, whipped back the curtains, and grabbed my rucksack from the floor. A muffled beeping emanated from the bag's side pocket. I pulled out my little battery-powered clock – that must have been what had woken me: my backup alarm. Thank goodness for my obsessive over-planning. *'Be prepared'*, as the Scout's motto goes, and I'd been a pretty decent Girl Scout. Top badge earner in my troop, thank you very much – so, in your face, Jenny McKenzie.

I plugged my phone into the portable charger I kept in my bedside drawer. It buzzed plaintively, a thin red line on the power icon showing it beginning to recharge.

Okay, focus. I looked at the clock: 6:23. Crap. I needed to be at the rendezvous point at 7am exactly. They had been extremely clear about that. '*Not 7:01, not ten seconds past seven, seven on the dot,*' the strange man in the tweed suit had said, jabbing the 'dot' in the air with the end of his pipe for emphasis.

Okay, remain calm. Sure, I'm not at my best under pressure, but now is not the time for a panic attack.

I took a deep breath. I needed to triage. I'd planned this morning's journey meticulously, including a target tube train time, backup tube train time and absolute final for-God's-sake-don't-leave-it-this-late tube train time. That last one departed in just thirteen minutes.

The tube station was ten minutes away, maybe six at a

sprint. That meant showering was right out; a quick flannel to the face and some roll-on would have to do. I pulled on clean underwear and snatched a top from a hanger.

Shoving a toothbrush into the corner of my mouth, I attempted to operate it with my tongue whilst I hurriedly pulled on a pair of tights, which—naturally—laddered immediately. Cursing, I quickly tugged on another pair, laddering those, too. Cursing even louder, I took out the toothbrush and rolled on a third pair, extremely carefully.

I'd packed my bag for the journey last night of course – I'm not insane. A quick glance in my rucksack confirmed the presence of the most crucial items on top of my neatly folded clothes: my purse, Travelcard, and most importantly, the triskele pendant.

I gazed at the Celtic symbol—a wooden triple spiral on a thin leather loop—and remembered the tweed-wearing man's gravely intoned instructions to never let it out of my sight. I slipped it around my neck; its weight reassuring against my chest.

I wrestled my long red hair into a hairband and flipped my skirt off its hanger on the back of the door. Trainers on, coat zipped up, and scarf thrown round my neck. A quick glance in the mirror; not great, but serviceable. I slid the phone and charger into my pocket before scooping up my rucksack and swinging it onto my back.

Then I was down the stairs and out the front door, letting it slam behind me with no concern for my Mum's sleeping habits. I wouldn't be back for a long while, so she'd have to send her usual complaints on a postcard.

I sprinted to the tube station under the dark grey, pre-dawn sky, the September morning's crisp, cool air filling my lungs. Stretching my lanky legs to their limit, I darted between the streetlamps' circles of light, wind whipping at my face. I ignored the, '*All right darlin*'s,' from a pair of construction workers at a pothole, as well as their generous advice to *'Cheer up'*, as it *'might never happen'*. I slalomed around their traffic cones and dashed up the road, dodging other early bird commuters, each lost in their own private world.

These were the inhabitants of twilight London; night staff heading wearily home and early risers out to attack the new day. I overtook a power-suited woman, her Mulberry handbag held in the crook of her arm like a shield as she alternated between sips of her cinnamon macchiato and instructions barked into her hands-free.

I raced around the corner, the tube station in sight now, and almost collided with a pair of drunk salesmen drifting home from an all-nighter. They stumbled along, arms around each other for stability as much as affection, triumphantly whooping their mantra of, *'Ten perceeeent!'* I moved aside just in time as one of them threw up violently against the side of a bus stop, splattering a poster of the latest girl band with half-digested vindaloo.

Panting and red-faced, I hurried into the tube station. A glance at the arrivals board told me that I had just one minute before my last-chance train departed. I slapped my Travelcard against the gate's card reader. Nothing. I tried again, more deliberately this time. Still nothing.

'S'broken,' sighed a bored voice from over my shoulder.

I turned to see the station guard regarding me from his cubicle, arms folded and lolling back in his chair.

'Sorry?'

He exhaled loudly and rolled his eyes. 'Network's down, gates aren't working,' he monotoned. 'There was a power cut.' Clearly, he'd been explaining this to people all morning and was amazed that they were still asking. To him, the public was one gelatinous mass of annoyances that got in the way of his daily duties of reading the *Sun* and being right about everything.

My eyes flicked quickly to the clock. Other commuters

were running up to the gates, slapping their passes and looking confused. I had to act fast. In my experience, when at the mercy of a jobsworth in a position of power, the quickest way out of the situation is to be unfailingly polite.

'Sorry, I'm in a bit of a rush. Can you help me get to the platform? Thank-you-sorry,' I stammered.

He gave me a pitying look and aimed a finger at the furthest gate, which had been left open.

'Thanks!' I said, racing through and down the steps to the platform.

Several other commuters ran with me, jostling each other in their haste. Behind me, I heard the same bored voice apprising the next commuter—'*S'broken*'—whilst ahead of me came the urgent beeping that signalled that the tube train doors were about to close.

I half-stumbled down the final three steps, nearly losing my balance to my overstuffed rucksack. I was at the back of a group of people running for the same set of closing doors. They leapt on board, then made a sudden dead stop, blocking my way despite having a fair bit of room in front of them. I've never understood why people do this – how can you not have empathy for someone in a situation that you were in *just two seconds ago*? I skidded to a stop to prevent a commuter pileup, and squeezed myself onboard, twisting sideways into a small gap as the beeping doors slammed shut a half-inch from my ear.

Naturally, I found myself wedged under a large man's sweaty underarm, so I was relieved when the driver's tannoy squawked into life, urging passengers to '*Please use the full length of the carriage*'.

A few people grumblingly complied, giving me a little more space to manoeuvre. But as I started to move forward, I realised that I was held fast around my neck – the end of my scarf was trapped in the doors. I carefully rotated myself out of its grip. Being strangled to death on the London

Underground would be a ridiculous way to die; knife crime was much more *de rigueur* these days.

Having released myself from the scarf's chokehold, I gave it a yank and it came free suddenly, propelling me further into the carriage, where I bumped up against the central pole. A middle-aged couple in the nearest seats gave me disapproving looks. Although, to be fair, they had the faces of people who'd settled on 'disapproving' as their default expression a good while ago, and rarely felt the need to stray from it.

'That one of those fidget spinners, is it?' asked the woman, seemingly to the world in general.

I looked down and realised that my triskele pendant had come loose and was dangling in front of my coat.

'Um, no,' I said, shoving it back inside. 'Just a necklace.'

Her husband eyed me suspiciously. 'These millennials. We didn't need all that rubbish when I was a lad. In our day we had *respect*.' He lifted his chin up as he emphasised the last word, triumphant in his assessment of all things fidgety and millennial.

Not that I was a millennial, of course. Millennials are in their thirties now. I was simply a member of the much-maligned 'YPT' – Young People Today. Now, usually I let these sorts of comments wash over me, but after the construction workers, the jobsworth station guard, and now this guy, my passive-aggression meter was flicking into the red. Added to which, of course, I was angry at myself for oversleeping and still a little giddy with adrenaline.

'Do you feel guilty?' I asked him, pointedly.

'What?'

'Well, as you say, your parents' generation did a great job bringing up their kids, but yours has failed to instil the same values. So, I'm asking: do you feel responsible *personally*, or do you just blame everyone else in your generation?'

Boom! Mic drop. #pwned.

Just imagine their faces if I'd said that out loud.

But in the diorama in my head they were sitting there slack-jawed whilst the rest of the carriage gave me a standing ovation.

The Tannoy squawked into life again: *'The next station is Hampstead. Please mind the gap.'* Okay, snap out of it Emily, I told myself – this is no time for daydreaming. I flipped back into crisis mode and pulled out my phone, which was now at 15% charge. I opened the GPS app, double-checked that the destination was still set and put the timer up on screen. I had just over eleven minutes to get to the rendezvous. I was going to be cutting it very close – but I could do this!

I leapt out of the tube as soon as the doors opened—*Please let passengers off the train first*—and ran down the pedestrian tunnel, weaving around slow-moving commuters like a pro. I took a quick right, a hard left, then turned sharply on my heel and doubled back to take a hard right instead, muttering 'Bollocksbollocksbollocks' under my breath.

I hit the escalators at top speed and bounded up them two steps at a time. A Rastafarian busker provided the soundtrack with an electro cover of Stevie Wonder's *Superstition* – quite apt, I thought, considering my destination.

But as I left the end of the escalator, something jerked at my left foot, almost sending me reeling. To my horror, I saw that my hastily tied shoelace was caught in the escalator's teeth. It quickly unfurled from its bow and was now dragging my foot back towards the revolving machinery. First my scarf, now this! Sure, I'm accident-prone, but two incidents in one morning? It hardly seemed fair. And now, along with the threat of being mangled from the toes up, I had a horrible view down the steep escalator, which was triggering my vertigo like nobody's business.

I yanked my leg away hard, freeing myself but snapping the lace off in the process. Cursing at my continued bad luck,

I pulled the frayed end taut and tied a hurried knot. It would have to do.

I emerged outside into the early morning light, oriented myself, and sprinted off towards the Heath. I prayed my shoelace would hold, consoling myself with the thought that at least nothing else could go wrong.

It began to rain.

Just spitting at first, but quickly getting heavier. There was an umbrella somewhere deep in my rucksack, but I dared not stop to rummage around for it. Wet strands of hair came free from my hairband and flopped across my face as I ran. I blew them away with the side of my mouth. I needed both hands free; one to hold my phone and the other to shield the screen from the rain. My eyes locked on the blue dot of the GPS as it guided me to my destination.

My phone's clock showed 06:57:03 as I entered Hampstead Heath. I had just under three minutes. I tried to fend off panic with my usual method of breaking tasks into small chunks. Don't think of the whole distance; concentrate on these next ten strides. Do them as fast as you can and count them as you go: *1-2-3-4-5-6-7-8-9-10*. Then the next ten. I was never the athletic type—give me a book and a cosy chair over a sports trophy any day—but I'd always been decent at cross country. My gangly legs made trouser shopping a nightmare, but here at least they gave me an advantage.

The rain turned into a downpour just as I reached the treeline of a heavily wooded area. I was thankful for the small provision of shelter, though the sound of the water hitting the leaves was deafening, especially when mixed with the cacophonous chirping of the birds sheltering in the canopy. Shivering from the cold, I swiped the hair out of my face and checked my phone through the mist of my heaving breath. One hundred yards to go. Two minutes left.

I dug into my last reserves of energy and took off again,

my calves complaining at the morning's unexpected cardio. Underfoot, slippery wet leaves became crunchy and dry as I entered the thicker wooded area.

Sixty seconds to go. The straps of my rucksack dug into my shoulders. Branches scratched at my face. *Forty seconds to go.* The dawn chorus filled the air, nature's alarm clock mocking me. *Twenty seconds.* I felt a stitch pressing into my side. *Twelve seconds.*

A wave of relief washed through me as the GPS app buzzed to signal that I was nearing my destination. A huge horse-chestnut tree appeared out of the gloom ahead, just as the tweed-wearing man had described. Spiky conker shells crunched under my boots as I stumbled, breathless, towards its trunk. I leaned out and slapped my hand against it, partly out of triumph, but mostly to stop myself collapsing in exhaustion. The trunk was old and knobbly, half covered in brambles. I laughed with relief as I felt the thick rough bark under my palm.

Three seconds.

At that moment the autumn sun emerged fully over the horizon, diffusing light through the mesh of branches and bathing the area in a golden hue. Everything felt at once more magical, yet more real. And with this change came a sudden clarity.

Oh God.

This whole thing's a prank, isn't it? I'm on a bloody prank show.

My heart sank as everything fell into place. It seemed so obvious now. The mysterious, tweed-clad gentleman with his crazy story about living myths and the secret bureau that controls them. How had I believed it, even for a minute? Christ, there were probably hidden cameras filming me *right now*. I had a horrific vision of Derren Brown appearing from behind a raspberry bush to give a smug lecture on 'Weak minds bending to the will of authority figures'.

Two seconds.

My fingers dug into the bark. I felt sick, and not just anxious: physically nauseous. The sunlight seemed to be growing stronger, somehow penetrating the dense tree trunk itself. The whole world glowed gold. What was happening? Was this a panic attack? I felt a surge of heat in my chest. God, not a cardiac arrest, surely? I'm only nineteen, too young to die! No, wait, the burning was coming from the *outside* of my chest. It was the triskele necklace; red hot and glowing. What the hell was going on?

One second.

The fillings in my teeth sang out. My vision blurred. There was a strange >*flüorgp*< noise.

And suddenly… I wasn't on Hampstead Heath anymore.

I wasn't even outside.

The light was different, the sounds had changed. Birdsong replaced by the background hum of conversation. There was a distinct smell of ozone and… wood polish?

A calm computerised voice spoke: 'Interphase transit complete.'

My hand was still leaning on something, but it wasn't bark now. It was firm, but soft, like… cotton? As my eyes refocused, I saw that, somehow, inexplicably, there was now a large figure standing in front of me, and my palm was pressed up against his broad, white-shirted chest. I quickly retracted my hand, apologising automatically as I did so, and heard a deep-throated chuckle.

I squinted up at him as my eyes adjusted to the light. He cut quite a striking figure; seven feet tall, smartly dressed in brown corduroy trousers, with thick orange braces over a starched cotton shirt that bulged and strained at the buttons struggling to contain his huge frame. But that wasn't the most striking thing about him. No, that was his face, which was covered in thick brown fur.

Also, he had a snout.

'Here,' smiled the creature, and handed me a towel. 'This may help'.

I took it gratefully and wiped the rain from my face, searching for the right thing to say but coming up empty.

'Terrible weather out there, isn't it?' he continued in his deep baritone, as if this was the most natural thing in the world. 'Can I just swipe your lanyard, miss?' He held up a small device and gestured at the still-glowing triskele around my neck.

I held it out on its leather strap, and his device made a reassuring *beep*.

'All present and correct,' he said with a nod, giving me a warm grin that displayed a row of canine teeth.

'Welcome to Myth Management.'

TWO

'THE NAME'S RUDY' SAID THE DOG-FACED MAN, HOLDING OUT HIS
hand. 'I'm the bureau's Administration Assistant, and I'll be
processing your onboarding today.'

I was flabbergasted. But I was also English, and my
politeness gene kicked in. 'Lovely to meet you,' I said. 'I'm
Emily. Emily Peasbridge.' I shook his hand, pretending not to
notice that it was hairy and damp like a dog's paw. He
noticed my pretending not to notice and gave a loud guffaw.

'Don't worry. Always a bit of a shock at first but you'll get
used to it,' Rudy said in a reassuring tone. 'Take a moment to
catch yeh breath whilst I finish your paperwork,' he advised,
then busied himself at his iPad, tapping at the screen with the
rubber end of a pencil.

I slid my rucksack off and patted down my wet hair with
the towel, fully taking in my surroundings for the first time.
We were standing in a large foyer with a green tiled floor and
wood-panelled walls, corridors branching off at all angles.
There was a circular reception desk in the centre where an
elderly lady sat, happily tap-tapping away at a typewriter.

We were surrounded by a hum of activity as tweed-suited
individuals marched purposefully from one connecting

corridor to another, carrying piles of papers, thumbing handheld devices, and conversing in polite but urgent tones about 'optimisation', 'targets' and 'ambassadorial visits'. Clearly, this tweed suit thing was an official uniform, as they were all dressed identically to the gentleman who had hired me.

The place had the vibe of an old-fashioned bureaucracy. I was reminded of the Ealing Studios films that I used to watch with my dad, curled up together on the sofa for one of our Sunday movie marathons.

'Is this another one from when you were a kid?' I'd asked him.

'No, princess,' he'd laughed. 'Even earlier than that, if you can imagine a time so ancient.'

Tilting my head down as I finished drying my hair, I noticed a pattern of symbols in a circle around my feet. Celtic runes, by the looks of it – they were partly obscured by the shallow puddle of water created by my dripping clothes. Bright shapes were reflected in the puddle, so I looked up to see where they were coming from.

My jaw dropped. High above us was a huge domed ceiling, upon which was painted a fresco that would put the Sistine Chapel to shame. This was also a panorama of deities, but not just Christian; these were from a multitude of religions, modern and historic, as well as creatures from myths and legend, all intertwined. Norse gods next to nymphs, Egyptian scarabs alongside Welsh dragons, poltergeists hovering above unicorns.

What's more, the figures seemed to be gently undulating, as if they had been painted on oil – and next to each one were constantly changing numbers and icons; data analytics on a celestial dashboard.

'Nice, eh?' said Rudy, who had finished his paperwork and was now admiring the ceiling with me. 'All the myths of the world, past and present. Logged, monitored and managed by the finest bureau history has ever known!' His chest swelled with pride – and it had been pretty damn swollen to begin with. 'The administrators of Myth Management run a very tight ship here. Nothing gets believed in without their say-so, believe me!

'And this is our HQ,' he said, gesturing around. 'It's where all the work gets done. Ambassadors from all the realms come here to break bread and consolidate contracts.'

It was all rather mind-boggling. 'Can I ask a stupid question?' I asked, though I wondered what would constitute a sensible question in the circumstances.

'Of course.'

'Are we still on Hampstead Heath?'

Rudy chuckled. 'Yes. And no.'

He spread out his hairy fingers, then locked them together. 'There are multiple realms of belief, all overlapping. The bureau carved out this slice for the HQ, since nobody seemed to be using it. So, we're neither here nor there, if you get my meaning.'

I didn't. 'Right,' I said.

'Don't worry, it'll all be explained during the induction this afternoon, and by wiser heads than mine. You finished with that towel?'

'Thanks,' I replied, handing it back. He flipped it over his left shoulder.

'Also, this is a secure area, so I need you to relinquish all digital devices.'

'Of course,' I said, switching off my phone and handing it over.

'Thank you kindly,' he said. 'The HQ's dampening fields should detect any malicious software, but you can't be too careful with the fate of the world at stake.'

'The fate of the world?' I asked.

'Come on, we'd better get moving. You were the last scheduled arrival; the other interns are already here.' He picked up my rucksack and swung it effortlessly over his shoulder.

'The dorms are this way,' he announced, pointing at one of the corridors. 'Hold up, though, what's Mavis after?'

The old lady at the reception desk was waving at us. 'Rudy?' she called out. 'Oh Rudy! Could you do me a favour, dear?'

We walked over and I got a better look at her; a kind face, excellent posture, and a rather impressive blonde beehive. She was clacking away at what seemed to be an old-fashioned typewriter, except where the paper should have been was a large computer monitor, which she peered at over her half-moon eyeglasses.

Behind her was a large black directory board covered with those little white plastic letters. I started to read a section of it: 'Fawns, fairies, forest creatures,' it said. 'Ghosts, ghouls, gremlins, giants.' Each was followed by a series of numbers and letters that, I assumed, corresponded to locations in the building.

'Mornin', Mavis.' Said Rudy. 'What can I do yeh for?'

'Administrator Thornhill has forgotten his papers again,' she replied with a hint of exasperation. 'He's in 3c with a delegation. Be a sport and pop this up to him, would you?' She hit one final key with a flourish and the printer next to her started ejecting paper at a frantic rate. She licked her thumb, and with a practiced move, slid the printouts into a thick manila folder, handing them over to Rudy, who took them with a friendly nod.

'All right, Emily; looks like we're going to go the scenic route,' said Rudy. 'We'll pop these upstairs, quick as you like, then get you to your dorm pronto.'

'Are you sure there's time?' I asked. 'I don't want to end up in the doghouse on my first day.'

I heard it as soon as I said it.

I could have kicked myself. Mavis stopped typing, the

huge room suddenly pin-drop silent as Rudy looked at me with a serious face. A big, hairy, serious dog face.

'Uh… no offence?' I ventured, smiling weakly.

Rudy threw his head back and roared with laughter. 'None taken, m'dear. Don't you worry, this won't take long.'

Mavis chuckled to herself and resumed typing. And with that, we headed off, Rudy striding ahead as I struggled to keep up.

'We're on the Ground Floor now, which is mainly meeting rooms and admin,' he explained as we entered a large wood-panelled corridor. 'First floor handles Contemporary Religions. Second Floor does Classical. Then there's World Myths on Floor Three, along with Chinese, Asian and Norse legends, and so on.'

I wasn't sure how 'and so on' made sense in this context, but then very little did at the moment, so I decided to just roll with it.

'Up the apples and pears!' Rudy said, bounding up a flight of wooden stairs three at a time, barely seeming to notice the weight of my backpack.

My mind raced to take it all in. The tweed-wearing man had explained a fair bit during my interview, but his talk of 'Managing mythical creatures' had seemed rather abstract at the time. Now that I was walking down a corridor with one of them, it felt rather more literal.

Talking of which, what sort of creature *was* Rudy? I had got top marks for my A-level Anthropology paper on 'The Psychological Resonance of World Myths' (one of the reasons I'd been flagged for recruitment, apparently), but I hadn't come across any dog people during my research. Well, I certainly wasn't going to ask him. I'd been science partners with Becky Lai for three years of high school, and never once asked whether she was of Korean or Chinese heritage, so I certainly wasn't going to ask Rudy what kind of mythical beast he was within five minutes of meeting him.

'Each department,' continued Rudy, oblivious to my train of thought, 'has its own dedicated team of administrators. You'll be meeting some of them later.'

I did my best to keep up as we hurried through a maze of corridors, past more fast-walking tweed-wearing bureaucrats, like a surreal version of *The West Wing* that had done a crossover with *Downton Abbey* and *Teen Wolf*.

Most of the bureaucrats ignored us, although one or two gave Rudy a friendly nod as they passed. To these he would tap his brow and call out a greeting: 'Good mornin', Mr Edwards!' 'Knowledge, Dr Hartford!'

'We've got two kitchens, three dining halls, and six libraries,' Rudy continued, striding ever onwards. 'The one on floor three is my favourite, it's got a lovely readin' nook next to the East window. There are two hundred meeting rooms and three dozen conference areas. And at the heart of the building: the Egosystem Control Room! Though that's not for the likes of us, of course – it's Administrator access only.'

'Oh, so you're not an Administrator?' I asked.

'Me? Hawww, no!' laughed Rudy. 'Strictly humans-only.' I wondered if I detected a flicker of resentment, but if so, it quickly vanished.

'Point of fact, there aren't many non-'uman staff at the bureau at all. But Administrator Champ and I go way back, and he put in a good word for me. That's why I'm the bureau's top Administration Assistant, wiv' all associated privileges.' He paused. 'Actually, I'm the *only* administration assistant.

'Anyway, I'll be lookin' after all the interns in the academy. Settlin' you in and keeping you out of trouble.'

We entered a large open-plan area that was positively buzzing with activity. There were dozens of desks arranged in neat rows, at each of which sat a woman tapping busily away at one of the same typewriter-laptop hybrids that I'd seen in the foyer. They were mostly middle-aged or older, and like

Mavis they had perfect posture and exuded a competent, no-nonsense attitude.

A river of tweedy bureaucrats flowed through the room, pausing at one or other of the desks to drop off or pick up manila folders, taking a moment to issue a request or make pleasantries, before speeding off again down another corridor.

'Secretarial pool,' explained Rudy. 'The beating heart of the organisation. When you're dealing with everything from Classical Gods and Monsters to Folk tales and Norse legends, there's no shortage of paperwork.'

We headed down another corridor, which had doors of different shapes and sizes. The one nearest us was made of thick metal, with a curved top and a round porthole set at head height. Each door wore a small blue plaque, which was adorned with neatly embossed white lettering. 'Administrator Burdett', this one said, and below that, in a larger font, 'Seafaring Myths'.

Just as we drew level, the door flung open and an administrator strode out, causing me to jump back in surprise. His tweed jacket was off, revealing a starched white shirt and green braces, and he wore thick, oily waders. Under one arm he held an ancient-looking diving helmet; the type with the circular glass window in the front. He treated us to a broad smile beneath a luxurious handlebar moustache.

'Ah, Rudy, excellent timing. Don't suppose I could borrow your…' he said, pointing to the towel that was still slung over Rudy's shoulder.

'Certainly, Mr B.' replied Rudy, tossing it over to him. 'How are talks going with Nessie?'

'Excellent,' he replied. Then, noticing me, 'I say, is this one of the interns?'

I opened my mouth to answer, but before I could say anything, he was slapping me on the shoulder with a wet hand, saying, 'Ah, very jolly! Best of luck – we expect great things!' Then, with a chirpy 'Catch you later!' he stepped back into the room, swinging the door shut behind him with a heavy clang.

'Did he say *Nessie*?' I asked. 'As in the Loch Ness Monster?' I tried to peek through the porthole, but Rudy ushered me on.

'No time. Almost there, now,' he said.

We continued down several more wood-panelled corridors, up one spiral staircase and down another, Rudy ducking under the occasional low beam. 'Don't know why they can't make these corridors bigger', he complained. 'We're in a bloomin' bubble dimension, it's not like we're going to run out of room.'

Rudy was still criticising the lack of architectural consideration for seven-foot-tall dog-people when we emerged into a large conference room, where I was greeted with the most astonishing sight yet.

All around the room stood groups of administrators, deep in conversation with mythological beings. To our left was a golem studying an item on a clipboard. Over to the right, a leprechaun was sharing a joke over a glass of wine. A pair of vampires were deep in conversation; one old and bent, with rat-like features and long fingernails, the other well-groomed and sparkling in a leather jacket. Above everyone's heads, a fairy and cherub weaved and dive-bombed each other, giggling happily as an exasperated administrator tried to coax them down with a broom.

My eyes were drawn to an imposing figure standing just metres away. He was large, blue-skinned, and pot-bellied. And he had an elephant's head. I recognised him immediately as the Hindu deity Ganesh. Hands behind his back, he was deep in conversation with a tweedy administrator. Noticing my stares, he offered a nod and a crinkly-eyed smile. Never having met an actual god before, I simply gawped back, slack-jawed.

I noticed that Ganesh—and indeed every creature here—wore a metal bracelet on his wrist that glowed with some strange golden energy. I was about to ask Rudy about them when one of the administrators, a short man with a pinched face, came striding over.

'Greenwood!' he growled at Rudy. 'There you are! Where's my report papers? I've been waiting nearly a quarter hour!'

'Apologies, Administrator Thornhill,' replied Rudy. 'I've got them right here.'

'I should think so, too', said Thornhill, snatching them from Rudy's hands. 'Try and be a bit more prompt in the future.' He noticed me standing behind Rudy and drew himself up to his full height, which didn't take long.

'Is this an intern? You know very well they shouldn't be in this area,' he huffed. 'Take her to the dorms at once.' With that, he spun on his heel and walked away.

I looked up at Rudy, who rolled his eyes good-naturedly. 'Come on, then,' he said.

We headed off down another bewildering series of passageways and staircases for several more minutes, Rudy whistling to himself and greeting various passers-by. Eventually, we reached a large set of doors, upon which a blue plaque read 'Apprentice Domicile'.

'Here we are, then,' said Rudy, pulling a green wooden triskele from his pocket and swiping it across an access panel. The doors swung open with a beep.

Inside was a large common room with sofas and beanbags, plus an open-plan kitchen area and a circular oak table. There was no one there, but excited chatter could be heard through the doors of several connecting rooms, and a kettle was boiling away on the kitchen counter.

'Looks like everyone's unpacking,' said Rudy, passing me my rucksack. 'You'd better do the same. Right after a much-needed cuppa, of course!' He tossed tea bags into three mugs, picked up the kettle as it started to whistle, and filled them up. 'Y'gotta pour it in just before it boils,' he said. 'It releases all the flavour.' He squeezed out the tea bags with the back of a spoon, flicked them into the bin, and presented me with a tray holding two of the steaming mugs and a small bowl of sugar cubes.

'Here you go. One for you and one for yeh roommate.'

'My what?' I asked.

'Roommate. Nice lass. You two are up the far end,' he said pointing. 'Dorm room 6. The penthouse suite, you might say.'

I knew the internship provided accommodation, of course, but it hadn't occurred to me that it would be shared. Well, I supposed it would be a relief to talk to someone else my age, not to mention someone who had been dropped into the same madhouse. So, lugging my rucksack over my shoulder with one hand and carrying the tray in the other, I made my way in the direction Rudy had pointed.

I passed rooms 4 and 5, but there was no number 6. I was about to shout back to Rudy when I noticed a narrow staircase in the corner. Great, I thought, more stairs. They led up steeply, then turned sharply on to a tiny landing area, with one final step up to a door, which was slightly ajar.

Unfortunately, rotating my body up and around in this narrow space had left me in an awkward position. The tea tray was balanced precariously in front of me, and my heavy backpack was digging into my shoulder and starting to slip off. Hoping to regain my balance, I shoved the door open with my knee whilst twisting my torso to try and slide the backpack further up my shoulder. At the same time, I suddenly realised that I was barging into a room unannounced, and yelped out a garbled, 'Hello! Sorry! Tea! Look out!' as I pirouetted through the door.

I was greeted with the sight of an unkempt figure in a Ramones T-shirt, giant headphones clasped over her ears as she air-guitared wildly, eyes shut tight behind some rather fetching black-rimmed glasses.

'Shot through the heart!' she howled, 'and you're too late!'

I couldn't stop myself from colliding with her. She opened her eyes and screamed in shock, falling backwards over an open suitcase and kicking the tray out of my hands with a purple-socked foot.

Bone china and Earl Grey enjoyed a brief moment of freedom mid-air, then crashed to the floor, pelting us with scalding tea and porcelain shrapnel.

'What the actual fuck?' the girl cried.

And that's how I met Izzy Hirway, who would be my Best Friend Forever.

THREE

THE GIRL TUGGED OFF HER HEADPHONES, STILL REELING FROM her encounter with the walking disaster that is Emily Peasbridge. Apologising profusely, I dropped my backpack and helped her up from the floor.

'God, no, my fault!' she insisted charitably. 'I can't hear anything with those bloody things on.'

After much apologising and counter-apologising we agreed an armistice and formed a search party to locate a tea towel and dustpan. Introductions were made on hands and knees as I scooped pieces of broken mug onto the tray and Izzy mopped up tea from the thick grey rug on the wooden floor. We were soon giggling from the ridiculousness of the situation.

'Bloody hell, what a 'mare!' said Izzy as we finished the clean-up operation. I detected a Northern accent – Yorkshire perhaps? She was smaller than me and a little curvier, light brown complexion (Indian heritage, I guessed), with short brunette hair parted over an oval face. She seemed very self-assured, and had a friendly way about her that immediately put me at ease.

'Well, I guess we just christened the room!' Izzy laughed.

'A bottle of champagne is more traditional, but what the hell.' She wrung out the wet tea towel in the sink of a small kitchenette that sat in a nook over the stairs.

'I suppose this is coming out of my first wage packet,' I sighed, dropping the broken pieces of mug into a wicker bin and looking around the space that I would be calling home for the next few months.

It was an attic room, about fifteen feet by twelve, with a full-height wall on one side and a sloping roof that started halfway across the ceiling and went down to a four-foot wall on the other side. Sunlight streamed in through a pair of hinged Velux skylights, illuminating a large oak wardrobe, two small wooden desks with chairs, and twin beds, one of which Izzy had now moved her suitcase onto. The writing desks had been positioned up against the shorter wall, where the sloping roof made it too low to stand.

The kitchenette over the stairs was just big enough for a sink, kettle and a small fridge. Across the room, in the opposite corner, was a rectangular boxed-off area with its own door. I peeped inside to find a slim shower unit and a loo. It was cosy and welcoming, though rather small for two people. I worried about how well we would get along in such close quarters. 'Penthouse suite, indeed,' I mused out loud.

'Yeah, it's amazing!' replied Izzy. 'Check out this view.' She flipped open a skylight and stood on tiptoe to peer out over the bottom edge of the window frame. I went over to the other skylight and did the same – although without the need to tiptoe.

It was indeed a magnificent view. We were at least seven stories up, I reckoned, overlooking a large circular courtyard. I could make out the tops of trees, and the sound of people and running water, but couldn't see directly down into it from this angle. On the other side, about sixty feet away, was what I at first thought was another building, but soon realised was part of this same HQ, which circled around the courtyard.

I could see the top few floors clearly: a mass of rustic red brickwork, square-paned sash windows, white-painted timber frames, parapets and Dutch gables – a jumbled mix of classic London Georgian, Victorian, and Edwardian architecture. The mossy, brown slate rooftop was punctuated with dormer windows, weathervanes, and chimney stacks of the type that you'd expect to see Mary Poppins twirling around. In the brightly lit rooms opposite, I could see tweed-suited figures at work.

'Wow, it's like *Rear Window*,' I gasped.

'What's that?' asked Izzy.

'One of these old movies I used to watch with my Dad. It's about this guy with a broken leg who sits at the window in his apartment and spies on his neighbours through a telescope.'

'Sounds a bit pervy,' mused Izzy. 'I'll have to check it out.'

We stood there for a moment, drinking in the view.

'So,' I asked. 'Where do your parents think you are?'

'I… told everyone I was going to University in St Andrews,' she replied. 'Far enough away to dissuade anyone from visiting. What about you?'

'Told my Mum I'd got a Digital Design apprenticeship in Seattle,' I said.

'Yeah, how's that going?'

'Pretty damn weird so far!' I laughed.

We were interrupted by Rudy's voice, ringing out from downstairs. 'Ten minutes, people!' came his booming baritone. 'I'll need you all out here in uniform, please.'

We snapped into action. Inside the large oak wardrobe, we found two sets of neatly-pressed uniforms: sturdy tights and a short-sleeved polo neck, both in dark green, plus a lighter green plaid skirt, which was short enough to walk comfortably in, but not too short. It even had pockets! We dressed quickly, put our triskele necklaces back on over the polo necks, and checked out our new duds in the wardrobe door's mirror. Not bad, I thought – the green worked pretty well with my pale complexion and red hair.

'Damn, we look pretty hot,' said Izzy, admiring her rear view. 'You know, in a sexy librarian way.'

'Is there any other sort of librarian?' I asked.

At the bottom of the wardrobes were two sturdy satchels with the letters 'MM' embroidered on the front. Each contained one large notepad, one pocket-sized notepad, a pack of slim black ballpoint pens, and a hardback copy of *Managing Myths* by Dr G Champ, PhD, ThD, MthD.

'Right then, let's go meet the other interns,' said Izzy. 'Try not to spill anything on them, okay?'

'Good tip, thanks,' I said, as we slung the bag straps over our shoulders and headed downstairs.

The common room was fizzing with excited conversation. I counted ten other interns; eight guys and two more girls, many of them clustered around the kitchen table where Rudy had laid out a spread of croissants and buns for breakfast (or was it brunch? Elevenses? I had completely lost track of time). Suddenly ravenous, I grabbed a teacake and scoffed it down.

Everyone was making small talk as they tried their hardest to look relaxed. Rudy was handing out thick marker pens and '*Hello, my name is…*' stickers, which we had to fill out and stick to our uniforms.

The boys' uniform was pretty much the same as ours, but with green tweed slacks instead of skirt and leggings. A wiry young man with stringy jet-black hair, whose nametag identified him as Neil, gave me a wide, friendly grin.

'Blimey, these uniforms, eh?' he said. 'Not sure about the colour – I usually only wear black.' He absent-mindedly scratched at a pentagram tattoo on his neck. 'Maybe I can still wear my pleather jacket. I'm going to ask Rudy if there's any wiggle room,' he said. 'Catch you later.'

The other two girls in the group were nearby, so Izzy and I went over to say hello. They were Kelly Bakewell, a large blonde girl who was positively bouncing with excitement, and Anna Ormskirk, who was wiry and stern-looking, eyeing the room with suspicion.

'I don't like the look of some of these guys,' Anna said dubiously.

'I dunno, a couple of them are rather dishy,' giggled Kelly.

'Humph,' snorted Anna. 'Well, I'll be keeping my hockey stick close at night.'

'Why did you bring a hockey stick?' I asked.

'Protection,' she replied, as if it was obvious. 'Always served me well, it has.'

A smugly handsome guy with wavy blonde hair swaggered over and introduced himself as Scott Munroe. 'Don't be nervous, ladies,' he winked. 'I'll look after you.'

Kelly giggled, and Izzy opened her mouth to say something, but we were interrupted by Rudy tapping a spoon on the edge of his mug to get our attention.

'Listen up!' he said. 'You lucky beggars are our first intake of new recruits in a long time. You'll be trained by the finest minds in Myth Management; each an expert in their field. Not only that, but you'll be mentored by the bureau's most senior administrator, Dr Champ himself!'

I caught Izzy's eye – that was the name on the book in our satchels, right? Rudy smiled and looked off into the middle distance. 'Ah, yes, a real 24-carat gent is our Administrator Champ – dependably reliable and reliably dependable, as I always say! You'll be meeting him this afternoon, but there's lots to do first, so let's begin the orientation, starting with a tour of your new workplace.'

With that, he shepherded us into an orderly queue, and we followed him downstairs to the ground floor, where, to my surprise, we exited into the foyer. It seemed that the 'scenic route' Rudy took me on earlier had been a loop around the whole building and right back to where we started.

Rudy led us down the corridors, pontificating enthusiastically as he went. I was at a definite advantage of course, having already had my own private tour, but the building was so large and labyrinthine that I don't think I recognised a single area I'd already seen.

He led us into one of the building's many libraries; a stunning area with a meticulously carved mahogany interior beneath a high-vaulted roof. Beautiful murals adorned the walls, and white marble busts perched on pillars alongside heavy illuminated manuscripts. There were ancient-looking benches and desks, intricately carved wooden columns, three huge standing globes showing locations of different classifications of mythical beings, and of course many, many rows of bookshelves.

At the end of each row there was a tablet (the iPad type, I mean, not the Moses ones). We watched as administrators would tap on one, scroll through a list of entries, then scoot off down an aisle or up a wheeled ladder to pluck a particular book from the shelves.

'This is total library porn,' said Izzy, in an awed whisper.

I winced.

'Sorry,' she teased. 'Did I offend your delicate sensibilities?'

'No, I just I hate that expression,' I whispered back. 'Food Porn, Space Porn, whatever. Not because it's vulgar, but because it's *inaccurate*. Porn is a cheap, clumsy thing that fills a base need. This,' I gestured around, 'is elegant, considered, graceful – a blood rush for the body *and* the mind. This is library *erotica*.'

'Fair enough,' laughed Izzy.

'Also,' I continued, 'you can't objectify something if it's already an object.'

A librarian sat in the corner at one of those typewriter-computer hybrids. I took the opportunity to ask Rudy why they used such devices, and indeed why they used paper books at all, when they had access to all this amazing tech.

'Bureaucracy moves slowly,' he explained. 'Seismic changes by increments. You can't stop progress, but you can't rush it either.' He paused for a moment. 'At least, not here you can't.'

He led us around the gargantuan library, recommending various books and waxing lyrical about the authors, many of whom had worked at Myth Management in what he called 'the grand old days'.

By one o'clock we were pretty wiped, so he took us for lunch in the canteen, where a jolly white-smocked dinner lady rolled out a trolley of thick-cut sandwiches and bowls of crisps. Izzy was chatting enthusiastically to a couple of other interns: a quiet Welsh guy called Arthur; and his well-coiffured dormmate, Ed. Poor Anna, meanwhile, had been cornered by a portly, bearded D&D type called Peregrine ('Call me Pez'), who was attempting to impress her with his knowledge of ornithological folk tales.

I can only do the socialising thing for so long before my introvert gene waves the white flag, so I took my cheese and pickle sarnie to a quiet corner and flicked through my copy of Dr Champ's *Managing Myths*. But my head was so swimming with new information that I was unable to take anything in, and gave up after reading the same opening paragraph three times.

* * *

AFTER LUNCH, Rudy continued the tour, showing off the Secretarial Pool, which was not at all where I remembered it being, and two other libraries. Then, checking a large gold pocket watch, he announced that it was 'Time to meet the senior staff – including Dr Champ himself!' So off we went down more endless corridors and up a spiral staircase, eventually reaching a large set of double-doors on one of the upper floors. Rudy tapped his triskele lanyard on an access panel, the doors slid open with a beep, and he ushered us inside.

We were in a large windowless conference room with a rather strange layout. The wall with the door in it bore a large set of shelves, straining with weighty tomes, but the opposite side was quite blank, except for a large gold 'MM' emblazoned on the wood panels in an elegant font.

Three long benches faced a small raised stage, upon which stood two men. The nearest of them, short and balding with a beard of speckled grey and a rather natty purple bow tie, gestured towards the benches, chirping, 'Come in, take a seat, welcome all'. The other man had a stern, severe face, and I realised with a jolt that it was Administrator Thornhill, the man who had rudely berated Rudy earlier.

Speaking of Rudy, he had gone straight to the back of the room, where he was now prodding at a laptop perched on a small table, glancing over at the large screen behind the stage, and mumbling to himself.

'Good afternoon, good afternoon!' said the grey-bearded man as the last of us squeezed on to the benches. He scribbled something on a clipboard, underlined it with a flourish, then stuffed it under his arm.

'Welcome to the academy. So wonderful to see all these new young faces – an injection of fresh blood and youthful energy for our venerable organisation.'

Thornhill nodded politely and Rudy clapped loudly from the back of the room. Of course – this must be the Dr Champ that Rudy had waxed lyrical about; senior administrator, hero of Myth Management, and author of the considerable tome weighing down our satchels.

'I am delighted to welcome you all here today,' he beamed at us, like a twinkly-eyed grandfather. 'Following a rigorous process of reviews, interviews and personality tests, you have been carefully selected for our apprenticeship programme. Over the following weeks and months, you will be learning the ways of the bureau; through lectures and study, but also on-the-job training as you shadow our administrators during their daily duties.

'You will also', he said, stroking his beard with his free hand, 'be expected to do a significant amount of research and report writing in the evenings and weekends in order to demonstrate a thorough understanding of our duties and responsibilities. It is for this reason—along with our organisation's obvious need for secrecy—that we have provided you with lodgings here for the duration. Communication with friends and family back home will be strictly scheduled, supervised, and monitored.'

He surveyed the room, gauging our reactions. 'This is a uniquely intensive and demanding programme, but then ours is a rather uncommon organisation, as I'm sure young Rudy here has already demonstrated.'

There was a smattering of nervous laughter.

'Now, I've been told that audio-visual presentations are the most effective way of imparting information to your generation,' he said, chuckling good-naturedly, 'so here is a short film that a few of our clever chaps made, providing an overview of our humble organisation.' He signalled to Rudy at the back of the room, the lights dimmed, and the monitor screen behind the stage lit up. A trumpet sounded as the title card appeared: bold white letters on a black background:

Welcome to
the Myth Management
Apprenticeship Programme

Rousing patriotic music played and the film faded in on a large group of tweed-wearing administrators, who saluted the camera enthusiastically. 'It's a man's life in Her Majesty's Bureau of Myth Management,' boomed the narrator.

Izzy leaned over. 'Are they taking the piss?' she whispered.

'For most of mankind's history,' continued the narration in a deep voice and clipped tone, 'we were subject to the whims of Gods, menaced by monsters of the Id, and battered by the storms of superstition.'

Ominous music played as the film changed to horrifying scenes of human sacrifice, witch burnings, and religious torture.

'Conceived in imagination, grown in tales told around campfires, and unleashed upon our collective ego,' the voice continued, 'humankind created these beings and then became subject to them, as their warring ideologies caused pain and suffering beyond measure. And so, to counter this threat, Her Majesty's government formed a new division – a department like no other,' boasted the voice-over, as the music swelled to a crescendo. The scene cut to a dashing figure wearing the familiar tweed uniform; around thirty years old, slim but broad shouldered, with a pipe clenched in his perfect teeth. He gazed earnestly into the camera.

'The department... of Myth Management!' said the man in the same firm, cut-glass accent, revealing himself as the narrator. He was very handsome in that old-fashioned English way, like a young Ralph Fiennes, with piercing blue eyes and excellent bone structure. I cringed a little at Myth Management's decision to use such a dreamboat actor to represent them in the film – talk about your fragile ego.

'The world needed someone to bring order to chaos,' he continued. 'Someone who could gaze unblinking into the abyss... and present it with a form to fill out!' He held up a clipboard dramatically.

'For our purpose was not to destroy these myths,' he continued, 'but to manage them.'

The film then cut to a series of shots of him interacting with mythical creatures as his narration continued:

'To stand unafraid, straight-backed and stiff-upper-lipped...'

He stood on a stepladder to shake hands with a yeti, who then gave the camera a thumbs-up.

'...before a multitude of gods and monsters...'

Now pointing at a chart of hieroglyphics as an Egyptian mummy pondered it with interest.

'...and ask them to form an orderly queue.'

Now rubber-stamping a pile of papers and handing them to a bemused looking cyclops.

The film then cut to a close-up as he took the pipe out of his mouth dramatically.

'What could be more proper? What could be more... British?' he asked, raising an eyebrow.

The film stopped suddenly, and the lights went up, leaving us blinking and momentarily disoriented.

'And we've been at it ever since,' continued the same voice, now from inside the room. 'Harnessing the psychic energy of the human subconscious and using it to catalogue legends, classify monsters, and administer gods.'

There, standing in the doorway, was the handsome man from the film; all six-foot-four of him, grinning broadly and gripping the stem of his pipe.

'Allow me to introduce myself,' he said. 'My name is Administrator Champ.'

FOUR

'So sorry I'm late,' said Champ, striding into the room. 'The Greco-Roman conference call overran, as usual.'

In one smooth movement, he slid off his tweed jacket and flung it towards a coat stand in the corner, where it hooked on perfectly. There was an impressed murmur from the room, though I noticed Thornhill giving a disdainful sniff.

'Knowledge, Director Hinson,' declared Champ, clasping the hand of the grey-bearded man, who beamed back at him in admiration. 'Professor Hinson here is the finest supervisor the bureau has ever had,' said Champ, turning to the room. 'Forty years of peace and prosperity under his watch, with efficiency up 12 percent this year alone!

'So, where have we got to?' asked Champ, stuffing his hands in his trouser pockets and stepping to the front of the stage. If anything, he was even more striking in the flesh. Well-groomed and square-jawed, with an intense, piercing gaze. He wore a mustard-yellow waistcoat over a white shirt and dapper red tie that framed his physique rather nicely. I caught Izzy's eye and we shared a subtle smile. Behind me, I heard Scott mutter 'Bloody hipsters'.

'Rudy, old bean, I assume you've given the new recruits the grand tour?' said Champ.

'Certainly have, Chief.'

'And you've obviously just seen the onboarding film. So,' he said, clapping his hands together energetically and grinning at us, 'I'm sure you have many questions.'

We looked around at each other, not sure where to start. Slowly, a hand went up.

'Yes, Miss… Bakewell?' said Champ, peering at Kelly's name tag.

'Oh, yes, thank you,' she stammered. 'I feel a little silly asking this after everything we've seen today, but… how exactly can myths be real if, as the film said, they came from our imagination?'

'A perfectly reasonable question, my dear,' said Champ. 'How can something be real and yet unreal? Well, one could also ask: how can light be both a wave and a particle? How can atoms exist in two places at once? Yet our finest scientific minds insist that it is so. As enlightened beings we must observe contrary states and accept them both to be true – passionately and logically. We must scoff at the very idea of deities, then invite them over to supper.'

Scott put up his hand. 'But if these creatures have caused so many problems,' he said, 'why can't we just, y'know, get rid of them?'

'Well, putting morality aside for a moment,' said Champ, raising an eyebrow, 'the pragmatic answer is that we need them just as much as they need us. Myths and legends are part of humanity's psyche, our genetic memory. A cult in ancient Egypt worshiped the scarab, '60s Britain gets Beatlemania – echoes reverberating through history.

'Myths, you see, are living metaphors. Universal stories that tell us who we are. We created them, so they are our responsibility. And so, we perform this vital task, maintaining the delicate balance of these mythological factions, in what we call the *egosystem*.'

Arthur, the Welsh lad, raised his hand. 'But how do you get them all to do what you want?'

'Aha!' said Champ, putting his hands behind his back. 'The breakthrough, you see, was realising that the egosystem itself is an energy source – and an exceptionally large one at that. Now, as we know, energy cannot be created, nor can it be destroyed. But with the right tools, it can be *managed*.'

'What tools?' asked Neil, he of the impressive neck tattoo.

'I'm sure you've heard the phrase, "Speak softly and carry a big stick"?' Champ asked, striding over to the large wall at the side of the room. 'Well, this is our big stick.'

He hit a button on a panel, and a split appeared in the wall down the centre of the MM logo. The sides of the wall slid away smoothly, revealing a full-height glass partition overlooking a huge open area. People started to stand up, straining to get a better look as bright light flooded into the room.

'Come on over and feast your eyes,' encouraged Champ. 'Gaze upon our works, ye mighty,' he chuckled.

We surged forward, pressing ourselves up against the thick pane of security glass. We were two storeys up, looking down into an enormous room inside the building, the centrepiece of which was a huge tree that seemed to be growing right out of the wooden floor. Its great trunk—easily six feet in diameter—reached up above us then split into three, branching off to fill the upper half of the area with its leafy canopy. Above that I could just make out a massive domed glass ceiling.

'It has many names,' said Champ. 'The Tree of Life. The Tree of Knowledge. The Tree of Illumination. It is an access point into the entire egosystem. A living database of the mythological world.'

'The bureau's founders,' explained Hinson, who had

joined us, along with Thornhill, 'developed methods of communicating with the tree, accessing the knowledge, the data, held within.'

I had my hand up against the glass and could feel the power emanating from the room, the low hum and soft pulsing vibration. It felt somehow familiar and reassuring. I had a sudden memory of being submerged contentedly in a warm bath, the muffled sound of my parents talking and laughing in the kitchen downstairs.

'At first, we used shaman and psychics – blunt instruments,' explained Champ. 'Then we developed cutting edge technology that could do the job faster and more effectively.' He gestured to various points around the trunk where screens and panels were embedded. A dozen or so lab-coated administrators were busy peering at the screens, cross-checking reams of readouts and tapping at keyboards. 'This enabled us to not just access the egosystem,' he declared, 'but to *control* it.'

'We call it MythTec,' injected Thornhill. 'It enables us to monitor and regulate the myriad of mythological realms, bringing balance to the egosystem.'

Champ turned to us and smiled solemnly. 'You've heard of the God in the machine? Well, we've put the machine in God.'

'We can access the data directly from the tree, reconfigure it, even download and store it for later analysis,' said Hinson. 'Ah, look – there's a download happening right now.' He pointed to a lab-coated technician who was reaching up and plucking an apple from the tree.

The technician scanned the apple with a handheld device, tapped at the screen, and printed out a small label, which he affixed to the apple. He then placed it in a circular transparent container and held it below the opening of a glass tube, which sucked it up and transported it at high speed along the edge of the room and out through a wall into some unseen storage area.

He tapped at his screen, pulled a little card from his pocket and scribbled on it, then placed that in one of the many reference card drawers that were arranged in concentric circles around the tree.

'These days we are mainly gardeners; pruning here, coaxing there. Removing the odd weed,' said Champ. 'Only certified Administrators are allowed into the Control Centre, of course, but I have brought a few items with me for demonstrative purposes. Gather round, if you will.'

The wall panels slid back into position over the glass as Champ crossed back over to the stage. Rudy wheeled over a small table supporting a wooden tray covered in a black velvet cloth. Onto this he was carefully positioning a peculiar set of items, including a triskele lanyard, a thick metal bracelet, and a pair of apples.

'Thank you, Rudy,' said Champ, taking position behind the table. 'All of our MythTec, including the devices you see here, are derived from the Tree. The triskele lanyard, for example, is carved from the Tree's wood, then implanted with technology configured to each user's aura.'

My hand automatically went to my lanyard, still hung around my neck.

'Then we have the diplomats' wristbands,' Champ continued, holding up an open metal bracelet. 'They are activated as so,' he said, closing it together with a snap.

It began glowing with that same golden energy that I had seen on Ganesh's wrist earlier.

'These enable mythological ambassadors to manifest in strictly controlled areas of our building for a defined period of time, so that we may conference with them in civilised surroundings.

'And finally, we have the Tree's data storage,' he said, gesturing to the apples. 'Our organic filing system. This one is empty,' he said, picking up a red apple, tossing it in the air and catching it. 'This one,' he continued, carefully holding up the other, which was green and glowing with a golden aura, 'is chock-full of mythological data.'

He placed it carefully back on the table.

'So,' he said, taking a third, reddish-green apple from his pocket. 'Who can tell me what this one is?'

There were a few shouts of 'empty', 'full', and 'half-full'.

'No', he said, taking a bite, 'this one's my lunch.'

Chuckling, he waved away the laughter and picked up an iPad-like device. 'We can scan them with our MythPads,' he said, holding the green apple up to the tablet device, which gave a reassuring beep. 'And we can even upload or download data into them, using these little widgets,' he continued, holding up what looked like a mini satellite dish, about an inch in diameter, with a sharp prong protruding from the bottom.

Champ carefully placed the items back into position on the tray and gave Rudy a little nod. 'You will have practical experience of all these wonderful contraptions,' he added, as Rudy retrieved the table and moved it to the side of the room, 'after you have first demonstrated mastery of the theory.'

Rudy tapped a few keys on the laptop and a large diagram appeared on the screen. It looked for all the world like a periodic table, but instead of chemical symbols, it showed colour coded groups of myths and legends.

'The pantheons are broad and deep,' said Champ. 'An Administrator must have a well-rounded understanding of them all, though they will specialise in a particular area. I, for example, am head of Greco-Roman Myths, an endlessly fascinating field. Golden fleeces, labours of Hercules, Greeks bearing gifts; I do think their legends have a certain *je ne sais quoi* – or should I say *particularis nescio qualitas*,' he chuckled.

Being a Latin nerd, I snorted loudly at this joke, then blushed as he caught my eye and gave me a broad smile.

'Not that it's been a cake walk, of course,' ruminated Champ. 'Remind me to tell you about our disastrous first meeting with the Harpies, or my many run-ins with Dionysus.

'So,' he said, 'we have the means, and now we shall discuss the method. All great strategies require an understanding of your opponent; who they are, how they think, what they desire. So, who here can tell me – what is it that mythical creatures *want*?'

We looked around at each other.

Ed raised a hand. 'Power?' he asked.

'Well, yes,' said Champ. 'Many of them want control over the human domain. After all, each once had their day in the sun – or their day *as* the sun, in some cases. But on a more fundamental level? What do they need to *survive*?'

I put up my hand.

'Yes?' asked Champ.

'To be believed in?' I ventured hesitantly.

He clapped his hands together in delight. 'Quite right!'

My stomach did a little cartwheel and Izzy affectionately nudged me in the ribs.

'And that's their weakness, isn't it?' he asked. 'They only endure when people *think* about them; when they exist in the cultural zeitgeist. But as the human race has become more educated, more secular, more cynical, how can they remain relevant in this brave new world?

'Well, the genius of the bureau was to realise that fighting this new status quo would be impossible, so instead we *embraced* it. If capitalism was our new God, then so be it! Let us use that to our advantage; let's make consumerism do the hard work for us.'

He nodded at Rudy, who hit another button, and the screen behind Champ refreshed to show a range of everyday products.

'You may have noticed how many brand names have

mythological origins,' said Champ. 'Now you know why! Every time someone wears Nike shoes, drinks a can of Sprite, or chews Trident gum, they are boosting our stats.'

He pointed to each item with the end of his pipe, as numbers whizzed upwards next to them and graphs appeared in the background, lines zagging upwards dramatically.

'Not to mention that many of the products are purchased... where?' he asked, turning to us with a questioning look.

'Uh... the internet?' ventured Kelly.

'Yes, but specifically?'

'Amazon!' said Izzy with a sudden realisation.

'You're damned right!' Champ cheered. 'Named after the river, but also evoking the mythical warrior women.'

He spread his arms wide. 'Everywhere we look, myths and legends are being kept alive in the products and services we use every day.' He scanned the room. 'Who can give me any other examples?'

'Mars bars, sir?' said Arthur, hesitantly.

'Indeed, named for the Roman God of War.'

'Olympus cameras?' suggested Anna.

'Quite right – and keeping with the Greco-Roman theme.'

'The Titans sports team?' ventured Pez.

'Yes, from what the Americans incorrectly call "football".'

'Sir, the Starbucks logo has a siren in it!' said Izzy.

'Good catch!' said Champ jabbing the air with his pipe. 'Symbols count as much as the names. Similarly, Versace's logo is a representation of Medusa. What else?'

There was a general hubbub as people shouted out other examples. This, I knew, was my chance to make a great first impression, but I'd need an answer that would really stand out from the crowd.

'Watching a Thor film made by Orion Pictures in The

Apollo theatre!' I said, almost stumbling over my words in the rush to get them out.

But, frustratingly, Champ hadn't heard – my voice had been drowned out in the clamour of shouted responses. I started again, but barely got the first words out before someone bellowed 'Nike!' right near my ear, making me wince.

'We've done that one,' yelled somebody else.

Before I could try again, a strong, confident voice rang out from behind me: 'A Thor film made by Orion Pictures at The Apollo cinema!' shouted Scott.

'Aha, a hat-trick!' cried Champ delightedly. 'Well done... Munroe, isn't it?'

I turned around in disbelief. 'Yes sir,' said Scott, grinning with pride. His dormmate Jim gave him a fist bump.

I couldn't believe it. He'd nicked my answer! I mean... hadn't he? There was no look of shame on his face. I suppose it was *possible* he could have come up with the exact same idea. But... while standing right behind me?

Damn it. I could tell that Champ was about to move on. I had one last chance – I needed another example, and quick. My brain did a frantic Google search and hit 'I'm feeling lucky' without stopping to check the results.

'Trojan condoms!' I shouted, much too loudly.

The whole room went silent for a second, then there was a ripple of stifled laughter. I could feel my face going bright red. Izzy stared at me, mouth agape.

Champ raised a single eyebrow. 'Well, yes,' he said coolly. 'A legitimate example, though a little close to the bone.'

This unfortunate phrasing proved too much for the group, who exploded with uproarious laughter. It took several minutes of Champ protesting and sternly rapping his pipe on the table to restore order. I attempted to play it off like I found it as funny as everyone else, though I'm sure my beetroot-red face betrayed me.

Hinson, looking embarrassed, busied himself scribbling on his clipboard, while Thornhill shook his head slowly.

'Come on now, I want your undivided attention!' Champ declared, clicking his fingers loudly as the last few sniggers died away. I tried to concentrate as he continued talking, but I was burning up with embarrassment. Feeling extremely self-conscious, I moved to the side of the room, leant up against the wall and rubbed my face with my hand.

And that's when I made my second, and much worse mistake.

You see, I had moved right next to the table—the one covered in MythTec devices that Rudy had wheeled out of the way—and as I bumped against it, I felt it rolling away on its castors. In a panic I leant out to grab it, slamming my hand down much too fast and hitting the edge of the tray. I watched in horror as the tray flipped up, throwing its contents into the air, including the glowing green apple, which—curse my terrible luck—had been perched right on the other end, and was catapulted several feet up in the air.

Time seemed to stop. I saw the apple hovering briefly at its zenith before starting to fall. The table rolling away on its castors. Hinson looking over in horror.

Then, with astonishing reflexes, Champ grabbed Hinson's clipboard and swung it out like a cricket bat, knocking the apple up in an arc over everyone's heads. It hit the back wall near the bookshelves, exploding in a cacophony of noise and light as it released its contents into the room: a very surprised looking gnome-like creature.

The gnome sat there for a moment amongst the glowing detritus of sticky apple pieces and dissipating golden energy. It was about a foot tall, with rough green skin and spiky features, ragged clothes draped on its bony frame.

Immediately, an alarm rang out and red strobing lights filled the room. 'Unscheduled release of a category four individual!' declared an electronic voice. 'Please remain calm.'

The interns looked around in panic. Hinson and Thornhill were rooted to the spot. The creature leapt up in alarm, clambered up the far end of the bookcase and started hurling hardbacks out into the room, screaming in a panicked, high-pitched tongue.

'Rudy – Catch and Collect; you know the drill!' shouted Champ, as he snatched up the remaining red apple from the floor, along with the tiny satellite dish device.

'Righto, Chief!' replied Rudy, cautiously approaching the gnome with his hands outstretched.

The creature screeched frightfully and hurled *Encyclopædia Mythica Vol IV* at Rudy. It was a particularly sturdy volume and it hit him right in the snout, causing him to swear loudly.

Rudy picked the book up and hurled it right back at the creature, which screamed and leaped off the bookshelf, grabbing a nearby light fitting on the ceiling. People scattered to the sides of the room as it dangled there for a moment. Then Rudy jumped up and seized it by the legs, pulling down with all his weight. Its body stretched out like an elastic band until it lost its grip and shot down, colliding hard with Rudy's chest.

He held the creature out at arm's length, grimacing in pain as it bit and clawed at him wildly. 'Ready, Chief?' he shouted.

'When you are,' replied Champ, as he jammed the prong of the satellite device into the red apple and twisted it. The device beeped loudly, and the apple changed to a pure white colour.

Rudy windmilled his arms, causing the goblin to abandon its attack as it was whirled around by its feet, arms outstretched helplessly. As Rudy's swing reached its apex, he let go, bowling the shrieking green creature directly at Champ, who held the apple outstretched in front of him.

A funnel of golden light flared from the little satellite dish, enveloping the creature, which twisted in the air, shrinking and folding in upon itself until it splintered into tiny colourful cubes of light that were sucked into the device.

The apple changed to green with a reassuring *ping*, and the alarm immediately cut off, soft light returning to the room. 'Incident closed,' said the electronic voice calmly. 'Please return to your duties.'

Hinson broke into spontaneous applause, which was joined very enthusiastically by the interns, and rather less so by Thornhill.

'Oh please, it was nothing,' said Champ modestly, unplugging the tiny satellite dish and handing the glowing green apple to Rudy, who took it very carefully in both hands.

'I'd better get this straight back to the Control room,' said Rudy, heading quickly past me out the door.

'Thank you, Rudy,' Champ called after him, then turned back to address the room. 'Now, settle down everyone. Accidents do happen.'

I stared at the floor in mortification. I had hit a level of embarrassment so extreme that I had almost entered a fugue state, disconnected from my physical body. Izzy put her hand on my arm reassuringly, but I couldn't meet her eye. I did, however, notice Hinson looking over at me with concern and Thornhill giving me a thin, patronising smile.

'Well, I hope you enjoyed our little impromptu demonstration,' said Champ in an upbeat tone, smoothing out his sleeves. 'Thankfully it was just a *dokkaebi*; a type of Korean goblin. Very interesting creatures, actually. And fairly harmless, though they can be rather messy little blighters.'

'You can consider yourself lucky,' interjected Hinson. 'It's not often that you get to see a live myth reacquisition, particularly by a hero of the bureau.'

'Well, yes,' said Champ, with a modest cough. 'Our days of battling myths are long behind us, thankfully. It's all paperwork these days. I'm quite sure you won't see anything as dramatic again – even the three of you who make it through the academy's probation. We run a pretty tight ship, as you'll see.'

Wait, what did he just say? I looked around the room and saw similar confused faces.

'Sorry, sir?' asked Kelly. 'What do you mean by "the three of us who make it through"?'

'You've all read your contracts of course,' said Hinson, surprised. 'It explains quite clearly in section 27b that three academy interns will be taken on as full apprentices at the end of the 12-week probation period.'

A dismayed murmuring filled the room and a sea of hands shot up.

'Wait, I didn't even have a section 27 in my copy!' complained Anna. 'I was just saying to Kelly earlier – I think I had pages missing.'

'Yeah, and my cover sheet says version 42.005, but Ed's says 42.016,' said Arthur.

'Oh dear, oh dear,' said Hinson, fiddling with his bow tie. 'I've spoken to HR about this several times. Not good at all.'

Administrator Thornhill stepped forward. 'Lapses in bureaucracy aside,' he said sternly, 'the situation is this: only three of you will be going forward to a full-time position. I will be keeping track of your performance with a strict points-based system, so only the finest candidates will move on to be Junior Administrators, and those less… suited,' he said, shooting me a disdainful look, 'will not.'

There followed much muttering and exchanging of nervous looks.

'I think that's enough excitement for one day,' interjected Champ, as Rudy arrived back through the door, wrapping a bandage around his arm. 'Rudy will take you to the dining hall for supper. I look forward to getting to know all of you over the coming months, whether you make it to the final three or not.'

He couldn't help glancing at me as he said this; not with malice, like Thornhill, but with pity.

Which somehow made it worse.

* * *

RUDY LED us all down to the staff canteen, seating us along a long table and serving up a dozen plates, each heaving with bangers and mash in a thick onion gravy. The clatter of cutlery mixed with the buzz of excited conversation as the interns processed the events of the day. But it could all have been happening behind frosted glass as far as I was concerned; I was trapped in my head, reliving the events of the last hour over and over, admonishing myself brutally.

I'd always been clumsy as a kid, but I had hoped it was an awkward phase that I'd grow out of. I prodded my mashed potato with a fork, unable to even think about eating while my stomach was knotted up like a year's worth of PMS had arrived at once.

When we returned, exhausted, to our dorm rooms after dinner, I took first turn in the bathroom. I washed myself and brushed my teeth in a daze, then put on my pyjamas and climbed into bed, utterly forlorn. After her turn in the bathroom, Izzy, who so far had wisely been giving me some space, came over and sat down next to me.

'Hey, you,' she said, giving me a friendly punch in the arm.

I gave her a half smile, which was the best I could muster.

'Come on, it wasn't that bad,' she said. 'Champ said it was just an accident, and there's plenty of time to redeem yourself. We've got three whole months before they make their decisions.'

I gave a deep sigh, feeling much too sorry for myself to respond.

'Look,' she said, upbeat, 'I promise you it's all going to seem better in the morning.'

Promise – the word dragged up a memory, unbidden; my dad holding me tight, his voice cracking, *'I promise I'm not going anywhere'*.

'Promise?' I snapped. 'You can't *promise* things you can't control. It's not possible, it's not ethical, it's not *fair*!'

Izzy leant back, shocked. Then she composed herself, stood up and walked over to her own bed. 'Okay, I suppose that's true,' she said calmly. 'But isn't it also true that when someone is just trying to help, you shouldn't be such a... total shit-gibbon.'

I opened my mouth to say something.

'Goodnight,' she said firmly, and switched off the light.

I lay there in the darkness, feeling quite wretched. I thought about how much can happen to a person in just one day. How quickly your fortunes can go from the greatest high to the deepest low. And, of course, how I was—undeniably— a total shit-gibbon.

FIVE

I was awoken the next morning by the sound of Izzy plonking a mug down next to my bed.

'Morning,' she said. 'Made you a tea.'

I looked up at her groggily. She was still in pyjamas, and had a towel draped round her neck.

'I'll take the first shower,' she said, her voice flat. 'There's some milk in the fridge, though I'm not sure I'd trust it.'

'Thanks,' I said meekly as she disappeared into the tiny bathroom. I heard the shower go on. The water pipes behind the walls made a low groaning sound, like a grumpy wookie.

I climbed out of bed slowly, shuddering as the events of the previous day came rushing back. I opened the mini-fridge and gave the milk a sniff. It seemed acceptable, so I stirred some into my tea, took a gulp, and sighed deeply. You've really screwed it up this time, Emily.

I was still wallowing in self-pity when Izzy exited the bathroom wearing a fluffy white dressing gown with an 'MM' embroidered on the front pocket. She sat at one of the desks, studiously ignoring me as she combed her damp hair.

'Look,' I said, clearing my throat, 'I just want to start by apologising. I was a total dick to you when you were only trying to help. I was incredibly embarrassed, so I put the shields up and then lashed out at completely the wrong person.'

Izzy put her brush down and regarded me carefully. 'You spend a lot of time in your own head, don't you?' she said, not unkindly.

Of course I do, I thought, with a surge of annoyance. Where else would I be – floating three feet outside of it? This had been a common refrain from my mum and my teachers; '*Stop spending so much time in your own head,*' or '*Stop overthinking things.*' Well, it's better than under-thinking them, if you ask me.

Not that I was stupid enough to bring this up now, of course.

'I'm afraid I've really gotten off on the wrong foot,' I said.

'Yeah, I know; I helped you mop up the tea, remember?'

I smiled half-heartedly. 'Perhaps I'm not cut out for this job. Maybe I should just quit while I'm behind and save myself from any more humiliation.'

'What? Are you mental?' exclaimed Izzy. 'You can't give up this *amazing* job because of one little balls up.'

'It was hardly little,' I protested. 'I yelled out the name of a popular condom brand then let a bloody goblin loose in the meeting room.'

'Yeah, that was pretty epic,' she grinned.

'And now look at me. I'm no doubt at the bottom of the rankings after just one day. I'm pretty sure that Scott guy nicked my idea. And I certainly don't fancy having to spend three months with a group of people who think I'm a hot mess.' I stared into my tea. 'I'm obviously not suited to this kind of high-pressure environment. I should just step aside and let someone èlse have a go.'

Izzy regarded me for a moment. 'You realise that's all just bullshit though, right?'

I looked up at her in surprise.

'The way I see it,' she said, pointing her hairbrush at me. 'Is that when life gives you crap, you have two options. One: let that crap pour all over you and just drown in it. Or two: scoop it up with both hands and shovel it into your methane-powered bullshit engine.'

'That's… very eloquent.'

'Too right. And I'll tell you what else; you've noticed how all the administrators here are men, right?'

'Pretty much, yeah. And all the secretaries are women.'

'Exactly. And look at the rest of the interns; there's twice as many guys as girls. That's some bullshit gender imbalance right there. There are clearly glass ceilings in need of smashing. So, you can't leave now, or you'd be letting down the sisterhood.'

I laughed, despite myself.

'And sure,' Izzy continued, leaning back in her chair, 'you were kind of a dick to me last night. So, yeah, I could spend weeks being pissed off at you whilst you act all awkward, trying to make it up to me. But you know what? Life's too short. I'm a pretty good judge of character – had to be, where I grew up – and I reckon you're basically a good person. Although, obviously, a bit of a dork.'

I was a little insulted, but couldn't really argue.

'So, I say we skip all that rubbish and go straight to being best friends. Starting right here and now: we're partners. Best buds. The dream team. We're going to win the top two places, let the rest of these losers scrap over third, and laugh as that arsehole Scott falls flat on his stupid symmetrical face. Are you with me?'

It was a damn fine speech. 'Yes. Absolutely. I mean, *hell* yes!' I said.

Izzy stood up triumphantly, spat in her hand and held it out. I clasped it firmly, making a mental note of where I had packed my wet wipes.

'Good. Then it's settled,' she said. She threw me a clean

towel. 'Come on, you dork. Day's a-wasting – we don't want to be late.'

* * *

WHILE THAT FIRST day had seemed to stretch out to an eternity, the following days passed in a blur of lectures, library studies, and late-night dorm conversations. As I had feared, I was indeed the butt of many jokes at first, but I did my best to pretend they didn't bother me.

'Just act confident,' Izzy would say. 'Fake it till you make it.' Unfortunately, I'd always been more of a 'Do it successfully several times and then concede that you're okay at it' type. But Izzy's infectious energy helped me tough it out, as did copious amounts of tea. God, why does tea always make things feel better? Is it just a British thing? And if so how do, say, Americans cope? Xanax, I suppose.

Izzy and I had a very similar work ethic, which was 100% commitment to the task at hand; and thank goodness, because we had one hell of a steep learning curve ahead of us. Myth Management—or 'the bureau' as the administrators often referred to it—managed a dizzying number of mythical realms, all grouped and codified in their bewilderingly complex, overlapping and cross-referenced classification system. Every species of deity, monster, being, and creature, be it religious, folkloric or allegorical, had its own unique multi-digit alphanumeric ID. As a veteran school librarian and Dewey Decimal System nerd, I took it as both a challenge and a labour of love to decipher the opaque hidden meanings behind their taxonomy.

Every day there was a different lecture from an administrator in one of the core fields, followed by mounds of research and essays to write for each. The lectures were held in one of a dozen conference rooms, each of which was named after a writer or artist from the world of myth, such as

Homer, Blake or Dumézil. 'See you at 3pm in Joseph Campbell', we'd say, and after a while it didn't even seem weird.

In the first week, Administrator Champ took us for Greco-Roman Myths, Administrator Burdett for Seafaring Legends, and Administrator Thornhill for Ancient Egyptian Mythology. We also had lectures from Administrator Singh; a tall, bearded, turban-wearing man who oversaw Indian Myths and Legends, and Administrator Hicc; a jolly, portly woman, who was responsible for Celtic Myths, and—as far as we could tell—was the only female administrator in the bureau.

There seemed, I noticed, to be a fair bit of interdepartmental rivalry. Administrator Champ would happily lecture for hours on the intricacies of what he called 'The Classics'—primarily his Greco-Roman specialism, of course—but he would also wax lyrical about gods and monsters from ancient Egyptian, East Asian, and Norse legends. On the other hand, he seemed quite dismissive of what he called the "Folklore of Modernity", such as ghosts, vampires, lycanthropes, and the like. Equally, the administrators of those departments regarded the "ancient" myths as a little dry and dusty.

The bureau also had associates that they would call on for specialist skills; a spectral detective who helped lost souls seek justice, a powerful wizard who ran an antiques shop on Portobello Road; and a witch's familiar fighting to avenge her slain coven.

Even after everything we'd seen, it was still difficult for some of us to get our heads around the idea that myths were alive and well and constrained by bureaucracy. But as Champ pointed out, 'Each stage of education is explaining that the stuff you were previously taught is a lie. Ask anyone who studied physics at high school, then university, then post-grad.'

I wasn't quite sure what to make of Champ at first. He was certainly very charming and charismatic, striding about with his hands behind his back and puffing away on his Billiard pipe (that's the style he had; I looked it up in the library's first edition of *Pipes and Pipe Smoking*). He was very fond of pithy but annoyingly vague sayings such as 'Myths are poetry, not prose, and must be attended to accordingly,' and he would punctuate his lectures with exclamations of 'jolly good!' or 'mustard!', talking and acting like someone from the 1940s.

I have long had a theory that everyone has an age that suits them, and they just stick with it. Some people, like my dad, acted like a teenager their whole life, even after they got kids and a mortgage, while others go straight to middle age on their twenty-first birthday. Champ was one of those, I reckoned; dressing like an old professor even though he was only in his late twenties. I passed this theory by Izzy during a tea break one day.

'Nah', she said. 'Champ looks barely thirty, but I reckon he's older. He's just got great genes – like Paul Rudd. He's still got his boyish good looks, but you can see in his eyes that he's been around the block a few times.'

'Oh aye, got a crush on the boss, have you?' I teased.

'Maybe a little,' she laughed. 'Haven't you?'

'Well, I can't deny he has a certain suave charm,' I conceded, 'but I'm not usually into the whole tweedy professor thing, all starched shirts and stiff upper lips. You'd really go for that?'

'God, yeah! Have you seen the bod he's hiding under that starched shirt? He can stiffen in my lips any day,' she said, and I laughed so hard I snorted tea up my nose.

* * *

Izzy and I both did well in the first week of classes. I got the second highest mark for Champ's first assignment, after Kelly Bakewell, who seemed to be a swot after my own heart. He noted my score with some surprise – one benefit, perhaps, of starting from such low expectations. By the second week I had even found the nerve to occasionally put my hand up during the Q&As, ignoring the stifled giggles from certain classmates, or whispers about certain brands of birth control.

Izzy, meanwhile, took a particular shine to Celtic myths. Administrator Hicc awarded her paper on Ley Lines an A+, telling the class it showed remarkable comprehension for one so young.

One of the strangest things about the bureau was its relationship with technology. The MythTec we'd witnessed in the egosystem Control Room was beyond anything I'd seen outside science fiction. Yet most administrators preferred to read from physical books during the lectures, and some even wrote on blackboards – with chalk!

There were no laptops or tablets for us either; we had to go old-school with our notebooks and pens. I actually quite liked this, and took great joy in organising and cross-referencing my lecture notes with a detailed system of colour-coded highlights, Post-Its and star stickers.

One of my exes used to call me 'Queen of the lists'. I'm not sure if he meant it as a compliment, but I wore it as a badge of pride. Lists bring order to chaos – or the illusion of order, at least. A good list is like a good queue, and queuing is a British institution.

At our desks in the evening, Izzy and I would compare notes, pulling off pen tops with our teeth to scribble annotations, double or triple-underline key areas, draw diagrams and doodle think-bubbles with follow-up questions. I found it all rather satisfying in a mild OCD way (not to minimise *actual* OCD of course, which is a genuinely debilitating condition, #woke).

One day, Rudy took us all for lunch in the atrium – the

large courtyard area at the centre of the building that we'd first seen from our dorm window. It was divided into three sections; a grassy area with wooden benches and a tree on a hill in the middle, a large deep-looking pond spanned by a bridge, and a small stone amphitheatre. A stone pathway twisted around them in a pattern that seemed familiar, although I couldn't quite place it.

'I often come here at the end of a long day to relax and feel the breeze in my fur,' Rudy explained. 'Administrators use the area to confer with plant elementals, or hold discussions with water-based species,' he added, gesturing to the pond.

As if on cue, a merman burst dramatically from the water, did a triple backflip to many 'Oohs' and 'Aahs' from the interns, and splashed back down again, showering us with a fine spray of water. Administrator Burdett, who was standing on the bridge in his waders, laughed loudly and gave us a cheery wave.

'Knowledge, Dr Burdett!' called out Rudy.

'Knowledge, Rudy,' he replied, then leant over the bridge to continue his conversation with the merman.

I had noticed how Rudy and the administrators used 'Knowledge' as a form of greeting and found it quite fascinating from an etymological and anthropological perspective. It seemed to indicate their attitude to life – like how other societal groups say 'Have a nice day', 'God be with you', or 'Your call is important to us. Please hold'.

I shared this hypothesis with Izzy. 'Oh,' she said, shrugging. 'I just thought it was short for *acknowledge*.'

Well, I guess it could be two things.

I peered up at the inside of the building, counting the storeys and looking for familiar windows or features, hoping to work out where our dorm room was. There was a huge clock face high up on one side, and a few pointed towers. But the building was such an architectural jumble of windows, ornate arches, and wrought ironwork that it was hard to distinguish one part of it from another.

* * *

As THE DAYS turned into weeks, the mysterious HQ began to feel less intimidating and more familiar; even homely. The daunting maze of wooden passageways that so baffled us at first became easier to navigate, then a fun place to explore during lunch breaks (we were confined to the dorms in the evenings).

The sight of a mythical creature in the HQ become commonplace enough that our initial sense of petrified awe was replaced by a kind of excited thrill, like the time I saw Benedict Cumberbatch shopping on Carnaby Street.

We weren't allowed to talk to the mythological ambassadors, but I once made eye contact with a tall, broad-shouldered elf in a corridor on level three. His elegant frame, long blonde hair, and piercing gaze left me rather weak at the knees for the rest of the afternoon, much to Izzy's amusement.

Rudy was a regular and most welcome presence, buoying our spirits with terrible puns, and keeping us well supplied with tea and biscuits. He would chaperone us between lectures, library visits, and lunch and dinner breaks, as well as answering our barrage of questions about the workings and history of the bureau. I asked him about an intriguing passage from Champ's textbook, *Managing Myths*, which read:

> *At one time, Myth Management's motto was,*
> *'Battle the monsters, save the world, file the paperwork'.*
> *These days, thankfully, it's mostly just the latter.*

Rudy explained that there had been decades of relative

quiet since a big conflict in the 1940s. Since then, there had only been a couple of 'Delta Level situations' – whatever that meant; he became frustratingly vague after that, quickly changing the subject.

I still hadn't worked out what type of mythological creature Rudy was, as he didn't seem to match any of the species that I'd found in the reference library. Izzy and I had a bet to see who could work it out first. Was he P'an Hu, the dog-headed man of Chinese myth? A member of the Adlet; the race of Inuit dog-people, perhaps? Or—and this was Izzy's favourite theory—a werewolf stuck mid-transformation?

Once, in the canteen, I'd seen him whispering to one of the dinner ladies about 'Leftovers for Ginger'. But when he saw me walking over, he quickly hurried off, clutching a small foil-wrapped parcel. No idea what that was about, but all rather intriguing.

In the evenings, Rudy was often to be found reading in a corner of the dorm common room. Izzy and I would often seek him out to chat or get help with some particularly obscure bureau regulation, as he had a wonderfully detailed knowledge of both the mythological world and Myth Management's operations.

One evening we were working on a report on Russian Folk Tales for Administrator Craggles, and Rudy had us spellbound with his explanation of the Rule of Three.

'Vladimir Propp wrote a wonderful book called *Morphology of the Folk Tale*,' he explained, chewing on what seemed to be a slice of tree bark. 'Wherein he postulated that any element in a folktale could be "*Negated twice so that it would repeat thrice*" – by which he meant, basically, that three time's a charm!' he chuckled.

'It's a pattern you'll see throughout mythology, if you're payin' attention. Genies granting three wishes. Cerberus, the three-headed dog. The 'sisters three' of Fate. And look at your triskeles,' he said, pointing at our lanyards. 'Three spirals joined at the centre. The triskele symbol has been around since the Bronze Age and has been used by everyone from the Greeks to the Celts. In the fifth century, Christians used it to represent the Holy Trinity – there's your rule of three again.'

We scribbled notes frantically. Scott swanned over as we were finishing up. 'Ah, rule of three,' he said knowledgeably. 'Yeah, that's where you divide your pictures into thirds – makes for a better composition, you see.'

'Oh, Scott,' I said, rolling my eyes. 'Stop humansplaining,' and Rudy had to resort to a sudden coughing fit to cover his laughter.

* * *

MY FAVOURITE PART of my new life was the evenings spent in the dorm room with Izzy, discussing the day's events, sharing notes and testing each other on trivia in readiness for one of the weekly tests. Spending that amount of time with someone can go one of two ways, but for us it was like a concentrated course of friendship, and soon we felt like we had known each other forever.

Every evening, it began to rain at 10pm precisely, a daily 20-minute burst designed to give the perfect amount of nourishment to the atrium's garden. It seemed that the MythTec controlling the bubble universe around our building included an ability to regulate the climate. I've always loved the sound of rain, and found the pitter-patter on the skylights wonderfully soothing.

At night, in the peaceful moments just before falling asleep, I noticed that the building seemed to creak gently back and forth, like a boat on the water. No, not a boat – once, on a school trip to Bruges I had climbed up into one of their huge old windmills and had felt the same gentle movement, as the huge wooden structure swayed slowly in the wind. The HQ had that same feeling; like an almost living thing; part of nature rather than a barrier from it.

At first, I had found this motion unsettling, but over time it became familiar, then reassuring, lulling my exhausted brain to sleep soon after my head hit the pillow.

SIX

By week six, Champ seemed satisfied enough with our progress to let us attend our first ambassadorial meeting. I was one of three assigned to shadow Administrator Thornhill for what he called his, 'Monthly confab with the 'Gyps' – his somewhat problematic name for the Ancient Egyptians.

The morning of the meeting, he sent me down to the Files Department on the basement floor to collect a pertinent file – one of their paperwork-stuffed manila folders. I walked down the badly lit stone corridor, past a series of empty storage rooms, until I arrived at an area that looked for all the world like an old-fashioned Post Office. Elderly ladies sat in a row of booths, numbers above their little windows, peering over their spectacles at paperwork or branding forms with large red stamps.

I coughed politely and one of them peered up at me.

'Yes dear?'

'Hello, I'm here to pick up a file.'

'Well, you'll have to wait a minute, it's like Piccadilly Circus in here today.'

I looked around the room. There was one other person there: an elderly administrator sitting arms crossed on a

bench against the far wall. He looked either asleep or dead –
only a sudden snore told me which.

'Take a number, dearie. We'll be with you as soon as
possible,' said the booth lady.

I pulled a number from the old wooden dispenser –
'789,004', it said. I looked at the readout above the booths:
'now serving 788,976'. I glanced around the room again – it
was definitely just me and the sleeping guy.

I sighed and took a seat. Myth Management prided
themselves on being what Champ called 'a perfect
bureaucratic machine, run with clockwork military precision',
yet I couldn't help but be frustrated by the endless red tape.
Luckily, I always came prepared. I took my library books
from my satchel and began researching the Egyptian
pantheon.

I have always found solace in the world of books. At
school I would camp out every break time at the library,
hoping to keep a low profile. I was not a cool kid – worse, I
was *uncool*, which at school was the greatest of crimes. It was
a disease everyone was petrified of catching, which they
demonstrated through a furious hatred at those afflicted.

It was partly my gangly, ungainly frame, but I was also
ridiculed for being a swot. I took comfort in the advice of my
favourite teacher, Mr Warren: 'For a few years they call you
swot. For the rest of your life, they call you sir!' And the hard
work had certainly paid off – whilst most of those classmates
were starting their first year of McJobs, I was... well, right
now I was sitting in a musty old basement, but you take my
general point.

There was a loud *ding* and the 'now serving' sign above
the row of booths rotated to show '789,004'. I walked up to
counter three, where an ancient-looking woman with purple
hair looked at me apprehensively.

'Yes?' she asked.

'Hello,' I smiled. 'Administrator Thornhill has sent me to

pick up ledger number…' I glanced at my notebook, '52ABX-32QJ.'

'Oh dear,' she said, squinting at me. 'This is most unusual. Standard procedure is to fill out a request form a fortnight in advance – he knows that.'

'I'm sorry,' I said. 'Is there anything you can do now?'

'Just a moment,' she sighed, and pottered off into a warehouse area behind her, which was lined floor to ceiling with filing cabinets, all rusty green metal and plastic handles. I wondered if Thornhill had sent me on a wild goose chase; set me up to fail. He'd certainly had a cruel sneer on his face when he sent me to get the file – but maybe he just had Resting Smirk Face.

The woman returned, tutting and grumbling, carrying a small wooden crate. She placed it on the counter and pulled out a huge stack of manila folders, each stuffed to overflowing with sheets of paper.

'It should be in here,' she said, then gasped in frustration. 'Oh no! They've used paper clips! I can't handle paper clips; you'll have to come back tomorrow.' She reached up and started to pull down the shutter of her booth.

'Wait!' I shouted.

She paused in surprise.

'I mean,' I said, giving her my friendliest smile, 'bloody paper clips, eh?'

She frowned at me, not moving her hand from the shutter.

'You ladies have such a demanding job,' I said. 'I was just saying the other day; you're the beating heart of the bureau – we'd be lost without you.'

'Well… it's certainly nice to be appreciated,' she said, her brow unfurrowing slightly.

'And now one of those big-shot administrators has asked us to retrieve a file at a moment's notice. Typical! The nerve, eh?'

'Don't get me started! It's all rush-rush-rush with those gentlemen.'

'Well, I for one think you're doing a grand job. And I totally understand that you can't help me right now,' I said, picking up my bag, 'So I'll just get out of your hair.'

'Well, I suppose… just give me a moment, dear,' she said, and returned to rifling through the papers, all the while expounding on the innate superiority of bulldog clips. Eventually she located the correct manila folder, stamped the cover with three different inks, and handed it over triumphantly.

'You're an absolute star!' I said, stuffing it into my bag. 'Thank you so much, I really appreciate your help.'

'Well, it's nice to see that some young people still have manners,' she beamed. 'And tell Administrator Thornhill that next time he wants a rush job, he can stick it right up his bottom.'

* * *

'She said what?' asked Thornhill, scowling as I handed him the thick file on the Egyptian myths.

'That she was happy to help, sir,' I repeated.

'Hmph,' he snorted, sliding the file under his arm. 'Very well.'

Thornhill, Scott, Jim and I were standing outside a conference room, ready for our first one-on-one with an actual bona-fide deity.

'You will sit in silence, observing only,' instructed Thornhill. 'These people are not like us; their traditions are strange, their beliefs deeply held. It is easy to anger them with some small action that, to you, may seem quite inconsequential, but to them, is reason enough for an Apocalypse.'

Right, I thought – so it's like living with your parents.

Thornhill swiped his triskele lanyard and we entered the room, taking our seats on one side of a thick wooden conference table. On the other side of the table lay a MythTec bracelet in front of a large chair. Behind that was an area of floor decorated with a circle of runic symbols, slightly overlapping the other side of the table.

'The representative will be arriving momentarily,' said Thornhill. 'It's one of the big boys today. I like to think I have a good rapport with them – so watch and learn.'

I've always thought that was a strange expression – '*I like to think*'. It seems to say, 'I enjoy believing this impressive thing about myself, but I don't want to examine it too much'. But there I go again, overthinking things; and this is certainly not the time or place to be taking things too literally.

Thornhill checked his watch. A low hum filled the room as a golden light emanated from the runes. 'Here we go,' he said. 'Remain calm, children.'

There was a flash, a crack and a whiff of ozone, and suddenly there he was – Ra, the Egyptian God of the Sun; seven feet tall, a muscular bronzed body wrapped in white robes, fierce black eyes regarding us from his falcon head. He held a sceptre in his left hand and an ankh in his right.

'Welcome, eternal one,' said Thornhill, bowing. 'Please join us once again in conference of the divine order.' As he spoke, hieroglyphics flashed up on the monitor attached to the wall; I recognised the symbols for balance, harmony and law, followed by the symbol of a suited figure with a briefcase and an outstretched hand.

Ra stared down at us imperiously, then leant his sceptre against the wall and placed his ankh on the table with a heavy thud. He picked up the MythTec bracelet, closing it over his wrist with a snap. It glowed with golden energy, and the colour from the runes on the floor dissipated. Ra pulled the chair back and sat down, the wood creaking under his weight.

'Let us begin,' he boomed in a voice that reverberated deep inside me, sending a shiver through my body and raising goose bumps on my legs. I couldn't tell if I was petrified or turned on. Possibly a little of both.

'First,' he began, 'we must talk about your increasing use of solar power. If you wish to continue receiving my heliacal blessing, I must insist on an increased...' He stopped abruptly, cocking his head. He stiffened, then moved his hands to the edge of the table, as if to rise. 'Wait – what time is it in this land, mortal?' he asked Thornhill, his eyes widening. Thornhill raised his eyebrows. 'Why, a little after four,' he said innocently, although I sensed a smile playing on his thin lips.

'In your month of November? I must...' Ra growled. But before he could finish, the runes on the floor lit up again, there was the smell of burning ozone, another golden flash of light, and suddenly, there behind him, appeared another, much larger being. It was a second Egyptian deity; this one female and wearing a dress of the deepest blue covered in vibrantly glowing points of light.

Ra turned in his chair, looking at her in horror as she opened her mouth impossibly wide, lips elongating, jaw stretching horrifically to reveal a black cavernous opening. She grasped him firmly by the shoulders, lifted him up effortlessly, and shovelled him, screaming, head-first into her gullet.

The other interns and I were screaming, too. Jim had fallen backwards out of his chair, and Scott was already at the locked door, yanking on the handle to no avail. I was pinned to my seat with fear. I looked over at Thornhill, who was sitting perfectly still, that same subtle smile on his lips. What the hell was going on?

The creature finished swallowing Ra, his feet wriggling as he went down. She burped loudly, ejecting the MythTec bracelet, which she caught as it flew up in the air, clasped it around her wrist, and calmly took her place at the table.

Thornhill checked his pocket watch with a flourish. 'How silly of me, it's sunset already,' he said smugly. He bowed his head at the new arrival. 'Forgive the young ones,' he said. 'They are not able to cope with the awesome beauty of…'

'Nut, goddess of the sky,' I interjected. Thornhill turned to look at me, surprised that I was still in my chair. 'Who, every night,' I continued, holding my voice as steady as I could, 'consumes the Sun God Ra.' I bowed to her and she inclined her head the tiniest fraction in return.

'Lovely to meet you', she said in a regal tone.

Thornhill's smile vanished; his face stony now. Clearly, he had intended to frighten us, a hazing to put the new recruits in our place. I refused to give him the satisfaction, and did my best to appear calm, despite my heart hammering against my ribcage and my stomach on the verge of returning my scrambled egg breakfast.

Scott and Jim quickly returned to their seats, mumbling excuses. Thornhill continued the meeting, though to be honest I didn't take much of it in. I was too giddy with the rush that came from holding my own against a bully.

* * *

Izzy was delighted when I regaled her with the story in our dorm that evening. 'You see,' she laughed, 'you just have to get out of your comfort zone.'

I positively glowed under her praise.

'Thornhill docked me three marks for "speaking out of turn",' I said. 'Totally worth it, though.'

'What? Oh, he's such an arsehole!'

'Yeah. I tried protesting that it wasn't fair, but he just said, 'Life isn't fair'. Which, I mean, obviously that's true, life *isn't* fair – but when people say that, they usually mean *they're* not being fair, and they're just using the randomness of existence as an excuse for their own shitty behaviour.'

'Yeah. People in positions of power acting like that is infuriating. You'd hope that adults would have it a bit more together by now, y'know?'

I shrugged. 'Adults are just kids who got older.'

'Well, you got one over on Thornhill anyway. What a nasty trick to pull. I bet he was extra pissed off that it was a girl who didn't fall for it, too. He's always so biased towards the boys in his lectures. Total misogynist.' She shook her head. 'Men like him – don't you just want to scream "*Fuck the patriarchy*" and kick them in the balls?'

'Well, I'm not really the screaming type,' I laughed. 'Anyway, we've got a test tomorrow, so let's get back to it.'

Izzy sat cross-legged at a desk under one of the skylights, holding her book in one hand and a cuppa in the other. I sat on my bed, propped up against a pillow with snacks. We had developed a habit of revising like this; asking each other questions and throwing seedless grapes into the other person's open mouth when they got an answer right. It often dissolved into fits of giggles, along with the occasional emergency Heimlich.

I have a very visual memory, so had taken to writing up key facts on notepaper and blue-tacking it to the walls at eye level near my bed. I would even stick some to the ceiling, so that they would be the last thing I saw before I slept, in the hope they would burn into my subconscious. Tonight's swot-session was on poltergeists, in preparation for Administrator Fletcher's lecture the next day.

'I get that ghosts are people who died with unfinished business,' I said, perusing my notes, 'but surely that's true of almost everyone?'

'I think it has to be, like, hugely important stuff,' said Izzy. 'Not just having left the heating on or missed the series finale of *Bake Off*. Remember Administrator Hicc telling us about that private detective who came back as a ghost to solve his own murder?'

'I suppose. But why are ghosts classified as non-human?' I asked. 'Seems a bit unfair to lose all your privileges just because your soul's gone a bit non-corporeal.'

'I dunno mate,' she replied noncommittally. 'To be honest I've hit a wall.' She yawned. 'I need to listen to some chill-out vibes or I'll never get to sleep tonight.' As was her habit, she pulled out her headphones and scrolled through her iPod.

'You listen to music more than anyone I've ever met,' I said, putting down my notebook and rubbing my eyes.

'Couldn't live without it,' she said. 'I had to fill out loads of forms and get special permission. They made me bring my old iPod because it's pre-Wi-Fi tech. Music helps me regulate my moods; gets me in the right zone, y'know? I've got over 7,000 songs on here, with playlists for every occasion. Like when we first met? I was jamming to some '80s Rock to pump me up for the first day.' She looked at me quizzically. 'Do you really not listen to music?'

'Not much. I'm more into TV and films. I'll get obsessed with a show, binge watch, scour the AV Club comments, and listen to all the podcasts. But I just don't have that kind of relationship with music.'

She shook her head at me. 'Okay, you need some education. I'm going to make you a playlist that will totally change your life.'

I pointed to her headphones. 'Can you really not hear a thing with those things on?'

'God, no! These are 100% noise-cancelling over-ear stereo headphones. Top of the range. Cost me a whole summer's wages from working the tills at Tesco, but it was totally worth it. Songs aren't just tunes, you know; they're messages out of the void, one soul communicating directly with another. Here, have a listen.'

She threw the headphones over, the cord snaking out in

the air behind them. I caught them clumsily. They were beautiful. Large but deceptively light, with a blue *BeezWax*™ logo on the side – as in, 'none of your beeswax', I presumed. I placed them carefully over my ears and found myself cocooned in an eerie silence; all the sounds of the world suddenly absent. Then, as if from all around me, an orchestra struck up, enveloping me completely, each note perfectly modulated, precisely pitched. A voice rang out, as if the singer were standing right there in the room, performing only for me.

'*Never gonna give you up*', it sang. '*Never gonna let you down. Never gonna run around and desert you.*'

Izzy was laughing herself silly.

'Very funny' I said, pulling the headphones off. I tossed them back, but as they left my hand I realised that I'd completely misjudged the throw. I watched with horror as they sailed right over her head – and out through the open skylight, the cord pinging out of the iPod and following after it like a snake.

'Oh shit!' I said, jumping up off the bed.

Izzy was immediately up at the skylight in our sloping roof, staring out into the evening darkness. I rushed over to the other skylight, cranked it right open and peered down. We could just make out the headphones in the dusk light, sitting perilously close to the edge of the roof, the cord dangling over the end of the tiles and out of sight.

'I'm so sorry!' I said. 'We need something to hook it with before it goes over.'

'I *need* those headphones, Em,' said Izzy, with panic in her voice. 'I'm not kidding.'

'Don't worry – I've got an idea!' I left Izzy staring worriedly out the window and ran down the narrow staircase and along to room 5, rapping loudly on the door with my knuckles.

Kelly opened the door in her pyjamas. 'Jeez, what's the emergency?' she said, rubbing her eyes.

'Is Anna there? I need to borrow her hockey stick.'

'Her hockey stick?' she asked incredulously. 'Bit late for a game, isn't it?'

'It's an emergency – no time to explain.'

'Oh, just give it her so she'll go away,' came Anna's annoyed voice from inside.

I raced back to the room, hockey stick in hand, and brandished it triumphantly at Izzy. 'We can hook it with this,' I cried.

Izzy looked dubious, but I climbed up on the desk under the skylight, knelt down and leaned out, the bottom edge of the window frame digging sharply into my stomach. I held the handle as close to the end as I could, and reached out the hooked end towards the headphones. But it was nowhere near close enough – they were still at least three feet away.

'Dammit,' said Izzy, watching from the other window. 'We need something longer. Maybe Rudy has a broom or something?'

A light wind started up and a crusty brown leaf blew across the roof, spun around slowly, then whipped off over the edge. I felt a drop of rain hit my bare arm. 'No time,' I said. 'It's almost ten o'clock; it'll be a downpour in a minute. Grab hold of my legs, I'm going to lean out further.'

'What? Hold on, don't you have vertigo? Let me try.'

'No. I'm taller. And besides, this is my fault, so I need to fix it.'

I gripped the wooden window frame tightly with my left hand and leant forward, stretching my right arm out as far as it would go. I now had a rather stunning view down the sloping roof into the atrium. From this angle I could see how the grassy hill, pond, and amphitheatre each took up exactly a third of the circular area, and that the winding stone pathways created a huge triskele symbol. Feeling dizzy, I forced myself to look away from the drop and focus on the headphones.

'Can you reach them?' asked Izzy, having wrapped her arms tightly around my thighs. 'Also, FYI, if you could not fart right now, that would be great.'

I chuckled, then yelped in shock at the sight of a pair of bright green eyes shining out from the evening dusk. There, sitting atop a brick chimney stack to my right, was a jet-black cat, regarding me with mild interest. It tilted its head, yawned, then stood up unhurriedly and hopped down the other side of the chimney – off to shelter from the rain perhaps, or just bored of these human shenanigans.

'You okay?' called Izzy from inside.

'Almost got it,' I replied as the rain started to increase, drops hitting my clothes with soft little pats and drumming a rising staccato on the window panes. I was tantalisingly close. The curve of the hockey stick was now almost touching the black rubber headband, so close that I feared I might knock it further away if I wasn't careful.

'I just need one more inch,' I said.

'Don't we all!' Izzy yelled back.

'I'm going to lean out a bit further, so hold me lower, okay? Above my knees.' I felt her grip shift, then tighten.

'This is silly, come back in,' said Izzy, concern starting to show in her voice. 'It's not worth getting squished for some silly bloody headphones.'

'Just a few more seconds,' I said, releasing my left hand from the window frame and leaning out further, stretching my body down the sloping roof, the cold hard tiles pressed beneath my chest. Holding the hockey stick as near the end as I dared, I twisted it sideways and slipped the curved end under the band of the headphones, hooking them precariously. 'I've got them!' I cried out in triumph.

'Thank God. Now just get back in here,' said Izzy.

I pressed my left hand to the damp tiles and pushed

myself back slowly, eyes locked on my prize, then reached back and found the window frame again, reassuring beneath my grip. Worried that the rain might be damaging Izzy's headphones, I swung the hockey stick up towards me. But just as they were getting near, I felt the stick begin to slip from my grasp.

'Oh crap!'

I felt a tug as Izzy, panicking, started to pull me back in. I made a split-second decision to let go of the hockey stick, whipping my hand across to the headphones and hooking them with one finger before they could fall. As I was pulled backwards into the room, I watched the hockey stick slide away down the roof.

Then suddenly I was back in the bright bedroom, Izzy's arms still wrapped around my legs as we fell backwards on the floor in a tangled heap of limbs.

'Ta-daaa!' I cried, holding up the headphones in triumph.

'Bloody hell, Em,' said Izzy, shaking her head and grinning at me. 'I thought I was supposed to be the reckless one.' She jumped up and pulled the skylight closed; the heavens had opened now, and the rain was beating down thunderously.

'You must be rubbing off on me.' I said, beaming back. I could feel my heart beating a mile a minute – what a rush! Maybe Izzy was right about this getting out of your comfort zone thing.

'Okay, just one problem,' I said. 'Who's going to tell Anna we lost her hockey stick?'

Izzy raised an eyebrow. 'What do you mean, "we"?' she asked.

* * *

AND SO, the days passed.

The Izzy and Emily mutual support group was really

paying off; we were tantalisingly close to the top of the leaderboard now. Kelly was in first place, with Scott—to my surprise—close behind her, then Izzy in third place, followed by me in fourth.

But more than the lectures with Champ or lunchtimes in the library with Rudy, it was those evenings that I remember most fondly: long conversations with Izzy, studying hard, and laughing until we cried. Watching her dance, loose-limbed and blissful, hips bobbing and arms weaving – so comfortable in her own skin, which somehow made me feel more comfortable in mine. I really felt like I had found a place where I belonged.

All of which is to say that, as we neared the half-way point of the trial period, things were going very well indeed. I was the happiest I'd ever been. I was settled, strong, and confident.

And completely unprepared for what came next.

SEVEN

'CHECK THIS OUT,' SAID IZZY, RUNNING UP TO ME ONE MORNING, waving a yellowing sheet of paper. 'I found an old personnel report for Rudy!'

'What? Have you been sneaking around trying to win our bet?'

'Absolutely not.'

I gave her a look.

'Okay, yes – but I wasn't sneaking around. I found it in the East Wing reference archives; it was just sitting there in an old filing cabinet with a rusty lock. But, hey, if you don't want to know what it says…' she teased.

'Alright, alright,' I laughed. 'So, come on then – what species is he?'

'It doesn't say.'

'What?'

'It's just really basic information, and loads of references to redacted files. But look – it shows his date of birth, and get this; it's *tomorrow*. He's turning fifty.'

'Blimey! What's that in dog years, about three hundred and something?'

'I don't think it works like that,' she laughed.

'We should make him a cake,' I said. 'I've seen him chatting to one of the canteen ladies a few times; I'm sure we can ask her to lend us the ingredients.'

'Brilliant!'

We sought out the dinner lady that lunchtime, and explained our plan. She was more than happy to help, even loaning us a recipe card from one of her books and measuring out the exact ingredients, wrapping them in silver foil parcels and placing them in a Tupperware tub.

To keep it a surprise, we mixed the cake in our room's tiny kitchenette that evening, which, being rather cramped, left us covered in white powder and looking like ghosts. Only when Rudy had left the common room late that evening did we dare sneak out and bake the cake in the oven.

The next morning, we got up early and surprised Rudy as he was setting up the communal table for breakfast, serenading him with a whispered rendition of Happy Birthday.

'Wot's this then?' he gawped. 'Why, chocolate cake with icing and candles and everything. You little monkeys, how did you know?'

'Female intuition,' we fibbed.

'Well, bless you. You've made an old dog quite emotional,' Rudy said, wiping away a tear. He glanced around to see if anyone else was up yet, then leaned in conspiratorially. 'Y'know, I prefer to keep this stuff on the down-low. I was going to cook m'self a special birthday dinner this evening, just on me lonesome as Champ's away on a trip – but why don't you two come join me? Shall we say seven-ish?'

Izzy lit up. 'Sounds great. Do you have booze?'

He chuckled. 'I might be able to dig out a bottle of plonk, yes.'

'Thank God,' said Izzy. 'I've not been sober this long since I was fourteen. When we get out of here, I need to have a retox month and flush my system with alcohol.'

The rest of the interns started to arrive for breakfast, so after a final whispered, 'Many happy returns', Izzy and I moved to the end of the table for our tea and toast. Izzy was giddy with excitement, and I was too, though I did have reservations. Sure, Rudy's room was only down the hall, but it was still technically outside the dorms, which meant breaking the 7pm curfew.

'Oh, come on,' said Izzy. 'Rudy will be able to swipe us back in afterwards. Anyway, rules are meant to be broken.'

'No, they're not,' I said. 'That's literally the opposite of what rules are for.'

'Come on, you dork,' laughed Izzy. 'I love this place, but everything's so serious all the time. I'm all for saving the world, but can't we have a bit of fun while we're at it?'

'But is it wise to go to a strange man's room in the evening?' I whispered. 'Rudy seems really friendly, but what if he's after… something else?'

'Oh sweetie,' said Izzy. 'In our entire time here have you ever caught Rudy staring at your tits?'

'Well, no,' I admitted.

'Or looking at my arse?'

'Again, no.'

'Exactly. And I have a really great arse.'

I laughed. She had a point; at one time or another I'd caught every guy here checking out one or other of the girls. Males are not subtle about such things, bless them.

'Come on, do it for me?' pleaded Izzy.

'All right.' I conceded.

'Great! Anyway, Rudy's probably not even interested in humans. You shouldn't be so homonormative.' She chomped on a slice of toast. 'As in *Homo Sapiens*, I mean – obvs.'

* * *

I DIDN'T SEE Izzy for the rest of the day as she was shadowing

Administrator Hicc on Celtic Myths while I was in the library working on my Egyptian Deities report for Thornhill. Deep in research, I only looked up when the bell rang at 6:45, signalling that it was time to pack up. I stuffed my books in my bag and raced up to the dorms, turning a sharp left down the twisting corridor to Rudy's room when I was sure nobody was looking.

Arriving outside the large oak door, I saw that Izzy wasn't there. She wouldn't have wanted to hang about where she could be seen, so perhaps she'd already gone inside. I could hear music playing, so gave the door a knock, and heard Rudy's friendly voice call out, 'Jus'aminit!'

I was feeling a little nervous again, then reprimanded myself for being so suspicious. Rudy had shown us nothing but kindness since we'd arrived. It was quite wrong of me to suspect him of being some kind of monster.

'Aaaagh!' I yelled, as the door opened to reveal Rudy, all seven feet of him, in a red-splattered apron, holding a huge knife in a blue-gloved hand, his eyes peering out from a hole in a white cotton mask that covered most of his face.

'Oh, boomin 'eck!' said Rudy, quickly pulling the mask down from his face. 'Sorry, I clean forgot I was wearing it.' He looked quite embarrassed.

'What even *is* that?' I asked in shock, my back pressed up against the corridor wall.

'It's a hair mask – for cooking!' he said. He held up his hands in apology, then, noticing the huge knife, quickly put it behind his back.

'I didn't want to get fur in your food, I know 'umans hate that.'

I stared at him. Well, that explained the blue rubber gloves. And at second glance, the red splatter on the apron was clearly Bolognese sauce. I burst into relieved laughter.

'Oh dear,' Rudy said. 'I'm not used to guests. I really could have chosen a less horrifying get-up. Come inside, quickly. Where's Izzy?'

'Is she not here yet?' I asked. 'We said we'd meet at your place; she's probably running late.'

'Well, come on in,' he said, turning and walking back inside. 'I won't bite.'

I followed him through the door into his living room, which was about twice the size of our dorm room. There was a large thick rug over a wooden floor, with a comfy looking sofa and chair arranged around a coffee table, all warmly lit by a trio of lamps set at different heights. A large octagonal domed skylight in the roof afforded a stunning view of the starry night sky.

The walls were bumpy and uneven, and I realised that they were interlaced with half embedded tree branches. I wondered how far we were from the Tree of Knowledge, and whether it reached this far into the building. There were a couple of large bookcases, and dozens of artfully scattered pictures of various shapes and sizes on the walls. One painting—a group of men playing poker around a circular table covered in green baize—looked curiously familiar.

'Welcome to the doghouse,' Rudy winked. 'Make yerself at home – I'm almost done.' He walked back to the open-plan kitchen, where he had something delicious-smelling bubbling away on the stove.

As was my habit when I entered someone's home, I immediately went to the bookshelves, so I could silently judge them. Rudy's shelves were groaning with thick hardbacks and various curious objects. I ran my fingers along the book spines: *Pride and Prejudice, Catch 22, Moby Dick*. He was certainly no slouch in the literature department – and some of these looked like first editions.

'You've got a wonderful library here, Rudy,' I said. 'But with all the bureau's tech, why do you have so many printed books when they take up so much space?'

'I like the smell,' he said from the kitchen.

'Of paper?'

'Of life! Experiences. Wisdom. You can't get that with eBooks. Pixels don't smell of anything.'

I moved to the highest shelf, which seemed to be non-fiction: Hobbes' *Leviathan*, Plato's *The Republic*, a cat's paw... 'Aaagh!'

I yelped out loud for the second time in five minutes at the sight of the jet-black cat lazily regarding me from atop the bookcase, one paw dangling casually over the edge. I recognised it immediately as the cat from on the rooftop. It seemed equally disinterested in me this time, lifting its head, blinking slowly, then settling back down and closing its eyes.

'That's Ginger,' Rudy said from the kitchen. 'I've had her since she was a kitten. Why'd you yell out? You're not allergic, are you?'

'No, I love cats. I'm just surprised you have one. I thought you'd be... more of a dog person.'

Rudy stopped stirring the food and looked over at me. I went red. Then he threw his head back and guffawed loudly. 'Ahh, never change, my angel.'

'I just meant...' I said, trying to explain myself, 'that a dog-person with a pet cat is a little... surprising.'

'Did you ever have pets?' he asked.

'Yeah, I had a Labrador when I was a kid.'

'So, you were a monkey-person with a pet wolf?'

He had me there.

We were interrupted by a sudden frantic knocking at the door. Izzy had arrived, full of apologies for being late – it seemed the Celtic practical had overrun.

'Right, this just needs to marinate for a while,' said Rudy, taking off his apron and gloves. 'I've put the kettle on for some tea. Builders' okay for you?'

We made agreeable noises. Izzy looked around the room, eyes wide. I pointed to Ginger on top of the bookcase.

'Dogs and cats living together,' I said. 'Total anarchy.'

'Take a pew on the sofa, I'll be right over,' said Rudy.

I took the opportunity to look at some more of his framed pictures. One in particular caught my eye; an old photo of Rudy as a child, standing with a group of administrators, one of whom had their hand on his shoulder.

Rudy exited the kitchen brandishing three teas in sturdy mugs, a plate of Hobnobs, and a bowl of Twiglets – result!

'Here we go,' he said, 'Fill your boots!'

He noticed me looking at the photo. 'That's me with Champ Senior, one of the founders of the bureau.'

The photo was faded, but I could see the resemblance; Champ's father had the same chiselled jawline and broad shoulders – he was even smoking the same style of pipe.

Izzy let out a sudden yelp from the other side of the room. 'Oh my God!' she exclaimed. 'Is this a '60s Dansette Bermuda?' She was staring at Rudy's red record player, which stood on its tall black legs next to the fireplace, serenading us with soft jazz.

'Ah, a fellow vinyl head!' replied Rudy, grinning ear-to-ear. 'Yes, indeed; it's the original model with the cloth-covered cabinet and brass plates. It can play 45s and 78s. Here, let me put somethin' special on,' he said, tracing a hairy finger along a shelf of LPs, selecting one, and sliding it out. He removed The Best of Bix Beiderbecke from the turntable, carefully returned it to its sleeve, and popped on the new record, deftly dropping the stylus in place.

'*Stop your messing around!*' it sang. '*Better think of your future!*'

'I know this,' said Izzy. 'This is ska, right?'

'Yeah – well, rocksteady.'

'*A message to you, Rudy!*' sang the chorus.

'That's how I got my name,' explained Rudy. 'Humans can't pronounce me real name, on account of them not havin' enough teeth.'

He sank back happily into the large comfy chair by the fireplace. Above it was a large framed poster bearing the legend, '*Same shit, different deity*'.

We munched on Twiglets, Izzy and Rudy enthusiastically debating the benefits of lacquer master discs, whatever they were. Ginger the cat appeared at my feet, twisting between my legs and looking up at me expectantly. I gave her a smile and she jumped onto my lap.

'She's usually wary of humans,' said Rudy as I stroked Ginger's back. 'She must sense your kind heart.' A timer buzzed in the kitchen. 'Right, dinner's ready,' he announced, standing up and moseying back to the stove. 'It's my signature dish: Quorn spag bol.'

He served up generous helpings in a set of white porcelain bowls. It was delicious, flavoured with garlic, onions, and mushrooms, and served with chunks of warm sourdough bread. He then poured out three large glasses of wine; fruity and brick-red in colour. 'From the bureau's own vineyard,' he said, proudly.

'Oh alcohol, how I have missed you,' said Izzy, taking a sip and closing her eyes in pleasure.

The album on the record player finished, stylus scratching at the empty grooves. 'Izzy, you're in charge of music for the evening,' said Rudy. 'Choose something and keep the tunes coming.'

'I get to DJ? Cool!' replied Izzy, flipping through the shelf of LPs, carefully selecting something, then putting it on.

As the evening went on and the booze took effect, I felt all the stresses of the internship slip away. You couldn't hope for two more amiable companions; Rudy holding forth on Ministry history, Izzy swaying in her seat to the music, conversation flowing as easily as the wine.

Ginger purred contentedly on my lap while we ate, but I was starting to get a cramp. I gently readjusted my legs, trying not to disturb her, but to no avail. She sat up and arched her back in a yawn, then jumped to the floor and sauntered over to Rudy, giving him a meaningful meow.

'What's that?' asked Rudy, looking down at her. 'Oh, yes.' He reached out and twisted the handle on a vertical steel rod, which opened a side window in the octagonal skylight above. Ginger hopped on a small desk, then a bookcase. She looked up, paused briefly to calculate the distance, then bounded up through the gap and out onto the rooftop.

'Off for her evening prowl,' explained Rudy.

Something on the desk caught my eye: a half-dismantled electronic device amongst a pile of tools and wooden boxes. 'Is that an Amazon Echo?' I asked.

'Mmm? Oh yeah, I was tinkering with it a while back. I had an idea about linking it up with the MythTec database, but I could never get it to work. HQ's dampening field, y'know.'

'You do electronic work too?' I asked. 'And all these books you read. You know more than most of the staff. I can't believe they won't let you be an administrator.'

Rudy smiled sadly. 'Champ keeps petitioning them to change the humans-only policy, bless him, but they won't budge.'

'Institutionalised speciesism – 's bullshit!' slurred Izzy.

'I keep submitting proposals, though,' said Rudy. 'I had this one idea, about taking a load of obscure old deities – gods of ploughing, and lute playing and the like – and reassigning them for the modern era. "Gods of Office Technology", I called it. People could pray to them for stronger Wi-Fi, or to prevent printer jams. Doubt the brass even read it. Ah, well, you can't fight the system,' he shrugged. 'More wine?'

'Please,' I said, holding up my glass. Rudy uncorked a new bottle and refilled us.

Izzy was looking at the wooden boxes on the table next to the electronic equipment. 'Rudy, what are these?' she asked, picking one up. It was beautifully carved, with an intricate pattern of interlocking triskele symbols whittled part of the way down one side.

'Just a hobby,' said Rudy. 'Helps me relax. I carve them from the wood of the Great Tree'. He gestured to the branches that wove along the walls.

'Hey,' he said, grinning. 'Why does no-one know how the Great Tree works?'

'I don't know,' I replied, puzzled.

'Because it's a Myth-Tree!' he said and threw his head back, guffawing with laughter and slapping his thigh.

I couldn't help but join in. It had been a long time since I'd heard a dad joke.

'Rudy,' I said suddenly. 'Can I ask you a question?'

'Course you can, pumpkin.'

'Your cat; why is she called Ginger?'

Rudy chuckled in surprise. 'Oh! Well, it's the Superstitions Department, y'see. They'd never let a black cat stay in the building. Too unlucky.' He paused for a second. 'Or is it too lucky? They can never seem to decide. Anyway, it's our little way of circumventing the red tape. She's smart enough to keep out of sight, and I call her Ginger in case anyone hears me mention her.'

'That's well devious,' said Izzy with an air of respect.

'And here was me', said Rudy, looking me right in the eye, 'thinking you were going to ask me why you can't find my species in the bureau's records.'

The song on the record player chose that moment to finish, and the room went suddenly quiet.

'Yeah, I know you've been checking up on me,' he said, scratching under his hairy chin.

Izzy and I started to apologise, but he smiled warmly and waved away our explanations. 'Don't worry, I understand. Can't resist a mystery, eh? Like a dog with a bone.'

He stood up, walked over to the kitchen, then ambled

back with a fresh bottle of wine, sinking back into the creaking chair with a sigh.

'Let's have another glass, children,' he said, pulling out the cork with his teeth. 'And I'll tell you a story. About my people. About the terrible thing that happened to them. And why you'll find no mention of us – not in any book, not in the bureau's records, not anywhere in the whole damn world.'

EIGHT

'They called us the shoggyhund,' said Rudy, pouring out the wine. 'The dog-men of ancient Briton. We were a peaceful people, keeping ourselves to ourselves, living in small tribes around the country, wherever deep woods gave sanctuary.'

He sat back and smiled softly. 'The woods were our cradle and our cathedral. Our god was the rustle of the wind through the leaves, the trickle of water in a spring. We believe that everything is alive; part of one giant consciousness. You, me, the animals, the birds in the trees. The trees themselves.

'I've studied humanity's finest philosophy books,' he gestured to his heaving bookshelves. 'You call it 'panpsychism' – the belief that reality itself is conscious. Although we saw it not so much as a belief, but an observation of simple truth.'

'Sounds like Buddhism,' said Izzy, leaning forward with a look of drunken concentration. 'Hey – what did the Buddhist say when he ordered a hotdog?' she asked, her eyes lighting up. '"Make me one with everything".' She snorted, spilling wine on her shirt.

'Yeah, that's a good 'un,' chuckled Rudy.

'But you've been here since you were a kid, right?' I said. 'What happened?'

'I don't remember much about my early years,' said Rudy, his eyes focused on some far away memory. 'Little flashes, mostly. Playing with the other kids in the forest. Lessons at the feet of the elders. My stridemother bouncing me on her knee. Life seemed simple, and good.'

He frowned into his glass, swirling the wine. 'But something was changing. We used to run into other groups of shoggyhund every so often, but we hadn't seen any for a year. And now our own tribe was shrinking. At first one or two were disappearing a month. Displaced, misplaced, nobody seemed to know. Then it was every week. The adults wouldn't talk about it in front of us, but I knew from their faces and their whispered conversations that something was terribly wrong.'

'Then one day I woke up and there were only three of us left. Me, my best friend Buru, and my older sister, Lola.' He paused for a moment at her name, then continued. 'She was running around the clearing in a panic, screaming for our parents. Then she stopped dead in her tracks and darted over to me with a terrified look in her eyes. She grabbed my arm and started to say something. But in the middle of her sentence—while she was looking *right at me*—she disappeared. No noise, no sudden rush of air, nothing. Just *gone*. Like she'd been edited out of reality.'

Rudy stared straight ahead as he talked, but he was somewhere else; somewhere far away and long ago. I felt Izzy shift closer on the sofa and take my hand.

'That's when the humans arrived,' said Rudy. 'They burst into the clearing, yelling loudly in their strange language. I'd never seen one up close before. They were petrifying, with their pale, hairless faces and their horrible second skin, flapping around them, all unnatural. Buru and I were frozen to the spot, wailing in fear.'

'The humans were shouting at each other frantically. One of them, their leader, sprinted over and started prodding me with strange metal things. I was terrified. I looked over at Buru, who was being picked up by another human. And just at that moment, he vanished. The human, his arms suddenly empty, looked over at us in horror. I screamed so loud, I'm sure it could be heard for miles. The leader pulled something out of his coat: a thick metal hoop. He clasped it around my wrist and it glowed a strange golden colour, burning my skin. That's the last thing I remember before I passed out.'

I hadn't dared to move or say a word until now. 'Those people,' I said. 'They were from Myth Management?'

'Yes. It was Champ Senior and a few others. I found out later that they had detected what was happening. He'd convinced the bureau to let him take some of their new MythTec devices and try and save a tribe of us, before it was too late. But they were slow getting the paperwork together, and by the time they arrived… it was just me left.'

'But I don't understand,' said Izzy, distressed. 'What happened to you all?'

'They were being forgotten,' I said, quietly.

'Aye,' said Rudy, nodding at me. 'The bureau called it a *Delta Level Incident*. You see, like all mythological races, we survive only when we are in the human consciousness. In the egosystem. Well, our kind had kept ourselves hidden for many generations – too well hidden, it turned out. Nobody told our stories, you see. So, we simply started to vanish. A trickle at first, then a flood. My family, my friends, everyone I ever knew or loved. An entire civilisation erased from the egosystem. If it wasn't for the bureau, I'd be gone too,' he said, rubbing the MythTec bracelet on his wrist.

'Shit,' said Izzy, wiping away a tear.

'They tried,' sighed Rudy sadly. 'Several times. But once a mythological race is gone from the ecosystem, there's no bringing it back. At least, no way we've found. There's still a lot about the Tree that we don't understand. All that remains of my people is in here now,' he said, tapping his head with a finger. 'The fading childhood memories of an old man. And when I go, they go with me. Like we were never here at all.'

'I'm so sorry,' I said.

'Not your fault,' said Rudy. 'Long time ago now, anyway.'

We all sat there in silence. I didn't know what to say. I mean, what *could* anyone say at a time like this?

Izzy leant forward. 'Rudy?' she asked, her voice soft.

'Yes, m'dear?'

'Do you have any weed?'

Rudy stared at her for a second, then threw his head back and laughed, a long cathartic roar.

'You girls keep me young, you know that?' he sighed, wiping his eyes with the back of his sleeve. 'No, I don't have any weed, not exactly. But I do have something even better, if you're interested?'

Izzy nodded enthusiastically. Before I could protest, she squeezed my hand and gave me a meaningful stare. 'Come on Em, you only live once.'

'Okay,' I said, hesitantly. 'Sure.'

Rudy chuckled, rubbed his hands together with delight, then reached down and slid a wooden box out from under his chair. This one was about six inches square, with a triskele symbol carved in the lid. He opened it up to reveal Rizla papers, a matchbox, some loose cigarettes, a rolling station, and what looked like a piece of ginger root.

'Can I roll?' asked Izzy.

'If you like,' smiled Rudy. Izzy took a paper and slid it into the roller, then gently tore open a cigarette, expertly crumbling it into the open paper. I tried to act like I had any idea what they were doing.

'Are these menthols?' asked Izzy.

'Yeah, fill 'em halfway,' said Rudy. He had taken the piece of root and was shaving it carefully with a small penknife that he had pulled from his pocket. Small curls peeled off into a pile on the open roof of the box.

'What is that?' I asked him, as casually as I could.

'We call it the *soul root*; it grows on trees whenever my people are near. Trees and shoggyhund are what y'call sympathetic; we know what each other needs, and we provide it. Ingesting a little bit of this helps us see the world as it is: connected and interdependent. The root system as a symbol of all life.'

'So, it's a fungus, like psilocybin – magic mushrooms?' I asked.

'You know your stuff, I see!' said Rudy.

'I'm not completely inexperienced,' I said, noting Izzy's impressed glance and deciding not to reveal that everything I knew about drugs came from a single podcast.

'And these are particularly sacred,' Rudy said, crumbling the shavings into the paper that Izzy had prepared, 'because they grew from the roots of the Great Tree itself.' He noted my worried expression. 'Don't worry, it's quite mild, really. Good trips only with this stuff.'

Rudy licked the paper and rolled the spliff tightly, holding it up to admire it for a moment in the lamp light. He picked up the yellow matchbox, extracted a match, and struck it with a flourish, lighting a cherry on the end of the roll-up. He took a long drag and held it for a moment before exhaling slowly through his huge nostrils. The air filled with a pleasant woody smell, like a campfire on an autumn evening.

'Me next,' said Izzy, her eyes sparkling with excitement. She took a deep drag, then sank back into the sofa, exhaling with a sigh of deep satisfaction. 'Oh yeah, that's the stuff.'

She handed me the spliff and I took it clumsily. I'd never even smoked a cigarette, but I was determined to keep my composure. I took a drag as best I could.

'Hold it in your lungs as long as you can,' advised Izzy.

I held it for a moment, then exhaled, coughing. Rudy

chuckled and held out his hand. I realised that I was supposed to hand him the spliff. We passed it round like this for a while. I honestly wasn't sure what effect it was having; I certainly felt very warm and fuzzy, but we were several bottles of wine down, so that was hardly unusual.

Rudy went to the kitchen for more snacks, and Izzy put another album on the record player.

'Goddamn,' she said wistfully. 'Can we just acknowledge for a moment that we are getting high in an impossible building with a dog-man from an extinct mythical race.' She took a long drag of the spliff then handed it over to me. 'This may well be the high point of our lives. So let it all in, honey. Soak it up.'

I took another drag as Rudy returned with a tray of biscuits.

'This place is amazing,' I agreed. 'Even with all the ridiculous archetypes. Champ with his tweed suit, umbrella, and pipe. I swear one time I saw him using a Pantone strip to check the colour of his tea. I mean, did this kind of England ever really exist? Sometimes I think it's as much of a myth as all the ghosts and goblins.'

'Well, here's to us myths, long may we prosper!' said Rudy, holding up his wine glass. We clinked and cheered happily.

'Thank you, girls, for the best birthday I've had in years,' he said warmly. 'In fact, hold on a mo.' He shuffled over to his workbench and rummaged around for a moment, then came back with another of his carved boxes, this one rectangular and about a foot long, covered in triskele symbols, with an 'MM' logo in its centre. He took an unopened bottle of wine and placed it carefully inside the box.

'In my culture,' he said, 'we don't receive gifts on our birthdays; we give them. It's to remind us of the importance of the tribe, without which we are nothing.' He held out the box to us ceremoniously. 'You are part of my tribe now.'

'Wow, Rudy. That's beautiful,' I said. We were both deeply moved.

'You two had better be getting back soon,' said Rudy. He reached over to a nearby drawer, pulled out a triskele, and threw it over. 'Here, borrow my spare lanyard; it'll get you back into your dorm. This old body can't keep up with you much longer,' he said, closing his eyes and leaning back into his chair with a contented sigh.

Izzy took another drag. 'Yeah, we're going to feel this in the morning,' she said. She stood up and stretched, arching her back, then went over to a window, tracing marks in the steamed-up glass with her finger and adding her initials below.

'If thirteen-year-old Izzy could see me now…' she mused, doodling a triskele shape. 'I spent years reading *Harry Potter* under the blankets with a torch, dreaming of a life of magic. And now look where I am.' She turned to me with a grin. 'Hey, do you think if Harry and Ron had gone to University, they'd have indulged in a bit of *experimentus*?'

I laughed. 'Izzy, you're sex mad.'

'Best sort of madness. Anyway, that's what uni is for – broadening your horizons,' she grinned.

'So, what about you, Emily Peasbridge? Is there someone special waiting for you back in the real world?'

I shook my head. 'No. There was this one guy a while back. I actually thought I was in love.' I snorted at the naivety of slightly-younger me. 'But it turned out he didn't really exist.'

'What? You mean, like, you were catfished?'

'No. He was just pretending to be someone he wasn't; to me, and to himself as well, I think. He talked a good game and I let my imagination do the rest, and between us we constructed the fictional man of my dreams.' I laughed and took another swig of wine. 'When the penny finally dropped, I had to mourn a man who was never really there, but who I was constantly reminded of, because he looked just like this dickhead I was dating.'

'Damn,' said Izzy. 'This is why I have a simple rule: don't get too attached. My last boyfriend was super-hot, but not very bright. He'd have to take his pants off to count to twenty-one. Not that I minded him taking his pants off, mind.'

'But, don't you want to meet your soulmate?' I asked.

Izzy snorted. 'People are always looking for their "one in a million". Do you know what the chances of that are?'

'One in a million?' I ventured.

'Exactly! And even if you found this amazing, perfect person, why would they be interested in you? You'd have to be *their* one in a million, but you're much more likely to be one of the other 999,999. That's just statistics.'

Rudy let out a loud snore, making us jump. His head was lolling back in the chair.

'Looks like our host's passed out,' said Izzy. 'Time to go. But first – I must wee!' She staggered off to Rudy's bathroom, swinging the door closed behind her.

I sat there for a moment, enjoying the quiet. I was pretty sure the tree root was kicking in now. The warm fuzzy feeling had deepened, and the room had begun to take on a lush texture as if it had been painted on a three-dimensional canvas. I'd watched enough movies to know that getting stoned could lead to philosophical musings on the nature of reality, but when you're living in a pocket dimension, that all seemed rather pedestrian.

My train of thought was interrupted by the bleep of a computer. 'You have one incoming message,' said a recorded voice, calm and business-like.

I looked around for the source. It seemed to be coming from Rudy's Amazon Echo; there was a neon blue light glowing around the base. But how? Didn't he say it wasn't working? In fact, I could see it wasn't even plugged in; the trimmed cord was there on the table, wires poking in the air. There was another beep, then a different voice spoke, clear and crisp in the silence of the room.

'Hello, Emily,' it said. And what a voice it was. Gentle, wise and kind, yet imbued with some strange sadness. The hairs rose on the back of my neck, and I felt a warm shiver run down my spine. Was this the tree root, or was this really happening?

'Hello?' I said. 'Sorry, but... are you the Amazon Echo?'

'The echo of an Amazon?' replied the voice, intrigued. 'No, I am no warrior woman, though the daughters of Ares are indeed my kin. Nor am I an echo, for my words are mine alone. A gift for those who are willing to listen.'

I leant forward on the sofa, and for a second thought I saw the flicker of a figure, there in the low lamp light of Rudy's living room.

'You can see me if you concentrate,' she said. 'As in all things, you just need to find the right perspective. Incline your head slightly to the left. No, not that much. Back a bit. A millimetre more. There.'

I could see her now, a figure sitting next to the table, her hand resting on the top of the Amazon Echo, its light shining through her fingers. She was an elderly black woman in a purple dress, with a knitted shawl draped around her shoulders. Curvy and large bosomed, with kind crinkly eyes and a gentle smile; she seemed only half there at first, like someone had turned down her opacity, but she became more substantial when I concentrated on her.

'Who are you?' I asked.

'I am an Oracle of Delphi,' she replied. 'You have heard of us, I'm sure.'

I had indeed. The legendary priestesses of Apollo, who

delivered prophecies of fame, fortune or impending catastrophe.

Looking at her, I was surprised to find that I felt no fear at all. Perhaps something in her voice convinced me that she meant no harm. Or maybe I was just stoned. I guess it could be two things.

'May I ask a question?' I said tentatively.

'It is what humans do', she nodded. 'You ask, we answer. The rest is up to you.'

'How are you manifesting here? The machine you are talking through is broken. And this building is protected by MythTec firewalls; it should be inaccessible.'

'Yes, your castle is guarded with strong magic. But yours is a remarkable mind, and tonight we felt it reach out, further than ever before. In the place where realms overlap, the gauze has thinned for a moment, creating a channel through which we may converse.'

'Okay, so—I'm not quite sure how to put this—but if you're Greek, why are you… a person of colour?'

'Because I assume the form that you expect,' she said. 'And you, my dear, watch too many movies.'

She'd got me there, of course; the wise old African-American is my generation's official Purveyor of Wisdom ™ (yes, I know there's another name for it, but I'm much too white to use it).

'Perhaps you would prefer this variant?' she asked. 'It's also very popular.' She morphed into a beaming Morgan Freeman, his freckled face gazing benignly across the room at me.

'I'm afraid I cannot stay long,' said Not-Morgan-Freeman, in his unmistakable velvety tones. 'I bring you prophesy. Great danger is coming. Listen closely, for if you are to survive, you must heed these warnings three.'

'Wait, what?' I said. I looked frantically around for a pen

and paper. 'Hold on.' I spied a battered old Biro on the coffee table, grabbed it, and pulled the top off with my teeth.

'One,' said the Oracle, morphing back into her old woman form once more. 'You must bury the bottle.'

I couldn't see any paper. Why wasn't there any damn paper?

'Two: you must open the glove box,' she continued.

I scrawled frantically on the underside of my forearm, green Biro marks against the blue veins: *bury bottle / open glove box*.

'And three: beware the breed that turns on you.'

'Wait,' I said. 'This makes no sense. What are these warnings about? Is something bad going to happen?'

'He is coming,' the Oracle intoned gravely. 'When you hear the sirens, it will already be too late. You will have reached the end of the line. The end will come when green turns to red.'

I felt myself sobering up fast. 'But you said this is a warning, right? We can do something to stop it?'

'Who is *we*?' she asked. 'Will you turn to your friends for help? The dog-man and the slip of a girl? One will be your lifelong companion. The other will soon be gone.'

I felt my stomach lurch. 'Rudy and Izzy? What do you mean? Is one of them going to die?'

'There must always be a sacrifice, it is the way of things,' she said calmly. There was no hint of malice; it was as if our fate was of no consequence.

'No,' I said fiercely. 'I won't let it happen!'

She tilted her head. 'You? What use is a silly little girl who spends too much time in her own head?'

I recoiled. It was exactly the phrase my Mum had used, so many times.

'Or perhaps you will put your faith in Administrator Champ?' she asked. 'His secret will be his undoing.'

I felt a fury rising in me now. 'What secret?' I demanded.

'*Who* is coming? Why do you speak in these riddles? You can't just sit there making cryptic comments while people suffer, or die, or—' I searched for an example, 'get slaughtered by a horse-full of Greek soldiers.'

She flinched.

'I'm sorry,' I said. 'Too soon?'

Her smile was gone now. 'I experience time in a non-linear fashion,' she said quietly. 'It is always too soon. And always too late.'

And with that, she was gone.

NINE

'MY POOR HEAD,' GROANED IZZY THE NEXT MORNING, RUBBING her temples. 'I was totally mortaled.' This was, I had learned, a rather wonderful Northern expression meaning to get so inebriated that you become vividly aware of you own mortality.

She slid from her bed and staggered to the bathroom, locking the door behind her. To give her privacy, I put her headphones on and turned up the volume.

I hadn't spoken to her about what I'd seen last night. I wasn't even sure if it had been real, or just a spliff-induced hallucination. We had left Rudy snoring away in his chair and crept back to the dorms, using Rudy's spare lanyard to get in. As soon as we were in our room, Izzy had collapsed on her bed and passed out. I had tried to do the same, but slept fitfully, mind racing, too full of adrenaline to get any decent rest.

I had been awake for the last few hours, the last part standing here at the skylight. I sipped my third mug of breakfast tea and watched the lights come on in the windows opposite, golden rectangles cut into the dark blue of the winter morning.

I had a sudden memory of sitting at my bedroom window as a kid, maybe six or seven years old, watching people moving around in the tower block opposite and realising that each tiny figure had a life as complicated and unique as my own. I had wanted to reach out and swap bodies with them, to travel in their shoes for a while. Then I worried that I already had. What if I'd been one of those kids looking over at my window, had reached out and swapped lives and memories into this body, and was now stuck being me forever?

'You thinking too much again?' said Izzy, emerging from the bathroom.

'Yeah,' I replied, hitting stop on her iPod.

'Have you been listening to that playlist I made you?' she asked.

'Just the first track so far; the Johnny Cash one. Hey, listen, I need to talk to you about something that happened last night.'

'Oh God, what did I say? Did I get a bit...?' she stammered. 'Look, you don't want to take me too seriously when I'm drunk.'

'No, nothing like that. You'd better sit down; you're not going to believe this.'

I recounted my experience with the Oracle, only leaving out the bit where she'd said that one of Rudy and Izzy would, 'Soon be gone'. I mean, that could mean anything, right? No point dwelling on it.

'Blimey,' said Izzy when I'd finished the tale. 'I can't believe I missed all that because I took a pee break and nodded off on the toilet. This is worse than that time at Glastonbury when I missed Wu-Tang's entire set because I was puking up in a Portaloo.'

'I think I should tell Champ,' I said.

'Whoa, hold on there, girl! Tell him what? That we were getting drunk and stoned at Rudy's place after curfew?'

'Okay, point taken,' I said, 'but this could be really important; we have to do *something*.'

'Yes, *we* should – you and me. It came to you, right, this Siri Seer? It told you that Champ had some big secret, that he couldn't help. And it chose *you*, out of everybody, to give the prophecies to. What were they again?'

'Beware the breed that turns on you. Open the glove box. Bury the bottle.'

'Breed could be a dog, like Rudy. Though I can't believe he'd ever hurt us.'

'Me neither.'

'Glove box; like in a car? There aren't any here. And I've no idea what the last one could mean.'

'Actually, I was thinking about that,' I said. 'There's this film that my dad loved to watch, one of his favourites. It's about a group of friends who bury a box of champagne together when they start college, then go and dig it up again after they graduate. My dad did the same thing with his friends at uni, and I always thought it'd be cool to do with my friends, too. And I guess this is my university, in a way, with the dorm rooms and all the coursework and everything.'

'I love it!' enthused Izzy. 'And it's perfect: we can use the box of wine that Rudy gave us, then dig it up when we pass our apprenticeships – which we totally will, because we rock.'

'Okay, but where would we bury it? I can't see them letting us dig a hole in the atrium garden.'

'No need. We're right next to Hampstead Heath. We'll just find a secluded spot under a tree.'

'Are you mental?' I exclaimed. 'We're not supposed to leave the building, it's against the rules.'

'Come on,' implored Izzy. 'We still have Rudy's spare lanyard, right? I bet that accesses the main entrance. Let's use it to nip out this evening, then just give it him back tomorrow.

I hesitated. Was this a stupid idea? Almost certainly. But I remembered what the Oracle had said about my friends being in danger. If that was true, and if this would help somehow, then the risk was worth it.

'Okay' I said. 'Let's do it.'

Izzy squealed with delight, then threw me a fresh towel. 'Come on, you dork,' she said, like she did every morning. 'Day's a-wasting – we don't want to be late!'

* * *

'ARE YOU SURE ABOUT THIS?' I asked Izzy, shifting the weight of the wooden box under my arm. It was just before 9pm. We had used Rudy's lanyard to exit the dorm area, then crept down the staircase that connected to the foyer. We were now crouched on the bottom step, peering furtively around the corner into the room.

'Of course,' said Izzy. 'The portals use ley line energy, remember; I did a whole report on it for Administrator Hicc. They're active for one second, every hour on the hour; if we use Rudy's lanyard at 9pm exactly, we can nip out, bury the box, and get back before anyone knows we we were gone.'

'Okay,' I sighed. I had spent the day getting more and more anxious about the idea, but I knew I'd never hear the end of it if I tried to back out now.

Thankfully, the foyer was deserted. The only movement came from the animated characters on the ceiling fresco, numbers spinning around their floating forms. On the floor a dozen feet away were the circle of runes that indicated the position of the entrance portal.

'Three minutes to go,' said Izzy, checking her watch.

A door opened abruptly across the way, and someone strode into the room, talking loudly to themselves. We shrank back against the wall. It was Mavis the receptionist.

'…Looked everywhere else, so it must be here,' she declared as she waddled over to the reception desk, her voluminous beehive swaying back and forth like a pendulum.

I took Izzy's arm. 'Let's go,' I mouthed.

Izzy frowned and shook her head. 'Two minutes,' she whispered, pointing at her watch.

For what seemed like an age, Mavis examined the contents of drawers and rifled through trays of papers, muttering 'Where can they be?' Then she caught sight of her reflection in the monitor and let out a yelp of surprised laughter. 'Oh, you daft apeth!' she said, pulling a pair of glasses from the front of her beehive and moving them down onto her nose. She turned away, chuckling, and headed back towards the door she'd come in by.

Izzy grabbed my wrist, whispered 'Now,' and to my horror pulled me to my feet and forward into the foyer.

Before I knew what was happening, we were sprinting towards the portal, feet moving as softly across the floor as we could, my eyes locked on Mavis' back as she headed towards her corridor. Thank goodness the poor old thing was half-deaf.

The floor was slippery with fresh polish and I almost fell, but Izzy kept pulling me forward, her hand vice-like around my wrist. We skidded the last few feet, sliding over the runes just as they lit up.

There was a >*flüorgp*< noise, a whiff of ozone, and suddenly we were crashing into huge piles of red and orange autumn leaves.

It took a moment for my eyes to adjust to the moonlight. It felt so strange to be back in Hampstead Heath. I looked up at the giant horse-chestnut tree that had been my entry point just a few weeks ago – though it felt like a lifetime.

'What a rush!' said Izzy, beaming.

'That was *too* close.'

'Aw, you worry too much. Come on, we've only got an hour, let's find a good spot.' She pulled out her torch to light the way. We moved quickly, hopping over roots and downed branches, half covered in a thick carpet of leaves that crunched underfoot. Then we were out into the open.

It was a crisp, cool evening, with a full moon and cloudless, starry sky. The Heath is a magical place at night. Paths illuminated by lamplight; figures silhouetted on the hill by the glow of the city, dogs barking happily and crows cawing from the treetops.

'Parliament Hill is that way,' I said. 'But that's no good; too open. Let's head North, past the boating lake, and up into the woods.'

'Righto,' conceded Izzy. 'You're the local.'

We trotted down the hill, jogged across an open area, then passed over an old stone bridge. There weren't many people about. A few late-night dog walkers, a sprinkling of couples out for a romantic stroll, the occasional man nipping furtively into a public toilet.

'We don't want to go much further,' I said, thinking about the time.

'How about up there?' suggested Izzy, pointing up the hill at a cluster of trees.

We climbed up the hill and forced our way through a tangle of shrubs and brambles. At the centre, we discovered a large willow tree, its drooping branches sweeping the ground.

'Perfect!' I said.

We pushed through its curtain of green and yellow leaves, emerging into a sheltered area beneath the dome of its umbrella-shaped canopy. I placed the box carefully on the ground while Izzy tied the torch to a low branch, pointing it downwards where it illuminated the ground, the leafy walls glowing soft and golden around us. I was reminded of Rudy's words; *'The woods were our cradle and our cathedral.'* A sacred space.

'Right – over to you,' said Izzy.

I pulled the book from my pocket: *Spells and Charms of Ancient England*, by Valerie Enth. 'Here goes,' I said. I flipped to the page we'd marked with a downturned corner and began to chant the words in as sombre and reverential a tone as I could manage.

The earth rumbled quietly, a muffled vibration under our feet. Loose pellets of earth were shaken from their place, slowly at first, then more forcefully. Two large tree roots stretched apart, pushing a small area of earth aside to create an opening a foot or so deep, pebbles and loose twigs falling into the rift.

'Told you we wouldn't need a shovel,' said Izzy, grinning.

The opening was easily big enough for Rudy's carved wooden box, which we picked up together and ceremoniously lowered inside. We then each pricked a finger with the safety pin Izzy had brought, letting a single drop of blood fall into the hole and onto the box.

'Together we bury this symbol of our friendship,' I said. 'Only when the two of us return together can it be reopened.'

Izzy then took the book and read out the second part of the spell. The roots slowly moved back towards each other again, closing the gap as if it had never been there. Izzy sucked her finger. I wrapped mine in a tissue.

'Now it's official,' said Izzy. 'A sacred pact: we graduate together or not at all.'

After a hug of celebration, we started heading back. I was moving quicker now without the bulky box under my arm, or perhaps I felt lighter for other reasons. Either way, we positively bounced along over the grass.

'I'm proud of you, Em,' said Izzy. 'Breaking the rules. Acting on your gut instinct.'

'I guess you bring out my reckless side,' I teased.

'Can I ask you something?' said Izzy.

'Of course,' I replied, wondering where this was going.

'You talk about your dad a lot, but only in the past tense. Is he...?'

'He died when I was twelve.' I said quietly.

'I'm sorry.'

'I only knew him through a kid's eyes. Hero-worshipped him, I suppose.'

'Your mum raised you on her own?'

'No, she remarried a few years later, so I had a stepdad. He's all right, I guess. Seems to make Mum happy, but...'

'He can't compete with a ghost?'

'Right,' I nodded.

'I bet you gave him a hard time.'

'Yeah. I used to wind him up by calling him Faux-Pa.'

'Oh my God,' said Izzy. 'You are *such* a nerd!'

'What about your parents?' I asked. 'You never really talk about them.'

'Actually… I don't usually talk about this because people make a big deal out of it, but I grew up in the foster system.'

'What? Oh my God, I'm so sorry. And I've been banging on about my Dad, I feel such a–'

'Shut that down right now,' ordered Izzy. 'That's exactly why I don't talk about it. I don't want people acting weird around me. It wasn't a great childhood, but it was fine. Some bits were even pretty good. I moved around a lot; met a lot of interesting people. Helped make me a great judge of character, remember?'

I nodded.

'If there's one thing I've learned, it's this: you make your own family. Like us.'

'Right.' I said. 'Absolutely. I just…'

I stopped suddenly, and looked around. I didn't recognise this part of the Heath. 'Hold on, are you sure this is the right way?' I asked.

'What? I was following you!'

'No, I was following you!'

'Oh shit.'

Izzy waved our torch around as we tried to get our bearings. We looked back along the path we'd walked down.

Was it the one we'd been down earlier? They all looked the same. Swearing under our breath, we ran back up to the top of the hill.

'Damn it, everything looks the same in the dark.'

'Look,' said Izzy, pointing into the middle distance. 'Where the path splits into three over there: we took the wrong fork. We've been heading in completely the wrong direction.'

'Crap. What's the time?' I asked.

'Five to ten,' she gasped, looking at her watch. 'Come on, we'd better leg it!'

We raced back up the path, found the right fork, then ran top speed down the hill and over the bridge. Here I was again, running for the portal in the half light. No GPS guiding me this time, but not on my own anymore. In fact, I felt less alone than I'd been in a long time. We laughed as we ran, I don't know why. Joyful and ridiculous as we were.

We crashed through the undergrowth towards the portal tree, arriving with seconds to spare. 'We made it,' panted Izzy as she pulled Rudy's spare lanyard out of her pocket. She grasped it tightly in one hand, grabbed my hand with the other, and we hugged the tree together, giggling hysterically as the light began to radiate from its trunk.

>*Flüorgp*<. Ozone. Wood Polish.

We were in the brightly lit foyer again. I looked around, half expecting Mavis to be standing there with her hands on her hips, but the room was deserted.

'See,' said Izzy as we caught our breath. 'Piece of piss.'

We crept up the stairs, swiped Rudy's access card over the reader, and quietly opened the door into the dorm area.

'Up late, aren't we?' asked Thornhill.

He was standing in the kitchen, quite still, his hands behind his back and a smirk of triumph on his face.

'I... we were just getting something from the library, I'd

left my notebook there and…' Izzy babbled, but Thornhill cut her off.

'Muddy in the library, was it?' he said, gesturing to our shoes. 'Funny thing; there I was, doing routine checks of ley line portals when I noticed an unscheduled transfer. Then another one popped up, right while I was looking. Had a hunch, and decided to pay the dorms a visit. So, tell me; what's that in your hand, Miss Peasbridge?'

I looked down at Rudy's lanyard. 'I can explain!'

'I look forward to it,' he said. 'Come with me, both of you.'

* * *

WE WERE SEPARATED, and I was taken to a room on the fifth floor, where I stewed and fretted for half an hour. Dammit, dammit, dammit. I knew this had been a mistake.

Now what would happen? I guess this was it: we'd both be expelled from the academy. And what about Rudy; would he be in trouble as well, for letting us take the lanyard?

The door opened and Thornhill entered, glowering.

'Administrator Champ has taken it upon himself to deal with the situation,' he said between gritted teeth. 'Come with me.'

He took me along the corridor and up to a thick oak door, which he rapped on loudly.

'Come in,' came Champ's voice. To my surprise, Thornhill then turned sharply on his heel and stalked away, clearly unhappy. Hesitantly, I opened the door.

It was a large study, bigger than Rudy's room, with a high roof. On one side was a large oak desk with a typewriter-monitor hybrid, piles of paperwork, a few strange ornaments and several books, each stuffed with dozens of bookmarks. The walls were lined with bookshelves and half a dozen display cabinets, within which a variety of exotic looking objects were exhibited, including a few that seemed to be deadly weapons.

A coat and umbrella hung on a stand to my left next to a large world map and a dozen old framed pictures. There was a huge bear rug in the centre of the room – at least, I assume it was a bear.

Champ was standing with his back to me, looking out of a large circular window that took up most of the height of the room, and which was divided into a familiar pattern. With a loud click, one of two large metal arms outside the window suddenly moved down a fraction, and I realised that the window was the inside of a huge clock face – the one I'd seen from the atrium garden.

'Good evening, Miss Peasbridge,' he said, turning around and fixing me with those piercing blue eyes. 'We need to have a little chat.'

He walked over to a small round table where a yellow teapot was sitting. 'Shall I be mother?' he asked, picking up the pot and pouring the hot tea into two small bone-china cups. He handed one over to me and the sweet, musky smell of Darjeeling wafted up to my nostrils.

As I waited for him to speak, my eyes were drawn to a shelf on the wall nearby, below a framed, faded map of Africa. Sitting on the shelf was a large glass box containing a battered white cricket glove; one of the long ones that has the forearm padding attached. A brass plaque on the front bore the legend: *Battle the monsters. Save the world. File the paperwork.* And then below that, on a red strip: *Break in case of emergency.*

'A family heirloom,' said Champ, noticing my interest. 'A relic of a more volatile time, but a symbol of the importance of our administration – and of adhering to our rules.' He took a sip of Darjeeling. 'Talking of which…'

He let the words hang in the air.

'Sir, it's entirely my fault,' I blurted. 'I took a spare lanyard from Rudy's room one afternoon, without his knowledge. Then I convinced Izzy—totally against her will—to join me for an evening on the Heath. I broke the rules, and I should be the one to pay the price.'

Champ raised an eyebrow. 'So, you take full responsibility? Nobody else was to blame?'

'Absolutely,' I nodded, trying to keep my voice steady and emotionless.

'Well, how peculiar,' he mused. 'Young Miss Hirway said it was all her idea.'

I stuttered, not knowing what to say.

'Now, loyalty to one's friends and colleagues is all very commendable,' Champ went on, 'but we can't have interns gallivanting around without permission. We must have standards, after all.'

My heart sank.

'On the other hand, no serious harm was done. And it's not to say I didn't play a little fast and loose with the rules in my youth,' he smiled kindly, then looked sadly into his cup. 'And undeniably, made my share of mistakes.'

His voice took on a serious tone. 'However, rules have been broken. There have been calls for your and Miss Hirway's immediate dismissal.'

I'm sure there have, I thought – and I could guess from whom.

'I do agree that an example must be made. Actions have consequences. So, here is my decision: I will not be expelling either of you from the academy at this time…'

A tremendous sense of relief washed through me.

'However, I am docking each of you exactly one third of your points. This drops you and Miss Hirway from the top of the leaderboard down to the lower rungs.'

I started to protest, but he raised a finger. 'It puts you at quite a disadvantage, yes. But not unwinnable. It will be a tough uphill struggle. So, Miss Peasbridge, it leaves one question: are you up to the task?'

'Yes, sir,' I said, holding myself up straight.

So, there we were, Izzy and I: halfway through probation, and right back at square one.

TEN

OVER THE NEXT WEEK, IZZY AND I REDOUBLED OUR EFFORTS. WE spent every lunchtime and evening in the library, then studied through to the early hours in our dorm room.

We hadn't been able to speak to Rudy alone, so I had no idea if he'd gotten in trouble, or even if the management knew we'd been in his quarters after curfew. I was pretty sure they didn't know about the booze and drugs, or we'd definitely have been out on our arses. Thornhill seemed particularly irritable during our lectures with him, although that wasn't much of a change.

Checking the schedule a few days later, I was thrilled to see that I'd be shadowing Administrator Champ for the first time. Also assigned to him that day were Neil, the goth (or perhaps he was a metalhead, I was never sure), and Anna, who had yet to forgive me for losing her hockey stick. We would be attending another ambassadorial conference, this time an arbitration between two opposing realms involved in a dispute.

'Righty-ho,' said Champ, when we met him outside a first-floor conference room. 'You've all done this before, so you know the drill. Keep your tongues in your head – that includes you, Miss Peasbridge; I've heard what happened with the Ancient Egyptians.'

I'm sure he had, I thought – Thornhill's version of it, anyway. Although I caught a flicker of amusement in his eyes when he spoke, so who knows.

Champ put his hand on the door handle, then paused and turned to us. 'Hold on a tick. How old are you again? Wait, silly question, ignore that. What religions are you?'

'Uh… broadly Judaeo-Christian, but sort of agnostic, I guess,' I said.

'Atheist,' stated Anna, flatly.

'Wiccan, sir,' said Neil, pointing to the pentagram tattoo on his neck. 'Why?'

Champ chuckled to himself. 'Okay, this will be fun,' he said, and opened the door.

Inside was a long oak table. The delegates from the two factions were already there; three at each side, arms folded, staring across at each other. Anna and I gasped. Neil swore under his breath. We could hardly believe our eyes.

How can I describe the scene? Let's start with who was sitting on the left-hand side. They were two tall, pale-skinned gentlemen, dressed all in white, with huge feathered wings growing from their backs and halos shimmering above their heads. On the chair between them was a crib. I couldn't see who was in it, but I could hear a baby gurgling and there was a small gleaming star hovering in the air above it, so I think it was pretty obvious; I mean – *Jesus*.

Then, on the right-hand side, was Santa Claus. Yep, Father bloody Christmas himself; the red suit, the big white beard, the whole shebang. He was flanked by two officious looking elves, who, like the angels, were carrying lawyer's briefcases and had come with their game faces on.

'Welcome all,' said Champ, taking his seat at the head of the table. We drew up stools just behind him, trying not to look too dumbfounded. 'So, we return to the matter of the Midwinter Festival…'

'*Christmas*,' interjected one of the angels, his voice taut and melodic, like the strumming of a harp.

'… and the correct balance of ownership for December 25th,' Champ continued, ignoring the interruption.

'I'm sure we can all agree that this Cold War has gone on too long – if you'll forgive the pun,' said Champ. 'But I know we can come to an amicable agreement.'

There was much disgruntled mumbling.

'If you will forgive me,' said an angel in a tone which implied that we bloody better had do. 'It is quite clear who Christmas day belongs to. *Christ. Mas.* It's right there in the name. Our claim dates back over two thousand years, whilst our honourable friends here,' he gestured across the desk, 'have merely appropriated a few German customs so they can sell plastic toys.'

'Oh aye?' said Santa, gruffly. 'Let's invite the Pagan delegation in, shall we? They might have something to say about cultural appropriation.'

A further hubbub broke out, growing louder until a tiny peach-skinned hand rose up from the crib. The room went pin-drop quiet as a baby, swaddled in blankets, rose gracefully upwards, glowing with heavenly light – quite literally. He was, without a doubt, the most beautiful thing I'd ever seen. My heart melted and my ovaries ached.

'Now, now,' said the baby in a voice so exquisite that tears sprang unbidden to my eyes. 'Don't make me pull rank here, *Saint* Nicholas.'

Santa shifted uncomfortably in his seat and turned his attention to our end of the table. 'Look, Champ, we've been very pleased with the Coca-Cola thing you guys organised. But it's a month away from the big date and I'm not seeing any new Santa movies hitting Netflix.'

'Ah, yes. Let's talk movies, shall we?' declared the other

angel, opening his briefcase and pulling out a series of charts. 'We've crunched the figures and there are twice as many Christmas movies featuring Santa Claus as there are for Our Most Holy Lord and Saviour. And that's not including *Die Hard*.'

'*Now I have a machine gun, ho ho ho,*' chuckled the shorter elf, making little finger guns, then going silent as Santa gave him a withering look.

'So, what I'm hearing is that you *both* want an increased share of the zeitgeist?' asked Champ.

They nodded vigorously. Clearly both sides saw themselves as hard done by. Champ tried being reasonable, but temperatures started to rise, and soon each side was waving printouts and shouting over each other about the decorations in Birmingham City Centre.

While they were arguing, an idea had been forming in my mind, which I'd been idly scribbling in my notebook. To my dismay, Champ noticed what I was doing and put his hand out for the notebook, his face impassive. I handed it over reluctantly, wondering how badly I'd managed to mess up this time. Champ studied it for a moment, then handed it back.

'Gentlemen, a moment please' he said, addressing the room. The bickering died down and they turned to him, arms folded. 'I find that every so often it can be beneficial to get a fresh pair of eyes on a situation. Young Peasbridge here has a suggestion, and in the spirit of there being no bad ideas, perhaps we should all hear it.'

All eyes turned to me, expectantly.

I froze. Was Champ trying to embarrass me, like Thornhill had? Surely not. I cleared my throat, steeling my nerves and trying not to make eye contact with two of the most important figures from my childhood.

'Well,' I stammered. 'Santa, that is, Mr Christmas, I mean

Father Christmas, has done very well recently with Elf on The Shelf, I believe? The little doll that watches kids to make sure they behave.'

'*So* cool,' enthused the shorter elf. The angels rolled their eyes.

'So, how about a religious equivalent?' I asked. 'A small doll of Baby Jesus in his crib that people can place on the mantelpiece. We could call it… *Your Own Personal Jesus*.'

'Johnny Cash. Nice,' nodded the nearest angel.

'Seems a little reductive if you ask me,' sniffed the other.

'The name's just a placeholder,' I said. 'We're looking for clickbait; something meme-ready that can go viral. Easy gags for the talk show hosts.'

'Interesting,' mused Baby Jesus.

'That's all very well for BJ, but what about us?' grumbled Santa.

'Well, that's the best bit,' I said. 'People will be taking sides—"*Are you Team Elf or Team Jesus?*"—which will add to both teams' egosystem metrics.'

'It's worked before,' interjected Champ. 'The War on Christmas did great numbers.'

Santa scratched at his beard while the taller elf whispered something in his ear. Baby Jesus glanced at one of the angels, who nodded back at him almost imperceptibly.

'Very well, Champ,' said Baby Jesus, floating back down into his crib. 'It's got my blessing.'

'Yeah, could be a goer, I reckon,' agreed Santa. 'And if this works out, you'll all be on my Good List.'

Champ beamed at me, and there was much back-patting and shaking of hands. And that's how I moved up three places on the leaderboard in one morning.

* * *

THE NEXT DAY we made our way to the atrium at the centre of the building. It was a warm late-autumn afternoon; a pleasant breeze ruffled the leaves in the trees and rippled across the surface of the pond. Champ had invited all twelve interns to attend an ambassadorial visit from the Realm of Albion, the coalition of Celtic and Old English Myths and Folklore.

He stood on the knoll beneath the sycamore tree, deep in conversation with a tall, silver-haired woman as we took our places on the wooden benches nearby.

After we were settled, Champ turned to us with a broad smile. 'We have a rare treat for you today. May I introduce you to an old friend of the bureau, the esteemed shaman, Ursula Wealdring. She will be leading us in a ritual meditation ceremony to celebrate the festival of Samhain.'

The Albion mythology, particularly the ley lines and tree worship, was clearly central to the bureau's MythTec. Perhaps, I thought, this was why they were allowed to perform one of their rituals right in the heart of the HQ.

There was a polite smattering of applause as Wealdring stepped forward. She was tall and slender, dressed in long robes of deep green. Although clearly of advancing years, she carried herself with a light and easy grace.

'Welcome, all!' she said 'Thank you so much for inviting me. I know you have spent weeks listening to endless lectures and perusing weighty tomes. Well, this afternoon will be a little different; a chance to experience our culture directly, not just through your eyes and ears, but with your heart, your mind and your soul.

'We need to make some room – so please lift these benches to one side so we can sit directly on the grass. That's it. Now let's remove our socks and shoes, and sit here on the grass, so we can feel nature against our skin.'

There was much giggling as we complied. Even Champ joined in, carefully untying his brown brogues and balling up his socks—yellow with blue stripes, I noted—then placing them in the hollow of the shoe and propping them up against the tree trunk.

Wealdring directed us all to sit cross-legged in a circle around her on the grass, arranged like a miniature Stonehenge.

'Everybody; gently rest your hands flat on the grass,' she instructed, her voice low and soothing. Out in the real world, London's grass would be dry and brittle at this time of year, but here in the HQ's microclimate it was thick and green, luxuriant beneath our palms.

'Now, without looking down, slowly move your hands in concentric circles,' she continued. 'Feel the blades of grass between your fingers. Keep going until you find a seed from the sycamore tree.' I moved them around and sure enough, my fingers soon discovered one of the wing-shaped drones – 'helicopter seeds' we called them when we were kids, because of the way they spun as they fell from the trees every autumn.

'Pick one up—that's right—and hold it in your open palm in front of you,' she continued. 'Now, close your eyes and concentrate on your breathing, long and deep. Just listen to my voice.'

She began chanting. I didn't recognise the language, if it was a language at all, but the sound was sweet and melodious, resonating on some deep, familiar frequency.

I became very aware of the heat of the sun on my face, the sound of the wind in the trees, and the delicate weight of the seed resting in my palm. The smell of incense pervaded the air. I inhaled deeply, feeling my lungs fill, my neck relax, and my muscles soften.

I've tried yoga a few times, but I could never really get into it. I couldn't quite get the hang of the 'emptying your mind' aspect. I always felt too self-conscious, too aware of how constructed it all was.

But this felt different. Perhaps it was the effect of the past few weeks, the new world that had opened before me, or maybe it was Izzy's constant advice to, 'Get out of my comfort zone'. Whatever it was, I felt an incredible sense of calm settle over me.

The chanting became louder and stronger, reverberating through the ground. I could feel an energy in the air, flowing around me and through me, reaching out like the roots of a tree searching for water.

The sycamore seed wiggled in my palm, tickling my skin. My eyes were still closed, but I felt it start to revolve, rotating in place, slowly at first, then faster. I knew, instinctively, that it wasn't the wind doing this. Some other elemental power was at work.

I felt the seed lift from my hand, leaving my palm empty and tingling. I chanced a brief glance, flicking an eye open for half a second, and saw it hovering an inch above my palm, spinning leisurely, like a rotor blade powering up.

I locked my eyes tightly, exhaled deeply through my nose, and concentrated on the chanting.

And then, all of a sudden, it wasn't just the seed that was floating.

Have you ever tried to sit down at the bottom of a swimming pool? It's almost impossible; you're pulled upwards and have to work hard just to balance yourself and not tip over. That's how it felt now, as if there was some unseen energy drawing me steadily up and out of my body.

I still had my eyes closed, yet somehow, I could see everything: the grassy hill, the leafy green sycamore tree, my fellow interns sitting cross-legged in the circle around me. My viewpoint was higher now, as if I was standing up, but I could still feel my legs crossed beneath me. I tipped forwards slightly and looked down. To my surprise I could see the top of my own head.

I was hovering above my body.

Bloody hell, I was having an out-of-body experience! Astral projection – a right load of mumbo jumbo, I would have told you a few months ago. But I could hardly be surprised that, here at least, it was as real as anything else.

My spirit, or soul, or consciousness—whatever you want to call it—had become unmoored from my body. But not completely. I felt the soft tug of some invisible connection, an umbilical cord tying me back to my earthly form.

I looked around at my fellow interns, each with their palms held out in front of them. Most of the helicopter seeds lay still, though one or two were shifting in their owner's hands.

I glanced over at Champ, his face placid. He had both palms outstretched, a sycamore twizzling in each like keys turning the locks of some ethereal machinery. Bloody show-off.

I could see groups of tiny floating particles clustered around everyone's bodies. It triggered a memory from childhood; I couldn't have been more than five or six, lying in bed and fascinated by the dust shining in the light of my bedside lamp. I'd sternly ordered my Dad to move the dust out of the way, and he'd laughed, explaining, 'It's always there, pumpkin, but you can only see it when there's a bright light in the darkness.'

The shaman's chanting continued, as if in encouragement. I found that if I concentrated hard enough and focused on a fixed point, I could move myself slowly in that direction, like a balloon pulled on a string. As I floated past Kelly, who was sitting to my left, I could sense the buzz of her thoughts, like the sounds of a lively dinner party emanating through a thin wall. It wasn't so much individual words or sentences; it was more feelings or a general attitude. An aura, I suppose you'd call it.

I floated back the other way, passing Neil; his aura screeching like a death metal guitar riff. I felt a tug as I approached Izzy and was pulled towards her like a magnet; so quickly, in fact, that I lost control and ploughed straight into her. Suddenly, I could feel her all around me – no, it was more like I *was* her, thinking her thoughts, experiencing her soul. I could see the world from her perspective; a glorious buffet of opportunities to gorge myself on. Her emotions burst like fireworks around me.

It felt so intimate – a terrible invasion of privacy. Embarrassed, I pulled away quickly, disconnecting from her and shooting backwards through the air – only to collide with another aura, this one much more powerful. Everything went sea blue as I was enveloped in its steady, potent energy, pulsing like the rolling tide of the ocean. I recognised the confidence and calm self-assurance of Administrator Champ. A peaceful self-belief, calm and rational, born not of arrogance, but experience.

It was overwhelming. I lost myself in him for a moment, almost forgetting who I was. I could feel his body, his arms – wait, was I moving his hands? Was that me doing it, or him? I could feel his thoughts. There was something concealed here, beneath the surface, something he needed to keep hidden.

A voice rang out, echoing all around me. 'Hullo? Who's there?'

Then the chanting stopped, and I was yanked backwards, out of Champ's mind, across the grass and crashing back into my own body. My eyes snapped open, my mind reeling. It was like waking from a vivid dream – for a second you are occupying two realities and it takes a moment to determine which is real.

Everything slowly came back into focus. Grass, sunlight, birdsong. The lesson was wrapping up, and the next few minutes were full of stretching and yawning, then an excited chatter as the other interns discussed their experience.

Izzy was blissed out, full of love for the world. She gave the shaman a big hug, then did the same to me, jabbering nineteen to the dozen about how connected she felt. I mumbled something in agreement, catching Champ's eye as he was shaking hands with the shaman. Had he detected someone in his head? If so, did he know it was me?

* * *

We went up to our dorm to freshen up and get ready for dinner. Izzy, complaining that she felt sweaty, hit the shower. I opened the nearest skylight, pushing it up as far as it would go, and sucked in a lungful of crisp, cool evening air. Dusk was falling outside, and lights were coming on in the rooms opposite. I was still feeling strange and tingly; not quite tuned in to the world.

On the desk was Izzy's iPod, lined up with the playlist she'd put together for me. What was it she'd said about being in the right frame of mind; opening yourself up to the music? Well, no time like the present, I thought. I put the headphones on and hit play.

A song kicked in, wrapping itself around me. I felt a warm shiver as the music enveloped me, buffeting me, lifting me. Could I do the same trick again, I wondered, without the shaman's chanting? Let's see.

My consciousness reached out, stretching its astral fingers. Immediately, I felt the tug of another soul; Izzy, in the shower. Flustered, I pulled away and flew upwards into the ceiling instead, melting through the plasterboard. I could feel little points of energy – mites crawling around in the wooden support beams. Then I was through the cold slate tiles and outside into the fresh early-evening air.

A bird flew off, startled. My nerve endings were like live wires. I could feel everything, a massive interconnected web of trees and animals and people. A black shape dropped down from a nearby chimney stack; it was Ginger of course. She sniffed the air in front of me, wrinkling her nose.

Then there was something else; something sharp and cold. I felt it slicing through the atmosphere; penetrating our reality. I don't know what it was, but I knew this: I didn't like it, not one bit.

I dropped back down into the room and into my body, yanking off the headphones. I heard a *>flüorgp<*, and the smell of burning ozone hit my nostrils. A shudder ran through me as I turned around.

There was a *thing* in the room with me. A creature. An interloper. It was leathery, hairy, and dank. Six feet tall, at least. The strong, sinewy torso of a man; the hairy legs and cloven hooves of a goat. Silver hair on his back. Horns protruding from his head. A thin mouth and cruel eyes.

He was extremely naked.

His hands were long and hairy, and capped with vicious-looking claws. His eyes were locked on a half-constructed electronic device that hung from a leather strap around his neck – was that MythTec? The creature looked up in surprise, then amazement and delight. Then his gaze fell on me, and his expression changed to one of cold malevolence.

A leer spread across his face. I didn't need to see his aura to understand his intention; that was horribly quite clear. He meant to kill me, and he looked like he would enjoy doing it.

I was rooted to the spot, paralysed with fear. He was standing between me and the door; there was no escape. This was it; this was how I was going to die.

I heard the sound of the shower switching off behind me, accompanied by the familiar groaning of the pipes in the walls. With a sickening horror I realised that Izzy was going to walk into the room just in time to see me eviscerated, and then she would be next.

A sudden anger surged through me. No, not anger; *rage*.

Adrenaline pumped through my veins. My ears went hot, my fists clenched. Before I knew what was happening, I found myself rushing at the creature, as his expression changed to one of almost comical surprise.

'Fuck the patriarchy!' I screamed at the top of my lungs, swinging my foot out as hard as I could and making contact between his legs.

Then I turned sharply, jumped up onto the desk, and flung myself head-first out through the open skylight.

ELEVEN

I REGRETTED IT IMMEDIATELY. I MEAN, WHAT THE HELL KIND OF A plan was this? Izzy was still going to walk out of the shower any minute, and then she'd be eviscerated, or eaten alive, or worse. Unless, of course, I'd gotten him mad enough to follow me out here. And then what?

I clung to the chimney stack that I'd scrambled to in a panic. The brickwork was cold and the edges crumbled beneath my grip. I tried not to look down or throw up as, shaking, I pulled myself around to the other side.

It was dusk already, the sky deep blue and darkening fast. Moonlight reflected off the grey slate roof tiles. I peered around the chimney stack, heart pounding. What was happening back in the dorm room? How long had it been since I jumped out? Five seconds? Ten?

Had I only saved myself, and sacrificed Izzy?

My answer came with a roar as the creature leapt up through the nearest skylight, howling, a murderous look on his face. I whipped my head back and flattened myself against the bricks, praying he hadn't seen me.

The roof rattled as he landed just feet away from me. I

could hear the sound of his cloven hooves and sharp fingernails, scraping on the tiles as he tried to find purchase.

I could see movement through the brightly-lit windows on the other side of the building as people calmly went about their business, oblivious to what was happening. I squinted: was that Champ in one of the offices? They couldn't see me out here in the dark, but if I screamed and waved, maybe I could get their attention? But that would give away my position, and there would be no chance of rescue before that thing got to me.

I closed my eyes and attempted to control my breathing, not daring to move a muscle. It wasn't easy, remaining motionless on a sloping roof; arms aching, legs trembling, gravity tugging at me. The old tiles were covered in patches of moss, slippery under my smooth-soled shoes.

I could hear him panting and growling, a low and threatening noise. He couldn't see me though; I was sure of it. He didn't know which direction I'd gone. As far as he knew, I could have hurled myself out the window and right over the edge.

Then everything went quiet. No growling, no panting, no sound of hooves on tiles. Had he gone?

I heard him sniff. Great deep, lung-filling inhalations. I'd never realised how threatening a sniff could sound, but this one was petrifying. And I was covered in sweat, stinking of fear.

There was a terrifying scrambling noise, and suddenly he had me. A hand seized my neck, claws scratching my throat. He dragged me from my hiding place, tendons flexing in his leathery arm as he lifted me bodily into the air.

He laughed, a short bark of triumph, baring his wolf-like teeth. I felt the stench of his hot breath in my face. I tried to stand on tiptoes to relieve the pressure around my neck, then gave up and kicked out frantically – but he twisted out of the way – he wouldn't be falling for that trick twice.

As he shifted his weight a tile gave way under one of his hooves, shooting out from under him and flying off down the sloped roof. He fell to one knee, bringing me crashing down with him, then let go as he slipped backwards.

He slid away quickly, almost to the edge of the roof, but threw his weight to one side, grabbing hold of a section of ironwork. A hoof slammed into the gutter, ripping it off the wall, sending wet leaves flying. He strained visibly as he held himself there for a moment, leaning forward to shift his centre of gravity.

He steadied himself and snorted, angry at his own carelessness. His eyes narrowed, cold and determined. He began pulling himself forward, careful and deliberate, making his way back towards me.

I turned, scrambling frantically on my hands and knees up the slope away from him, then flung myself over the peak of the roof. I scanned the rooftops of the circular building, looking for a way out. A jumble of architecture spread out in both directions: cast-iron railings, clusters of chimney stacks, gables, aerials and weathervanes. No windows. No doorways. No escape hatches.

The area to my left seemed a little flatter. Decision made, I forced my trembling legs to stand, then set off, running along the thin-beamed rooftops as fast as I dared. My vertigo was screaming at me, but not as loud as the fear of what was behind me. I forced myself to concentrate on the few metres in front of my feet. Pretend it's an obstacle course at school; leap over those chimney pots, vault over these railings – thank God for three years of compulsory gymnastics.

I could hear him behind me now, but I didn't dare turn and look. On firm ground he'd have caught me in seconds, but up here maybe I had a chance.

A sudden thought occurred to me – Rudy! He was bigger, stronger and hairier than this creature. He was my best hope. But where was Rudy's room? I pictured the route from our dorm room, down the stairs to the main area, out and along the corridor; then tried to map that on to the rooftop.

Shit. I was heading in the wrong direction.

As I reached a cluster of huge old TV aerials, I heard a snarl behind me and felt hot air on the back of my neck. Desperately, I grabbed the largest aerial and dived to one side, using it to swing myself around. It bent dangerously, making a horrible creaking noise as my feet scrambled on the sloping roof.

The huge dark shape of the creature passed by on the other side, and he snorted furiously as he realised what I'd done, hooves scraping as he slid to a stop. I let go of the aerial and it sprang backwards, the spiky top section hitting the creature solidly in the face, enraging him even further, but buying me a few more seconds.

I ran full tilt back the way I'd just came. I knew the terrain now, but then so did he. In the near distance I could see the golden light coming up through my dorm skylights, and beyond that, what I desperately hoped was the silhouette of Rudy's octagonal glass dome.

I sprinted across the flatter surfaces, treating the ridges as balance beams, vaulting over a chimney stack – then, with a crack, something cold and hard hit me in the back of the head.

I fell, landing hard on my side and sliding down the sloping roof. I rolled over on to my front, arms flailing in panic. My fingers found the edge of a wooden frame and I clung on for dear life. Looking up, I almost wanted to laugh – it was the skylight to my room. I was right back where I started.

The creature strolled along the roof towards me. Walking carefully, no need to rush. He tossed a roof tile in his hand nonchalantly.

'Work smarter, not harder,' he said, as if reprimanding himself. 'You had me quite worked up there. Acting like a dumb animal.' His voice was like sandpaper, but his tone was clipped and polite.

'Took me a moment to start thinking clearly. Well, "That's on me" as you humans say.' He tossed the tile off the side of the roof. 'Time to wipe up the mess.' He began moving down the slope towards me, his narrow eyes fixed on mine.

An incongruous sound drifted up through the skylight; a melody, slightly off-key. As if someone with headphones on was singing along to music.

He tilted his head, listening. 'What's that? Ah, you have a little friend. Well, I'll have to see to her, too, of course. But first things first.' He shifted down the last couple of feet, lifted a leg, and planted his hoof on my forehead, ready to push.

'Time for you to "pop off", little English girl.'

I let go of the window frame.

I slid backwards rapidly, my hands pressed flat against the tiles, trying to slow myself as much as I could. I hit the edge and my legs went over, feet scrambling frantically. One foot found something – an overhang of some sort. I pushed against it as hard as I could, barely managing to keep myself from falling further.

'Oh, you dreary mortals,' sighed the creature, shaking his head. 'Always clinging to your tiny little lives. I don't know why you bother.' He moved steadily down towards me, leaning back for balance, hooves scraping the tiles.

My fingernails dug into the rooftop, tips white with pressure. My leg was burning with effort. He bent down and reached forward with a hairy clawed hand. This was it.

Then something small, furry and jet-black flew through the air. It landed on his head, screeching and clawing at his face. Ginger! God bless you!

At the same time, I noticed something lying in the gutter next to me; something long and wooden with a hook at the end.

The creature howled in pain and ripped the cat from his

head, hurling it across the rooftops. I shifted my weight on my leg, grabbed the hockey stick, and swung it desperately at his legs. The hook caught around one of his ankles and I pulled hard, yanking his leg out from under him. He fell backwards onto the roof, slamming his head hard and sliding down right past me. For a split second we locked eyes—his wide with shock and anger—then he was over the edge and gone.

God knew where I got the energy from, but somehow I clambered up from the precipice, pushing with my legs, belly flat against the tiles, muscles screaming. I reached out with the hockey stick and hooked it over the edge of the skylight's window frame, pulling myself upwards and onto my knees.

Convinced I would collapse at any minute, I used the last of my strength to hurl myself towards the open skylight, plunging through it headfirst. I tumbled through into the bright light and warmth of the room.

I collided with Izzy, who was walking underneath right at that moment. We crashed to the floor together, Izzy dropping her mug of tea, which shattered over the carpet.

She pulled her headphones off and looked at me in shock. 'Jesus!' she said, holding the broken mug handle. 'Why do you keep *doing* that?'

* * *

THE REST of the evening was a mess. I had to explain what had happened several times, first in broken gasps of breath to Izzy, then to Rudy after Izzy half-carried me downstairs, yelling for help. The rest of the interns had already gone to the dining hall, so Rudy called for Champ, who arrived with Director Hinson and Administrators Thornhill and Hicc in tow.

Rudy gave them the gist of what happened, and everybody started barking questions at once. Administrator

Hicc shushed them, wrapping a blanket around my shoulders and checking me over for cuts and bruises. 'Can't you see the poor thing's in shock,' she reprimanded.

Thornhill started to protest, but Hinson acquiesced. 'Quite right, quite right!' he said, and went to put the kettle on. Izzy sat next to me, her arm around my shoulders.

Champ sent Rudy down to the atrium to check for any signs of an intruder – such as, for example, the body of a half-goat, half-man creature splattered all over the ground. Then he made me go through the story one more time, slowly and deliberately. I told him everything, except for the bit about Ginger, as I didn't want to get Rudy into trouble.

Champ asked a lot of questions: what the creature looked like, the device around its neck, the way it had spoken. When he finished, he sat back and lit his pipe, staring at me intently.

'Quite remarkable,' he said, puffing away. 'It seems you've been very brave. And very lucky.'

'What?' exploded Thornhill. 'You can't seriously believe this ridiculous story? There's no way anything could penetrate the HQ's defences. The girl was obviously messing around where she shouldn't be, and has made up this ludicrous tale as a cover.'

Rudy arrived back in the room, breathing heavily.

'Anything?' asked Champ calmly, looking over at him.

'Nothing, Chief. I double-checked the whole area. No blood or sign of an impact, neither.'

'See?' exclaimed Thornhill, triumphantly. 'Explain that, young lady.'

'Emily said that thing had a MythTec device, didn't she?' interjected Izzy. 'That's how it got in, and it must have used it again when it fell from the roof.'

'Hogwash!' scoffed Thornhill. 'We've never had a breach of this kind. Nothing showed up on the monitors. In fact, the only issues we've had recently were caused by these very two young ladies!' he said, pointing at us angrily. 'An unapproved expedition to the outside world, and a goblin released into a conference room.'

'Very well, Thornhill,' said Hinson. 'You've made your opinion quite clear.' He turned to Champ. 'What do you think, old friend?'

Champ sucked on the end of his pipe. 'The young lady believes it happened,' he said, steadily. 'And I believe her.'

'But—' began Thornhill.

'Administrator Thornhill's quite right, though,' said Champ, cutting him off. 'We've never had a breach like this. We need to take it very seriously. Increase security, change all the passwords, strengthen the firewalls.'

'Agreed,' said Hinson. 'However, I think we should keep this to ourselves. No use panicking the other interns.'

'Yes, sir, whatever you think is best,' said Thornhill between clenched teeth. He turned to me. 'There'll be a lot of paperwork for you to fill out. Expect it first thing in the morning.' He glanced over at Champ, who was now deep in conversation with Hinson, then turned back to us. 'Two screw-ups already, ladies. Three strikes and you're out.'

WE'D BEEN ORDERED to keep mum on the attack, but that didn't stop Izzy and me doing a bit of research under the radar. During lunch break the following day, I retreated to a window nook in the library on floor three, arms heavy with reference material. Izzy turned up twenty minutes later, out of breath.

'Sorry I'm late, I was stuck in the loos with Kelly. Poor thing was crying her eyes out.'

'Oh no. Why?'

'It's that arsehole, Scott. He's broken her heart.'

'They were hooking up? I had no idea. Didn't think she was his type.'

'No, that's the thing,' said Izzy. 'He'd been hanging out with her a lot, being all handsome and flirty, and suggesting they pair up for revision sessions. But she looked at his last couple of reports and it's all her work; he'd been ripping her off.'

'I *knew* it! That's what he did to me on the first day.'

'He denied it, of course. Said they were just, "Bouncing ideas off each other". Sounds like it was all bouncing one-way, though.'

'What a dickhead.'

'Yeah. Anyway, we've got bigger fish to fry; how's it going with the research?'

'Good,' I said. I swivelled a book around on the table—a large hardback volume of *Alban's Compendium of Greco-Roman Myths*—and pointed to an entry under 'S':

Satyrs (Greek: σάτυρος sátyros) – creatures of the wild, part man and part beast, having the legs of a horse or goat.

'Is that what you saw?' asked Izzy, pointing at the accompanying illustration.

'I think so. Although he was older – a silverback.'

We carried on reading:

Satyrs first appeared in Greek literature around the 8th century BC. They are closely associated with Dionysus, the Greek god of wine and celebration.

'Dionysus – didn't Champ say something in one of our lectures about having run-ins with him?' I asked.

'Yeah, I think so. And listen to this…'

Satyrs revel in wine, music and dancing. Known for their animalistic behaviour, these muscle-bound creatures have been known to drunkenly rip apart villages, trampling crops and looting food. They are famous for their insatiable lust, rarely take no for an answer, and are often depicted with a permanent erection.

'Holy shit', said Izzy. 'These guys are the original fuckbois!'

I laughed, then shuddered. Izzy put the book down and gave me a hug.

'I still can't believe what you did,' she said. 'You saved my life with that crazy stunt. Promise me you'll never do something that stupid again.'

'I very much hope I don't have to.'

She stared at the illustration. 'What the hell was that thing doing here, anyway? How did he bypass the security?'

'I don't know, but it must be to do with the device he was holding. The book says they're feral and animalistic, but the one I tangled with wasn't like that; he was smart, intelligent.'

'Do you think they've got their own MythTec?' asked Izzy.

'I don't know,' I sighed. 'But if they do… we're all in a lot of trouble.'

TWELVE

'Road trip!' cried Administrator Champ, beaming at us.

It was a week after the rooftop incident, and Izzy, Scott and I had been assigned to shadow Champ for the afternoon. We were standing in a large underground garage in the North Wing basement. Champ wore a long tweed overcoat and held an umbrella in the crook of his arm. Behind him was a row of vehicles, each covered by a crisp white tarpaulin.

'Where are we going, sir?' asked Izzy eagerly.

'An ambassadorial meeting. Well, more of a meeting to arrange future meetings, actually. It won't be particularly eventful, but everything is a learning opportunity.'

'But why aren't we doing it here, in a conference room?' Scott asked.

'Well, it's an unusual case. We've been contacted by a group that's been a bit stand-offish of late. A faction of the Greco-Roman myths,' he said, catching my eye. 'They've reached out to us for a conference, so we thought—for various reasons—we should hold it on neutral territory. We'll even be travelling there by conventional means, rather than using a ley line. Ah, there's our driver now.'

Rudy strolled up, whistling, and gave Champ a little salute. 'Afternoon, Chief!' He pulled the sheet from one of the vehicles, revealing the gleaming chassis of a classic London black cab.

'Hop in,' said Rudy cheerfully, sliding into the driver's seat and switching on the yellow roof light. He rolled down the driver's window and stuck his elbow out. 'Won't go south of the river at this time, guv'nor!' he said, much to his own amusement.

'Rudy's driving us?' I asked in surprise. 'Won't that... attract attention?'

Rudy gave me a wink. 'Initiating RDF,' he said, flicking a couple of switches above his head. The taxi's windscreen shimmered for a moment, then Rudy's visage changed to that of a middle-aged man in a cloth cap.

'RDF: Reality Distortion Field,' explained Champ proudly. 'Cutting-edge MythTec. It manipulates the electrochemical signals sent to the brain's occipital lobe, persuading the observer to ignore anything unusual and replacing it with the expected. Hence, from outside the cab, Rudy looks just like a regular human driver.'

'A man sees what he wants to see,' said Rudy, 'and disregards the rest.'

We all climbed in the back, Izzy, Scott and I sliding next to each other on the big leather seat while Champ took the fold-down chair opposite.

Rudy turned on the ignition and the engine purred into life. He flicked another switch on the dashboard and the steering wheel lit up: a giant triskele symbol in a leather-coated outer ring.

A calm computerised voice came over the garage loudspeakers: 'Interphase transit initiated. Please proceed to automotive departure port.'

The car rolled forward towards a large circle of runes carved into the garage's stone floor, coming to a stop directly over them as they began to glow. Rudy pulled up the handbrake but kept the engine revving.

'Fasten your seatbelts,' he ordered.

We strapped in as the taxi began to vibrate, the engine roaring as the wheels spun in place. Rudy slid into second gear, pumped the accelerator, and kept his hand on the parking brake, holding us in position.

'Here we go!' he shouted.

A flash of light, the smell of ozone mixed with burning rubber, and… >*FLÜORGP*<.

Rudy released the brake and we shot forward, materialising on a Hampstead backstreet, tyres finding traction on the tarmac as we sped forward. I looked back through the rear window to see a ramshackle row of old council garages behind us, a glow fading around the front of one of them. Large blue letters were painted on the white garage door: *Keep clear: exit in use at all times*.

We raced through London at breakneck pace, Rudy taking easily to the role of black cab driver, judging by his nominal adherence to road traffic regulations. The reality distortion field seemed to be doing its job; none of the pedestrians paid us any mind, although I noticed a toddler in a buggy staring at us wide-eyed, and later a pair of dogs we passed barked excitedly, straining at their owner's leash.

On the way, Champ held forth on his favourite subject, the Greco-Roman myths. He spoke fondly about them all – except one: Dionysus, the god of wine and ecstasy.

'Sounds pretty good to me,' said Scott.

'In moderation, yes,' agreed Champ. 'But given enough power, Dionysus makes men weak-minded. Drives them to madness and chaos. Our bureau stands in direct opposition to that. We bring civility, order and peace. He would tear all that down if he could.

'It's not Dionysus or his people that we're meeting today, of course,' Champ assured us. 'This will just be a small diplomatic party representing the Greco-Roman pantheon as a whole. One more step in an incremental process. They are not a people amenable to change. It's ironic really; the ancient Greeks understood the importance of progress, but their gods are locked in amber. Ah – here we are!'

Rudy screeched up alongside the pavement and we looked up through wrought iron gates at our destination; the enormous quadrangle of the British Museum, pale white against a clear blue sky. We clambered out, Champ instructing Rudy to return for us in one hour, and he pulled away quickly with a cheery wave, tires squealing.

We made our way across the forecourt towards the South entrance, a row of impressive stone columns topped by a triangle pediment. The elaborate sculptured figures of The Progress of Civilisation gazed down at us as we made our way up the huge stone steps. Inside was the great court, the huge bright-white inner courtyard with its spectacular glass roof.

'Magnificent, isn't it?' grinned Champ. 'Eight million objects displayed across 800,000 square feet, in a building older than the entire USA. Almost puts our HQ to shame, eh? Keep up now.'

He sprinted up steps and along corridors until we reached the section of the museum dedicated to Greece and Rome. At the end was a door that had been roped off, with a sign in front declaring, 'Closed for emergency refurbishments.' A smartly-uniformed guard put out his hand as we approached, but Champ flashed some identification at him, and he saluted sharply, pulling back the rope.

The four of us walked into the middle of a large room, surrounded by marble statues, glass cabinets of ancient vases and pottery, and walls displaying enormous faded murals.

'The ambassadors will be arriving any minute,' said Champ, looking at his watch.

We stood in silent anticipation, Scott shuffling his feet,

Izzy and I eyeing each other nervously. All that talk of Dionysus had us quite on edge. But Champ knew what he was doing, right?

'Here we go,' he said. The lights flickered briefly, the room's temperature seemed to go up for a moment, and then... nothing.

I wasn't sure what I was expecting, but there were no cyclopean ambassadors, no winged horses, not even some dude in a toga.

Champ looked around, puzzled, and checked his watch again. As he was doing so, something caught my eye – a series of figures painted on a giant Greek vase to my left. I recognised them immediately as satyrs. They were dancing around the central figure of Dionysus, a huge bearded man wearing an ivy and grape wreath, and holding a pinecone staff.

But it was the character next to him, the one at Dionysus' shoulder, whispering conspiratorially into his ear, that sent a jolt of fear through me. The painting showed him looking directly out at us, and I recognised his malevolent expression immediately; it was the silverback from the rooftop.

I read the museum label:

Silenus, companion and mentor to Dionysus, and commander of the satyr army.

So, now I knew his name.

Before I could say anything, Champ's voice rang out. 'I say! Did anyone notice this when we came in?'

He was pointing his umbrella at an empty plinth in the middle of the room. No, not quite empty; on it sat a small piece of folded paper. 'I'm sure that wasn't there earlier,' he said as we gathered round. He gave it a gentle poke with the end of his brolly. It didn't explode or burst into flame or anything, so he picked it up and unfolded it.

Inside was written, in a bold calligraphic hand, five words:

'Beware of Greeks bearing gifts.'

It was the same message that the Oracle had given me; no coincidence, I'm sure.

'Oh dear,' said Champ.

'What does it mean?' asked Scott, as Izzy and I exchanged a worried look.

'A warning, perhaps,' he replied. 'Or a threat.'

'I'll signal Rudy to pick us up,' said Champ. 'We must return to HQ immediately.'

We raced out of the room, back through the museum, out through the doors, and down the steps towards the street. Rudy pulled up just as we got there, and we piled into the back of the cab.

'What's up, Chief?' asked Rudy.

'A bad feeling in my gut, old friend. Make haste for Hampstead, and don't spare the horses.'

Rudy tore off, speeding through the streets of Bloomsbury and up towards St Pancras. My mind was racing. I'd never said anything to Champ about the Oracle, and I was now beginning to think that this had been a terrible mistake. Sure, I hadn't wanted to get Izzy or Rudy in trouble—and there had been that talk about Champ's secret—but if I was honest, I'd been protecting myself. It was time to own up and face the music.

'Administrator Champ,' I said, 'there's something I need to tell you…'

'One moment,' he replied. 'I need to speak to HQ'. He flipped open the front of a box by his seat and pulled out a black telephone receiver on a spiral cord. He listened for a moment, frowning. 'Rudy, I'm getting a dead line. Do a system check, will you?'

Rudy tapped at a screen on the front dashboard. 'I'm picking up a lot of interference. Power surges all over the egosystem. Seems to be disrupting communications. Very strange.'

We passed Camden Market, then under the green steel bridge of Camden Lock. Outside, I noticed people on the pavements acting strangely – tilting their heads as if listening for something. As we drove further up the road towards Chalk Farm there seemed to be more of them, swaying together as if in some kind of trance. I could hear music, growing louder, but muffled by the cab's thick windows.

'Hey, look,' shouted Scott, noticing more people up ahead. They were dancing, swinging their limbs around with gleeful abandon. 'It's one of those flash mobs – brilliant!'

I saw him reach out and, before I could protest, hit the button to lower his window. The effect was immediate; intoxicating music filled the taxi. I felt dizzy, ecstatic, and nauseous all at once. We all felt it; Champ looked bewildered, Izzy's eyes were wide with wonder, Scott was grinning like a fool. Up front in the driving seat, Rudy threw his head back and howled. Was he angry? In Pain? No, I realised; he was singing.

The music was enchanting us, invading our senses, making us lose control. The cab began to drift across the lane. I unlocked my seatbelt and dived over to Scott's side of the car, reaching out for the window control. As I pressed the button, Izzy let out a panicked yell from behind me – too late.

The vehicle lurched sideways as if yanked by an invisible cord. I was thrown sideways, landing face-first in Champ's chest and getting an unexpected mouthful of tweed waistcoat.

Then we flipped over.

For a surreal moment I found myself twisting, weightless, in the air, gawping stupidly at Izzy and Scott, their bodies straining against their taut seatbelts. My mind flashed to a video I'd seen of Tom Cruise in the 'vomit comet', filming scenes for one of the *Mission Impossible* movies. 'Thanks, brain,' I thought. 'That's a really useful memory to be bringing up right now. Great crisis management – thumbs-up emoji.'

Then gravity jealously snatched me back down, slamming my soft body against hard metal, and everything went black.

I DON'T KNOW how long I was unconscious, but when I came to, my head was throbbing. There was a high-pitched ringing in my ears, accompanied by a rhythmic thumping. Everything looked strange. Shattered glass everywhere. Why was the floor so weird? It took me a moment to realise that the cab was upside-down.

I could taste blood in my mouth. Oh my God, it was mine! Wait, of course it was mine – who else's would it be? People don't go around bleeding into each other's mouths now, do they? Or maybe they do. I don't know, I've lived a pretty sheltered life.

It occurred to me that I might be suffering from a concussion.

I shook my head, trying to clear my thoughts. I needed to concentrate, to take stock of the situation. Looking around, I saw Izzy's bag lying on the floor. But there was nobody else in the cab – not here in the back, or up front in the driving seat. Surely they hadn't all just abandoned me?

Spots danced in my eyes as I squinted out through the broken side window. There were dozens of people in the street near the car, all dancing strangely, as if not in control of their own bodies.

I couldn't see Scott or Rudy, but I locked in on Izzy immediately. She was in the middle of the road, dancing and twirling like I'd seen her do so many times in the dorm, but now in a strange jerking, drunken manner. Her mouth was open wide, laughing or shouting I think, although I couldn't hear anything over the deafening ringing in my ears.

And there was Champ, staggering around with his hands clasped over his ears, a look of fierce concentration on his face, as if from some massive effort. Then he looked up, staring at something out of my line of sight, and his expression changed to horror. He dropped his hands from his ears and ran full tilt towards Izzy, grabbing hold of her and flinging her to one side.

The next moment a huge red blur filled my vision as the 388 to Hackney Wick thundered past, out of control, sideswiping an abandoned car and careering off down the road.

On the opposite side of the street I saw Izzy and Champ climbing to their feet. They seemed unhurt, but were both laughing now, and dancing, too. They staggered away together, joining the ever-growing crowd, all heading in the same direction.

The ringing in my ears began to recede. I realised that the loud rhythmic thumping—which I'd thought was the frantic beating of my heart—was actually coming from outside the vehicle. It was the enchanting music emanating through the air – a baseline so loud that the gravel on the road vibrated in time.

As the music became clearer, I could feel it reverberating deep in my soul. My legs began to tingle. My fingers drummed on the metal roof. My God, this music! It pulsated within me, its strands coursing through my bloodstream. Beyoncé would claw her eyes out for this tune.

I had to find a way to block it out before it controlled me, too. But how? Another concussion? No, stupid idea. My eyes fell on Izzy's bag on the floor—well, ceiling—of the cab. I turned it upside-down, spilling out its contents, then rifled through them frantically.

'Come on Izzy, tell me you brought it with you...'

Yes! I pulled on her noise-cancelling headphones. Yet, somehow, I could still hear the music; an enchanted earworm burying into my head. I grabbed the iPod, hit 'random shuffle' and turned the volume up to max. The Bee Gee's *Staying Alive* blasted into my ears, almost deafeningly loud, drowning out all other noise. This was probably going to give me tinnitus, but at least I wouldn't turn into a zombie.

I crawled out of the car window and wobbled to my feet. I could see the taxi's skid marks across the road behind me, and the impact where it had hit the curb and the red post box before turning over.

I gazed around at the surrounding chaos. Izzy, Champ, Scott and Rudy were nowhere to be seen, but the crowd of dancing, laughing, glassy-eyed people was growing every minute.

They were flowing towards the circular brick building that I now recognised as the Camden Roundhouse, looming up like an island at the centre of the seething mass. The crowd moved inexorably towards it, drawn in like the tide by the irresistible music emanating from within.

I stared up at the huge posters on the sides of the building, advertising the current show – the hot girl band of the moment: *Sirenz*.

'You've got to be kidding me,' I said.

THIRTEEN

I WOVE MY WAY BETWEEN THE WRECKED AND ABANDONED CARS surrounding the building, dodging the spaced-out people who grabbed at me, laughing. My friends were in that building, enslaved by some mythological power – I knew I must help them, though I had no idea how.

I squeezed through the crowd that were pouring through the entrance, hands held protectively over Izzy's headphones in case they were knocked free. Inside was pandemonium. I couldn't hear the sirens' music, but I could feel it reverberating through the floor, and smell it in the heady stench of sweat in the air.

The girl band was up on stage, faces enraptured and glowing with a strange purple energy. Around them was a seething mass of gyrating bodies, drenched in sweat and vomit and god knows what else. Teens who'd come to party mixed with sharp-suited businesspeople, bearded hipsters, and Lycra-clad bicycle couriers who had been passing by and drawn in by the enchantment.

Those nearest the stage, who had been there the longest, had a look of desperation in their eyes. They were dancing to the point of exhaustion. If I didn't do something quickly, there were going to be heart attacks, or deaths from dehydration.

The song on Izzy's iPod finished and it jumped to the next one: an electro-punk cover of '80s pop standard, *The Rhythm is Going to Get You*. In the half-second gap between the tracks I could feel the lure of the sirens' song, even through the noise-cancelling headphones.

I looked around desperately. Up to my left, bright light was emanating through the long window of the control room. Of course – kill the power, stop the music! Simple.

I located a door marked 'Staff Only' and yanked at the handle – locked, dammit. I scanned the area until I spotted a man in a hi-vis security jacket, who was dancing nearby, vacant-eyed and drooling. I took him by the hands and twirled him around towards the door.

He hugged me, totally blissed out, a string of saliva trailing sideways from the corner of his mouth. Grimacing, I reached into his pocket, found the fob for the door, and swiped it against the panel. A light went green and the door released. I pulled it open with one hand whilst twirling the man away into the crowd, then slipped inside and made my way up the stairs.

The control room was a mess of cables and overturned boxes, with equipment strewn all over the floor. There was nobody here. Whoever was running the show was no doubt now down on the dance floor, caught in the spell.

The huge control panel was covered in a confusing array of knobs and switches. I started flicking some of the more important looking ones, but it didn't seem to make any difference. Then I found the plug sockets and pulled them all out, one after the other – click, click, click. The lights on the control panels faded to black and the system shut down. I whooped in triumph.

I looked out through the wide glass window, down onto the main floor. What the hell? The people were still dancing, the girl band singers were still glowing. Of course; it was mythical energy magnifying their voices, not electricity.

Now what? I mustn't panic; my friends needed me. I scanned the crowd and spotted Rudy right away; Izzy was sitting on his shoulders, arms waving back and forth with the music. They both had that horrible vacant look on their eyes. Near the stage was Scott, grinning stupidly, arms wrapped around a young woman with a similar intoxicated expression. And – yes! There was Champ, near the middle of the throng.

I knew what I had to do. I began searching the room, rummaging frantically through the clutter of equipment until I found what I was looking for: an audio splitter and another pair of bulky, professional-looking headphones.

I took a deep breath, braced myself, and unplugged Izzy's headphones from the iPod. As soon as Izzy's music stopped, I could hear the sirens' intoxicating song penetrating the headphones, calling to me – I think it was getting stronger. It took all my willpower to ignore it, my hands trembling as I plugged the splitter into the iPod, then both sets of headphones into the splitter.

To my relief, Izzy's music returned, flushing my brain with Muse's electronic/classical/progressive rock mashup *Unsustainable* (yeah, I'd been learning some stuff).

I ran back downstairs and pushed through the crowd, making my way towards Champ. Dozens of sweaty faces gazed at me or through me, lost in the ecstasy of their mythical mosh pit. I made it to Champ, grabbed hold of him by his collar, and wrangled the second pair of headphones onto his head.

His expression changed slightly, Izzy's music now fighting with the sirens' song. But Champ still looked half-lobotomised. Had he been under the sirens' influence too long? Was my attempt to free him of the spell too little, too late?

A light flashed on Izzy's iPod: 'Low battery'.

Come on, Emily – think! Maybe different music would help; something more his style? I scrolled through Izzy's app – she had 10,000 songs, right? There must be something suitable here. Aha! I pulled up *Land of Hope and Glory* and blasted it full volume into Champ's ears.

His eyes refocused. His expression changed, first to surprise, then recognition and appreciation. He put his hand on my shoulder and grinned. Administrator Champ was back on the case – he'd know what to do! I looked at the flashing battery light. Whatever it was, we'd better do it fast.

Champ surveyed the scene grimly, quickly taking in the situation while dancers jostled and bashed into us from all sides. We tried to keep them at bay, one hand clamped firmly over our headphones – our lifelines to sanity.

He tapped me on the shoulder and started gesticulating rapidly. I realised he must be using sign language, and shook my head apologetically.

A huge bearded hipster bashed into me, almost knocking me off my feet. Champ shoved him back, pulling me close and pointed to the stage, which was about fifteen feet away through a heaving mass of revellers. I understood – we needed to get over to the girl band.

We linked arms so as not to get pulled too far apart. If our headphones were yanked from the splitter, we were done for. We tried to make a parting through the crowd, but barely made any headway; it was just too tightly packed. Champ and I had to grab hold of each other just to stop ourselves from being knocked over – breaking several bureau guidelines on appropriate co-worker interactions.

It was no good – there was simply no way through. The last dozen feet were packed solid, writhing bodies tightly compressed, arms raised gleefully in the air. Champ looked at them, then turned to me and—to my great surprise—grasped me firmly around the waist. He lifted me bodily up into the air, then turned me sideways and laid me down on top of the crowd.

I felt dozens of hands lifting me, supporting me, tickling and groping. I shuddered. In a flash, Champ was up there next to me, linking his arm with mine.

Following some subconscious impulse, the hands below us began sliding us along, manoeuvring us towards the stage. Crowd surfing on zombies; what a way to spend a Thursday afternoon. We reached the stage and Champ clambered onto it, then hauled me up as I kicked out at a hand that had made its way halfway up my thigh.

There was the girl band: three mini-skirted figures with varying hair colours, all glowing with energy. Their mouths were stretched open in song, eyes as vacant as the revellers below. I looked at Champ questioningly – now what?

Staying close together, we scrambled into the wings at the side of the stage. Leaning up against one side was a white board with a marker pen attached on a string – the 'idiot board' that stagehands use to communicate with performers. Champ grabbed it and began scribbling a message in thick black pen: *Singers possessed by sirens. Must break spell.*

I nodded, took the pen and wrote one word: *How?*

Champ searched through his coat pockets for a moment, then pulled out two red apples, one in each hand. He held them up triumphantly, then handed one to me.

He checked through his other pockets, finding a pencil, a pipe and a handkerchief, none of which seemed to be what he was looking for. He frowned, then clicked his fingers, reached into his front jacket pocket, and pulled out one of the little satellite-dish shaped funnels. He flipped it open and jammed its spike into the apple I was holding.

Champ took me by the shoulders and guided me back out onto the stage. Even in the midst of this chaos, he was using it as a teaching moment. He positioned me six feet away from the sirens—close enough to feel the tremendous heat emanating from them—and lifted my arm, aiming the apple with its little metal funnel right at the singers.

I felt the air around us shift as a new power source was introduced. Champ held me close, supporting my arm. The purple glow around the sirens began to shimmer, then swirl, twisting in the air, drawn towards the apple like smoke being sucked into an extraction vent.

The singers' energy field flickered. I saw the white glaze over their eyes begin to fade as their expressions changed. I could sense their confusion and fear as their human minds started to switch back on. It was working!

Then the golden funnel of energy lurched away from the apple, rearing up as if alive. It swelled, changing colour to an angry red, then lashed out, whipping around us. It flashed and crackled; a lightning storm on stage.

Champ took the apple from my grasp, held it out in both hands, and stepped forward, moving it towards the sirens. It trembled in his grip, as if forced away by some invisible shield – then it exploded with a crack of thunder, knocking Champ backwards into my arms and splattering us both with apple juice.

We lay there on the floor of the stage, the tiny metal funnel spinning like a top in front of us. The singers were back in the grip of the mythical energy, which had returned to its purple colour, wrapping around them even tighter than before.

We climbed back to our feet. Champ looked troubled, his confidence shaken. He wiped apple juice off his hands with his handkerchief and picked up the satellite dish. Grabbing the whiteboard, he wrote: *Too far gone! MythTec alone cannot reverse the enchantment.*

I showed him Izzy's iPod screen; the red battery indicator was flashing. We had barely five minutes left, I reckoned.

Champ took the pen and wrote again: *Human minds floating away. Must bring them back.*

I nodded.

Champ scribbled frantically: *Remind them who they are. Human needs and desires.* Then underneath that, in capitals: *WHAT DO THEY WANT?*

He underlined the last sentence twice and looked at me imploringly. Of course; the aspirations of young female pop stars was hardly Champ's area. It was up to me. I racked my brain. I mean, I wasn't really an expert here either. What do members of a girl band want more than anything else? Fame? Adoration? No, they had both of those in spades. There must be something else – something I could use.

An idea popped into my head. Quite ridiculous, really. Probably wouldn't work. But what the hell, it was worth a try.

I would need someone from the crowd; a particular type. I scanned the audience desperately, looking for a likely candidate. My eyes fell on Scott, who was right near the edge of the stage. I sighed. Yeah; he'd do.

I pointed him out to Champ and motioned that we needed him up here with us. Champ clearly didn't know why, but he didn't question it. We knelt over the edge, each grabbing one of Scott's arms, and awkwardly hoisted him up.

'Ready?' mouthed Champ, over-enunciating so I could read his lips.

I nodded.

He pulled out his second apple, holding the metal funnel at the ready.

Scott was hugging me, blissed out. He ran a hand through my hair, murmuring sweet nothings. I was thankful I couldn't hear what they were.

Champ fixed my eye, mouthed, 'Good luck!' and jammed the funnel into the apple. He dropped to one knee, bracing himself, and pointed it at the girl band.

Once again, the lights flickered, and the energy prickled in the air. The glow waned for a moment, feeling the tug of the apple. I heard the music on the headphones waver and start to fade. The battery was finally dying. Time's up.

I twisted Scott around so he was facing the girl band. As I saw their eyes start to clear again, I shoved him forward and bellowed at them at the top of my lungs: 'HEY GIRLS! THIS GUY'S A RICH FOOTBALLER!'

I saw a flicker of recognition in one of the girls' faces, then another. The energy around them was fluctuating again, taking on a red tint. Then their eyes began to fade again. My heart sank – was it too late?

Suddenly the red haired singer's expression changed. Some primal emotion had been accessed; an elemental reaction triggered. Her eyes cleared and her brow furrowed in determination.

'Hey! I saw 'im first!' she screamed, lunging forward and throwing her arms around Scott.

This seemed to jolt the other two out of their reverie, and they too became suddenly animated. 'Gerroutovit!' shouted the taller one, grabbing at the first singer's long hair and yanking it back.

'Oy! Leave some for me!' shrieked the brunette, leaping onto Scott and wrapping her legs around his waist, causing all four of them to topple to the floor in a writhing heap.

With their singing interrupted, the purple energy was suddenly untethered. It whipped around us furiously, tugging at my clothes and pulling out my headphones. Static electricity filled the air, and I felt a powerful energy rush through my body. Light bulbs popped. A speaker exploded, showering us in sparks.

Champ was kneeling in the eye of the storm, holding the apple above his head with both hands, holding on to it for dear life as it pulsed and vibrated. Purple energy whirled around him, whipping his coat about dramatically. His bulky headphones had been pulled from his head and were twirling around in the wind, the cord tangling around his neck. Sparks from the speaker had hit his coat, setting the tail end on fire.

Then, with a final lurch and an ear-popping screech, the energy was sucked down into the apple, swirling like water down a plughole until every bit of it was gone. The wind stopped and Champ's headphones hit the floor with a thud.

The apple made a low *ping* sound and turned green.

The deafening cacophony of the energy storm had been replaced by an eerie silence that hung over the whole venue. People who had been dancing and thrashing around just moments ago were now looking at each other in confusion, woozy and bewildered, coming down from one hell of a high.

Champ pulled off his coat and stamped out the fire, then held up the red apple in triumph, beaming at me. 'Excellent work, Intern Peasbridge. But I don't understand; what did you do?'

I grinned back at him. 'These manufactured girl bands – most of them just want to be WAGs!'

Champ shook his head, befuddled. 'I have no idea what you are talking about', he laughed, 'but jolly well done.'

'Help!' came Scott's plaintive cry from beneath a tangle of girl band limbs.

The tall blonde singer stood up, staggered over to the edge of the stage and threw up violently. We helped the redhead and brunette up from the floor, then saw to Scott, who didn't seem sure whether this was the worst thing that had ever happened to him, or the best.

Champ went to the front of the stage and addressed the crowd in a commanding but soothing tone. 'No need to be alarmed,' he called out. 'Everything is under control. Please make your way calmly to the exits, assisting each other as best you can. Emergency services are on the way.'

Rubbing their eyes and murmuring groggily, the crowd started to shuffle towards the exits. 'This one's going to take a boatload of paperwork,' Champ muttered, turning back to us.

Izzy, cheeks flushed, had clambered down from Rudy's shoulders, and the two of them pushed their way towards us, against the flow of the crowd. As he passed one dazed hipster, Rudy nimbly swiped the pork pie hat from the man's head and placed it on his own, pulling it down as far as it would go. It was hardly the most convincing disguise, but thankfully everyone seemed too out of it to be paying much attention.

I jumped down from the stage, followed by Scott and Champ, rushing up to Izzy and hugging her tightly.

'Are you okay?' she asked. 'What happened? Hey, is that my iPod?'

'Will someone please tell me what *the hell is going on*?' demanded Scott.

'A mythological manifestation,' said Champ grimly. 'Creatures of legend taking form in the human world. I've not seen anything like this in a very long time. We must get back to headquarters immediately!'

A chill ran through me as I remembered the Oracle's words: *'When you hear the sirens, it will already be too late.'*

FOURTEEN

RUDY SHOULDER-BARGED THE EMERGENCY EXIT, POPPING THE BAR with a snap and nearly taking the door off its hinges.

'Oops, sorry!' he apologised, as we emerged, squinting, into the afternoon sunlight.

We were in an alleyway down one side of the Camden Roundhouse. At the end of the alley, about twenty feet away, we could see a section of the main road, clogged with abandoned vehicles. In the distance came the wail of ambulances and police cars.

'I'll see if the taxi is salvageable,' said Rudy. Before anyone could stop him, he sprinted off towards the road, leaping onto a car roof on all fours, then bounding across the rooftops of other broken vehicles.

'Wait, Rudy, the civilians will see you!' Champ shouted after him. 'Ah well,' he sighed, 'I don't suppose it'll make much of a difference now.'

Champ checked each of us for injuries, and before we knew it Rudy was running back, carrying two bags and an umbrella.

'No good, I'm afraid,' he said. 'The cab's caput, and the road's blocked in all directions. I retrieved our stuff, though.' He handed Champ his umbrella and Izzy her satchel.

'Very well,' nodded Champ, hooking his umbrella over the crook in his arm. 'I'm initiating Emergency Regulation A13-983.'

'Opening a ley line directly into headquarters?' asked Rudy. 'Are you sure, Chief? I mean, the paperwork alone…'

'Desperate times call for desperate measures,' Champ replied. 'Rudy, my briefcase, please.'

Rudy handed him the other bag; a brown suede briefcase with 'MM' embossed on the side. Champ noticed that Rudy was using his left hand.

'Your right arm; is it broken?' Champ asked.

'Just sprained, Chief,' said Rudy, rubbing it. 'Happened when the car flipped over. I'll be fine.'

Champ nodded. 'Good man.' He popped open the bag's clasp, pulled out a MythPad, and started tapping away at it. 'Does everyone still have their lanyards?' he asked.

I grasped the leather rope around my neck and pulled out my triskele. Izzy, Scott and Rudy showed theirs, too.

'All undamaged?' asked Champ, peering at them. 'Good. Thank heaven for small mercies.'

He continued tapping at the MythPad, filling in several forms, then entering a password. He knelt down and placed it on the floor, face up. Golden beams of light shot out from around its edges, burning a circle of Celtic runes onto the dirty ground around it. We stepped back as the symbols on the floor began to sizzle. Our triskeles glowed and I could see Champ's doing the same, its light shining through the fabric of his waistcoat.

Ping. 'Emergency Portal activated,' said a calm computerised voice.

'One person at a time,' said Champ. 'Rudy, you first, then I'll send through each of the interns. Orderly queue, please.'

Rudy stepped into the circle, sniffing suspiciously, his

nostrils twitching. 'Hold up!' he said. 'Something's…' but before he could finish, we heard the familiar >*flüorgp*< sound and he vanished in a puff of ozone.

Where he'd been standing a moment before there was now just a triskele-shaped swirl of purple smoke. It floated in the air for a moment before abruptly bursting into flame. The MythPad gave off a piercing screech of feedback, then shut down.

'System overload,' said the computerised voice. 'Rebooting.'

'Damn!' swore Champ.

'What was that?' I exclaimed. 'Is Rudy okay? Did he get through?'

'Yes,' replied Champ, examining the MythPad, 'but the portal collapsed behind him.'

'Then open another one,' shrieked Scott. 'We… need to get the girls back safely.'

Izzy rolled her eyes.

'No good,' said Champ, tapping at the device. 'The whole system is inaccessible. We're completely locked out.'

'What do we do now, sir?' asked Izzy.

'Hold on a minute,' I said. I ran over to a large green recycling bank at the side of the alley and climbed up onto it. 'Look!' I shouted, pointing. 'Chalk Farm tube station's over there. Hampstead is only two stops away.'

'Public transport?' said Champ dubiously.

'The ley line's down,' I said. 'We'll have to take the Northern.'

'Very well,' he nodded. 'Lead on, Miss Peasbridge.'

We headed out of the alleyway and merged into the crowd that was still exiting the building, nursing injuries and hugging each other.

As we lurched across the road towards the tube station, we passed a young man sitting on the bonnet of a car, holding his bleeding head. Champ stopped for a second, pulling out his handkerchief and putting it in the man's hand, which he placed against the wound. 'Help is coming,' he said in a reassuring tone, as the wail of the ambulances grew nearer.

'I hate to leave them', he said as we hurried onwards. 'But who knows what's happening at HQ – we must make haste.'

I knew Chalk Farm station well; the wedge-shaped building that sat on the intersection between Belsize Park and Primrose Hill. We ran in through the entrance, Champ sliding up to the barriers and tapping his pipe on a round yellow Oyster reader. All the gates sprang open at once, and he darted through, the rest of us following close behind.

We clattered down the escalators, Scott yelling, 'Stand on the right', at slow-moving tourists whilst Champ apologised to everyone he passed; 'Excuse us', 'Official business', 'So sorry.'

'Which way?' Izzy asked as we reached the bottom.

'Northbound – Edgware branch,' I shouted, pointing. We raced down the circular corridor tunnel, lined with its mosaic of beige tiles, passing posters advertising Nike trainers, Starbucks coffee, and the latest album from *Sirenz*.

The corridor split in two at the end. Scott sprinted ahead confidently, urging us onward down the right fork, then left at the next junction. Something about the tunnels was bothering me, but I couldn't put my finger on it.

'Are you sure this is the right direction, Mr Munroe?' asked Champ.

Scott stopped and looked around. 'Yeah, it's definitely this way,' he said, then turned around and looked back the way we came. 'Or this way…'

'Hey,' said Izzy in a worried tone. 'Where are all the other commuters? The tube's usually packed, but there's only the four of us here.'

'Maybe it's been evacuated?' said Scott. 'Because of the accident?'

Izzy frowned. 'I didn't hear any announcements.'

'I don't like this one bit,' said Champ. 'We are going to retrace our steps.' He pointed his umbrella down the corridor. 'Get behind me, please. We will move quickly but carefully.'

We marched back to the previous intersection, but when we got there it looked different to a moment ago. It branched into four corridors – hadn't it been three before?

'The station's layout has changed,' mused Champ. 'Most peculiar.'

'Not good, man,' said Scott, starting to panic. 'Not good.'

I looked down each of the corridors and suddenly realised what had been bothering me. 'Look!' I said. 'The tile patterns on the walls are all different. That one has the beige squares, right? But the one next to it has rectangular tiles with yellow stripes, and that one has a black and green pattern.'

'So?' snorted Scott. 'Hardly the time for interior design criticism!'

I ignored him. 'And the tiles on that one have the Sherlock Holmes silhouettes, which you only get in Baker Street.'

'Emily's right,' said Izzy. 'It's like all the tube stations have been mixed up together. How is that even possible?'

Champ was staring at an information poster on the wall. 'I believe this may provide the answer,' he said solemnly.

It was the tube map – but not the one we were used to, with its thick coloured lines and circles denoting the stations; this one was a confusing network of intercommunicating paths and passages. At a dozen or so places were large red dots, each bearing the legend, 'You are here'.

'It's a maze!' cried Scott. 'We're trapped in a maze!'

'Not a maze,' said Champ, pointing to the foreboding symbol of a bull's head at the very centre of the diagram. 'A labyrinth.'

As if on cue, a monstrous roar reverberated down one of the corridors, echoing off the tiled walls.

'And that, I believe, would be the Minotaur,' said Champ.

'What?' cried Scott. 'Bloody hell, you *have* to get us out of here!'

'I certainly intend to,' Champ replied calmly. 'Hold this a moment, would you?' he said, handing Scott his umbrella.

He took off his tweed jacket and removed his mustard-coloured waistcoat, then tugged at it to find the end of a thread. He wound the end around a screw protruding from a corner of the poster frame, then handed the waistcoat to Izzy.

'Be a dear and unfurl this as we go,' he asked. He folded his jacket over his arm and retrieved the umbrella from Scott.

'Right, let's...' he began, but he was interrupted by another sound echoing down a different corridor. It was shouting and yelling this time, followed by the scream of a young child.

'Form a line behind me,' ordered Champ. 'It seems there are other people trapped down here with us, and they need our help.'

'Wait,' said Scott, appalled. 'We're going *towards* the screaming? This is not our problem, guys!'

'Of course it is,' said Izzy, proudly. 'We're Administrators from Myth Management!'

Champ looked at her, raising an eyebrow.

'...in training,' she added, somewhat less dramatically.

Another scream reverberated down the hall. Champ cocked his head to one side, then pointed down the right-hand corridor. 'This way,' he commanded, and strode off, leading us further into the labyrinth, his umbrella held out in front of him like a sword.

Scott stayed at the back, muttering under his breath, then, hearing screams echoing from behind us, quickly moved to the middle. 'Stay close to me, girls,' he said, unconvincingly. I wished Rudy was still with us.

Izzy unwound the thread from Champ's waistcoat as we went, hooking it around handrails or poster frames whenever we reached a junction, being very careful not to snap it. 'I don't know how long this is going to last, guys,' she said.

Every time we thought we were getting closer to the yells and screams they seemed to come from a different direction. Were we getting nearer, or further away?

Another huge roar echoed down the corridor – but this one was different. It kept going, getting deeper and louder. 'That's no monster', I said, relieved. 'That's a tube train.'

'We must be near a platform,' said Izzy.

I could feel the wind whipping down the corridor at us, forced along by the oncoming train. Then something small and grey darted towards us, scampering between my ankles.

'Agh! Tube rat!' I yelled.

'Oh, Emily, it's just a little mouse,' chuckled Izzy. Then she and Scott started screaming as dozens more came pouring around the corner, scurrying over our feet, fleeing desperately from whatever was back down there.

'Keep moving!' Champ ordered, leading us onwards.

The wind was blasting our faces even harder now and the noise was deafening. We turned a sharp corner and found ourselves on a tube platform as a train barrelled past, only a few feet away. Wheels screeched against steel rails in an anguished wail that reminded me of the pipes in our dorm room walls – how I wished I was back there now.

Champ was shouting something over the cacophony, but I could barely hear him. Then the tube train disappeared into the tunnel, newspapers blowing in its wake, and we were left in a sudden silence.

'Administrator, I'm afraid we've run out of waistcoat,' said Izzy, tying the end of the mustard-coloured thread to a wooden bench.

'End of the line,' I whispered under my breath.

The Tannoy crackled to life – or perhaps it had been on the whole time, but we hadn't been able to hear it. It spat out a mismatched jumble of recorded announcements: *'Please mind the delay,'* it said calmly. *'Due to passenger action, tickets will be accepted on planned engineering works.'*

There was another scream, much closer now, followed by a yell for help. From around the long, curved platform came a family of four, barrelling towards us at top speed.

'A bear!' wailed the man. 'A bear's escaped from the zoo! Run for your lives!'

He was dressed in a garish Hawaiian shirt and clutched a suitcase with a straw donkey strapped to the front. His wife was right behind him, dragging two young boys along by their arms.

'It's not a bear, it's a monster!' wailed the eldest child, a petrified nine-year old.

'Yeah! Monster! Best holiday *EVER!*' shouted his delighted younger brother.

'Over here!' yelled Champ. 'Get behind me, please'.

They ran past us, then skidded to a stop, the petrified adults gasping for breath. I gave them my best reassuring smile.

'Are you the transport police?' asked the mother, hugging her children close.

'Not exactly,' I said.

'Don't worry, we're professionals,' said Champ. 'We'll soon have the situation under control.' He started moving slowly along the platform.

'I should probably stay here and look after these civilians,' suggested Scott.

Champ ignored him and carried on inching along the curved platform, his umbrella pointed out in front, while Izzy and I followed close behind. As more of the platform slowly came into view, a huge dark shape revealed itself, and my heart leapt into my throat.

The Minotaur – eight feet tall, with jet-black leathery skin and ferocious red eyes. The head of a bull set upon the body of a steroid-addicted mountain gorilla. Its deadly-looking horns glinted under the fluorescent lighting as it thrashed around in a circle, confused and furious.

The stench of it hit me even from a distance: sweat, blood, and fear. Its torso was bare, but its bottom half was clad in a bizarre patchwork of human clothes, as though someone had sewn together random scraps of suit trousers, jeans, and what looked like a tartan skirt.

We stared at the beast in awe.

'I don't suppose you've got any more apples?' I whispered to Champ.

'Sadly not,' he replied.

Above the creature's head, a digital arrivals board updated, the fluorescent orange dots forming the words 'Train Approaching'. There was a distant rumble and screech of metal. The wind whipped up again, disturbing a discarded can of Sprite, which rolled off the edge of the platform and onto the tracks.

'You'd better take this,' whispered Champ, handing me his umbrella. 'If the train stops, get everyone onto it,' he instructed, not taking his eyes off the Minotaur.

'What are you going to do?' I asked.

'I'm going to take the bull by the horns,' he replied, adjusting the jacket draped over his arm.

Really, I thought: puns? At a time like this?

At that moment, the Minotaur looked up, noticing us for the first time. Its blood red eyes narrowed, and twin plumes of steam snorted from its huge nostrils.

It bellowed—more in anguish than anger—then it shifted its weight, put its head down, and charged right for us.

FIFTEEN

EVERYTHING WENT INTO SLOW MOTION AS THE MINOTAUR rushed towards us on all fours, its massive leathery torso heaving, clothes tearing around its rippling muscles.

The train clattered into the station alongside it as if in a race, quickly overtaking the creature at first, then drawing level as it slowed down, brakes screeching. And there was Champ, off like a shot, running head-on at the Minotaur, a beast three times his size. Was it bravery or stupidity? I really couldn't say.

I squinted as the front of the train shot by, blasting me with wind and dirt. Champ had almost reached the Minotaur; he had his jacket taut between his hands, holding it up in front of him like a bullfighter's cloak. The creature roared, but as razor-sharp horns met tweed, Champ placed his foot on a bench and flipped acrobatically over the beast's head. The jacket remained pinned on the prongs of its horns, covering the Minotaur's eyes and obscuring its vision.

Landing in a perfect dismount on the other side, Champ turned, wedged his back against the platform wall, and jammed both feet against the Minotaur's rear. He shoved as hard as he could, pushing the beast forward and slamming its head into the side of the still-moving tube train with a resounding clang. The movement of the train twisted the Minotaur's head to the side, pulling it over, then slamming the beast to the floor.

'Holy shit!' shouted Izzy. I enthusiastically concurred.

Champ removed his torn jacket from the unconscious Minotaur's horns. We stared at the beast lying with its head next to the words, 'MIND THE...', painted in faded yellow stripes on the platform floor.

It had been a strange day.

The Tannoy resumed its jumbled narration: '*Stand clear of the replacement bus services,*' it squawked. '*A good service is operating on all other gaps.*'

The train doors beeped open, revealing a half-dozen bewildered passengers. 'Excuse me,' said one man, leaning out. 'Is this Mornington Crescent?' Then, 'Oh my!' as he noticed the unconscious beast lying at his feet.

'Everyone on the train, please,' instructed Champ loudly. 'This stop is not in service.' He looked over at us. 'Tactical withdrawal, chaps – let's get these people away before our friend wakes up.'

I looked behind us. Scott was already on board, yelling in a panicked voice at the family of holidaymakers, who were still standing on the platform, mouths agape.

Izzy and I ran back and jostled them in through the nearest set of doors, which, preparing to close, had already begun their urgent beeping.

We sat them down in the seats as the train slowly began to move, its engine straining. There was a commotion coming from further down the carriage, next to the other set of doors. To my relief I saw that Champ had gotten on board safely, and was now trying to calm the alarmed group of passengers.

'Just what do you think you're playing at?' complained an

officious-looking woman, jabbing at Champ's chest. 'Some of us have important jobs to get to, you know!'

'I can assure you that the situation is quite under control, madam,' replied Champ in a placid tone. 'If you'd like to take a seat on these…' he frowned in distaste, 'rather gaudily patterned seats, I'm sure we can get you all to your destinations forthwith.'

As we pulled away, I could see the platform through the moving carousel of carriage windows. For a second I thought I saw something: a dark shape rising from the floor. Then we entered the tunnel, and the view through the windows became a dark blur.

'Administrator Champ?' I said. 'I think…'

But I didn't get to finish. A terrifying roar came thundering down the tunnel. The Minotaur had woken up, and it did not sound happy. I wondered what the average speed of a tube train was, and whether that could be matched by an eight-foot pissed-off bull-monster with a score to settle.

The woman stopped mid-rant, her finger stalled in the air, her face suddenly white. Champ took charge immediately, ordering everyone in our carriage to move up towards the front section of the train. Terrifying roars echoed down the tunnel behind us, punctuating his instructions. He didn't need to ask twice.

Izzy, Scott, and I herded the passengers into the next carriage as quickly as we could. There are several types of tube trains in service on the London Underground, and this one was from the older stock; the ones that had small connecting doors between carriages. Unfortunately, this meant that we had to open our door, reach across the small gap between the carriages, then open the other one before stepping over the rattling gap. This created a bottleneck as passengers fussed and panicked.

We ushered them across, instructing them not to look

down at the track whooshing dangerously by beneath their feet. A man near the back of the crush frowned, jabbing his finger at a sticker on the door's sliding window. 'This states quite clearly that the doors are not to be used in transit,' he stated officiously. Another roar echoed from the back of the train, followed by the sound of metal being ripped apart.

'Up to you, mate,' said Scott as he jumped between carriages.

The man followed him quickly, his objections soon forgotten.

'That's the lot, keep them moving,' boomed Champ, who had stayed at the back of the group, checking for stragglers. 'Excellent work, interns. Grace under pressure,' he said, trying to keep our spirits up. 'A bit of on-the-job training, eh?'

We shepherded everyone up along the next carriage, which was mostly empty, then into the one after that, bringing extra passengers along as we went. All the time we could hear crashing and metal scraping noises coming from the rear.

'That thing must be hanging onto the back of the train,' I said. 'Trying to claw its way in.'

There was a loud clang, and the scraping noises stopped. Then a roar of victory mixed with the thundering of the train.

'It's through!' yelled Izzy.

We stared back along the tube train, trying to get a decent view through the gaps of the connecting doors. The winding track swung the carriages in and out of view, but every so often they lined up and we could make out the Minotaur's huge bulk thundering its way towards us.

The beast's head scraped the ceiling, smashing overhead lights with its horns and sending sparks flying. The snaking track and flickering neon conspired to create a nightmarish vision where the beast was visible only every so often, revealed like lightning flashes in a storm – nearer each time.

Thankfully, the beast was so large that it could barely fit

through the connecting doors. It had to hurl itself against the metal frames until they bent enough for it to force itself through. The train fishtailed around another corner. I don't know which was worse: being able to see it behind us as it gained in fits and bursts, or only being able to hear the roaring and the anguished wail of twisting metal.

The last of the passengers jumped across the gap into the next carriage, followed closely by Scott. I put one foot across the divide and stepped over, looking back, past Champ, just as the train straightened up again.

I could see the Minotaur clearly now – just one carriage away. Blood was smeared down one side of its colossal head. It looked furious.

'This is the last carriage!' Izzy shouted from up ahead. I turned to look. She was right – there was nowhere left to go.

I heard a click behind me and turned to see Champ closing the connecting door from the other side. I stared at him through the sliding window.

'As soon as you hit the next station, evacuate the train,' he ordered. 'I'll keep our friend here busy.' Then he turned and made his way slowly back down the carriage, towards the crashes and roars, once again armed with nothing but his umbrella.

I felt a hand on my arm; it was Scott, pulling me back. 'Come on, we've got to go,' he yelled. 'This is crazy. We're not trained for this.'

I watched Champ as he disappeared into the flickering lights of the carriage.

'Emily,' said Scott, his voice suddenly low and calm.

'What?'

He looked me in the eyes, his expression serious. I could tell what he was thinking – this was his big moment, just like in the movies.

'Do you trust me?' he asked.

'No.'

'Then take my hand!' he exclaimed, grabbing my wrist.

He paused for a second, surprised. 'Wait – what did you say?'

'Of course I don't trust you, Scott,' I replied, pulling my hand away. 'You have the morals of a velociraptor.'

He puffed his chest out indignantly. 'You know what your problem is, don't you?'

'Yes,' I said calmly. Then I turned away, opened the door and marched back into the lower carriage, with no idea what I was going to do next.

* * *

I WAS HALF-WAY to Champ when the Minotaur burst through the bent door frames and into the carriage, bellowing at the top of its lungs. Seething with fury, it hurtled towards Champ, crashing through vertical steel poles, pinging them out like toothpicks.

Champ wasn't about to attempt the bullfighter routine again. Even if the beast was dumb enough to fall for the same trick twice, there was no room to manoeuvre in such a confined space. Instead, he planted one foot firmly behind him and pointed his umbrella at the approaching creature. Aha! I'd been wondering what his Myth Management umbrella would do; fire a tranquilliser dart, or a MythTec laser beam, I expected.

Champ popped open the umbrella and began spinning it around quickly. 'You are getting sleepy,' he commanded.

Christ.

The Minotaur smacked the umbrella out of Champ's hands, snorting with anger, then picked him up by the front of his shirt. It hurled Champ against a window, which shattered with the impact, breaking into a pattern of tiny glass squares. The pieces showered down around Champ as he fell hard onto the row of chairs, striking his head on an armrest.

Champ's body lay slumped and unmoving. The Minotaur ripped a handrail from the ceiling, stood over Champ, and lifted it up, ready to strike.

It seemed pretty surprised when the fire extinguisher foam hit it.

I had spotted the bright red extinguisher in the wall compartment when I'd entered the carriage, and had grabbed it instinctively. Not that it did much good; I'd managed to blind the beast for a moment, but now it would turn its wrath on me.

Wiping the foam from its face with the back of a huge leathery hand, the Minotaur stared at me in almost comical disbelief. I lifted the fire extinguisher up, ready to use it as a club, but didn't get the chance. The beast lunged in my direction, gripped me by the throat, and lifted me up in the air, leaving my feet dangling. Then it slammed me against the tube's sliding doors, which I felt buckle behind me.

I grabbed hold of the creature's muscular arm with both hands, trying to relieve the pressure on my throat. *Choking to death on a tube carriage would be a ridiculous way to go,* I thought, with a surreal sense of déjà vu.

I couldn't breathe. My mind was whirling, synapses firing desperately, thoughts bouncing around my skull with nowhere to go. The Minotaur could crush my neck in an instant. Why was I still alive? Was it toying with me? Or was it something else – could I detect some hesitation?

I felt my consciousness slipping away, my mind only half-tethered to my body. Wait, I told myself – *use this*! Remember the meditation session in the garden. Close your eyes, reach out, make a connection.

I felt its aura immediately – well, I could hardly miss it. It was huge and chaotic; a tumultuous whirlpool of emotions. I could sense the rage emanating from it like a physical force. But there was also confusion, frustration... helplessness.

I could hear a cacophony of voices, all screaming at once: 'Stand on the left, dammit!' 'I'm going to be late!' 'Goddamn boss, can't treat me like this!' 'So bloody crowded I can't even think!'

Maybe it could hear me, too? 'Be calm,' I said in my mind, as soothingly as I could. 'I hear you. I feel your pain. I understand.' I opened myself up, attempting to touch its aura with my own, trying to envelop it in a kind of astral hug.

I felt a shift immediately. Its aura seemed to soften. The snorting of air from those huge nostrils slowed. 'I'm here to help,' I said, more confident now. 'You don't have to be scared.'

I felt the grip on my throat relax slightly. I opened my eyes; the Minotaur was staring at me, chest heaving slowly. I looked back into its eyes, full of compassion. It lowered me to the ground gently and let go of my neck, then sank to its knees.

Part of me wanted to run, then. But I fought the instinct and leant forward, embracing the beast tightly, feeling the pumping of its colossal heart.

'You can rest now.' I said, my voice croaking. 'It's over. Everything is going to be okay.'

The creature let out a long, strange wail of exhaustion. It shuddered under me, then its body seemed to somehow shift and separate, coming apart in my arms.

I stepped back in shock and watched as a glowing gold energy dissipated from it, and its form separated into five human figures—three men and two women—who slumped to the floor, unconscious.

Champ climbed down from the row of seats, his mouth agape. 'Good lord!' he said, holding his injured head. 'A full reversal, with no MythTec! How did you manage it?'

At that moment, Scott reappeared, wielding the

holidaymaker's suitcase above him like a weapon. 'Stand back,' he bellowed dramatically. 'I'll save you!' Then, looking around, 'Oh, has he gone? Well, lucky for him, really.'

'Yeah, great timing,' I said, checking the unconscious commuters' pulses, then moving each of them into the recovery position. They were murmuring to themselves, starting to regain consciousness.

Light burst through the carriage windows as the train pulled into the next station. The driver's voice came over the intercom. 'The next station is… uh… Cockfosters?' he said, with some confusion. 'This train will definitely be terminating here.'

'Cockfosters?' Scott said. 'That's not even on the same line.'

'Labyrinth got us all tangled up,' said Champ. 'But it looks like everything's back to normal now,' he gestured to the tube map on the wall outside, which had returned to its usual design.

The doors beeped and slid open. 'All passengers please disembark,' came the driver's voice over the Tannoy. Nobody needed any encouragement; they were pouring out of the front carriage, yelling at each other and heading for the stairs.

Izzy came running down the platform, the family of holidaymakers in tow. 'Em!' she gasped. 'Are you okay? What happened?'

'We had a little trouble', said Scott causally. 'The Minotaur's gone now – but it hasn't heard the last of Scott Munroe.'

'It hasn't heard the first of you,' I muttered.

'Can I have my suitcase back, please?' asked the dad, pointing at it.

'Oh, yeah – here you go,' said Scott.

'Look, I don't really understand what just happened,' said the dad. 'But I think we owe you our lives. So, thank you.'

He pulled the straw donkey from the strap on the front of

the suitcase. The toy had a goofy look on its face and was wearing a T-shirt bearing the slogan, 'I love Cyprus'.

'Here,' he said. 'This was going to be for Grannie Mary, but you can have it.' He thrust it into Scott's arms, then hurried his family down the platform, joining the other passengers in the scrum for the exits.

'Another illegal breach of mythological energy,' said Champ, shaking his head angrily. 'It shouldn't even be possible. First the sirens, now the Minotaur. Both Greco-Roman myths. There's no doubt now; my old adversary Dionysus is behind this.'

Izzy was looking at Champ's MythPad, which she'd been carrying in her bag since we left the Roundhouse. 'Look, it's rebooted,' she exclaimed. 'And the ley lines are back up!'

'Excellent! No time to waste,' said Champ, taking it from her and entering his password. He placed the MythPad on the ground and the purple lasers shot out as before, creating glowing symbols on the carriage floor.

'We can't be sure it'll stay open,' said Champ. 'So as soon as the portal is active, we're all going through together. Link arms – that's it. On three, we'll jump into the circle. Ready?'

I held on to them tight, Champ on one side and Izzy on the other, Scott opposite.

'One!' called out Champ.

Our triskele lanyards glowed.

'Two!'

A bright golden light enveloped the carriage.

'Three!'

Ping went the MythPad, and we jumped forward. I felt the familiar energy swirling around us, twisting my stomach.

>*Flüorgp*<. Ozone. Wood polish.

We collapsed in a tangled heap on the floor of the HQ foyer.

Alarms were blaring all around us as panicking

administrators rushed back and forth, an agitated flock of tweed, yelling contradictory instructions at each other.

Up on the ceiling, the fresco of myths and legends was awash in a sea of red warning messages, each screaming for our attention in all-caps.

'Out of the frying pan…' said Izzy, not letting go of my arm.

SIXTEEN

'Chief! Girls! Thank goodness you're all okay!' gasped Rudy, running over to us, his right arm in a sling. 'I've been trying to get a lock on you, but couldn't-', he stopped short, noticing Champ's bloodied shirt. 'Blimey, what happened to you?'

'No time to explain,' said Champ. 'What's the status here?'

'It's bad, Chief. Power surges all over London. You got through just in time; Director Hinson has ordered a full lockdown.'

Champ picked up the MythPad from the floor and handed it to Izzy. 'Look after this again, please, Ms Hirway,' he said. He grabbed a long tweed coat from a nearby stand and pulled it on in one smooth movement.

'We're experiencing an Alpha Level Incident,' he said. 'To the Control Room at once – you too, Rudy, I don't want us getting separated again.'

The five of us raced along the corridors, Champ's coat billowing around him dramatically. Administrators and secretaries stampeded past, faces ashen with fear, folders of documents clutched to their chests and loose papers fluttering behind them. Red strobe lights flashed in every corridor, accompanied by the urgent wail of klaxons.

We ran as fast as we could, Champ leading us along winding corridors and into an area of the building I'd never seen before. Soon we arrived at the entrance to the Control Room: two huge interlocking steel doors that sat incongruously in the wood-panelled wall.

A pair of large blue-uniformed security guards stood either side of the doors. They eyed me and the other interns suspiciously, then their eyes fell on Rudy.

'No non-humans,' said one guard, pointing at him.

'He's with me,' declared Champ as he marched towards the door, not slowing down.

'But sir, our orders…'

'Damn your orders – make way!'

The guards looked at each other, then one shrugged and hit a button. The huge doors slid open and we piled through into the Control Room, the entrance slamming shut behind us.

The room was even more chaotic than the rest of the building. A dozen white-suited technicians fretted at control panels, pulling levers and turning dials desperately. Others darted between the many bookshelves, filing cabinets, and reference card drawers that were arranged in concentric circles around the tree, frantically leafing through books or flipping through binder-clad manuals.

I stood rooted to the spot, gazing up in awe at the gigantic tree that grew up through the floor and spread out above us, its leafy canopy barely contained by the domed glass ceiling.

I'd seen the Tree of Knowledge before, of course, back on my first day, which seemed like a lifetime ago now. But that had been from the other side of the thick Perspex window; this was a completely different experience. The Tree's power permeated everything, washing over and through me. Even through the screeching of the alarms I could hear its background hum, like the murmur of a million far-away voices.

I saw from her expression that Izzy could feel it, too. Rudy looked over at me, smiling serenely. 'A cathedral,' he said, a tear in his eye. His MythTec bracelet was glowing red and beeping shrilly, adding another alarm to the cacophony in the room.

'Switch that alarm off,' ordered Champ. 'Switch all of them off, damn it, I can't hear myself think.'

A technician tapped at a control panel and the room turned mercifully quiet.

Thornhill and Director Hinson looked up in surprise. They were standing on a raised steel platform around the base of the tree's huge trunk, where the main control panel was situated.

'Champ!' shouted Hinson with obvious relief. 'Thank goodness you're here.'

'Nice of you to join us,' said Thornhill tersely. 'Whilst you've been off on a jolly with your interns, we've been countering multiple breaches all across the egosystem.'

'Yes, we experienced a couple of them first-hand,' replied Champ, striding over.

He leapt up the metal steps onto the platform, studied the monitors keenly, then quickly took control, issuing instructions to white-robed technicians in his steady, commanding voice. He moved swiftly from one terminal to another, his fingers moving rapidly at the keyboards, flipping switches and twirling dials, like a conductor who could play all the instruments.

'Dionysus is behind this, I'm sure of it,' Champ intoned gravely. 'I believe he's made alliances with other myths and is sowing confusion across the city.'

'But why?' asked Hinson, flabbergasted. 'And how is this even possible? Our MythTec should have the entire egosystem locked down.'

Champ shook his head. 'Clearly, he has found a way to penetrate our defences. Intern Peasbridge warned us that one of Dionysus' men had accessed the building,' he said, looking at me. 'But we didn't take it seriously enough.'

Thornhill slammed his fist on a control panel. 'Dionysus must be crazy!' he raged. 'He'll never get away with this. Once we regain control, the penalties against his realm will be extreme. A hundred years of sanctions, his influence reduced to a trickle for generations.'

Champ stopped, his fingers hovering over a keyboard. 'But he knows that, doesn't he? So… why do this? Even for someone as impetuous as Dionysus, it doesn't make sense.'

'Everything's going to be fine,' said Hinson. 'No need to panic. Dionysus can't make any permanent changes to the egosystem without access to the Tree – and there's no way he's getting in here.'

'And even if he did, there are rules, precedents…' said Champ, turning and scanning the room with a worried look. His face went white as his eyes landed on Scott, and the souvenir donkey that he was still holding under his arm.

'Oh no,' Champ whispered.

The stuffed donkey vibrated under Scott's arm. Something inside it began to pulsate and glow. I stared at it, a horrible, sickly feeling developing in the pit of my stomach as realisation dawned.

A wooden horse.

A gift from Greece.

The echo of a story, an ancient path well-trodden.

Scott dropped the donkey in alarm, but instead of falling to the floor, it stayed hovering there in mid-air, its belly swelling unnaturally. He took several steps backwards, his mouth agape.

With a sudden bang, the donkey burst apart, scattering us with fragments of straw and pieces of torn T-shirt. A strange object the size of a cricket ball was floating there now, glowing with purple energy. It was a peculiar looking thing; absurd and unnatural. It looked for all the world as if someone had 3D printed a computer icon of a bunch of grapes; seven perfect circles around a stalk bearing a single green leaf, all encompassed by a thick black outline.

'Grab it,' shouted Champ, bounding down the steps from the raised platform towards us.

Izzy and I were rooted to the spot in shock. Scott had backed up several feet against a row of filing cabinets. From the corner of my eye, I saw the blur of Rudy running towards us, arms outstretched to grasp the floating icon. It flared brightly just as he got close, and he yelped in pain as it burnt his hands.

The icon shot rapidly up into the air, out of reach, and hung there for a moment, spinning slowly as if orientating itself. Then it surged across the room, heading straight for the Tree of Knowledge.

Champ, who had almost reached us now, skidded to a halt as the glowing purple object streaked over his head. He leapt up and grasped wildly for it as it passed, but only succeeded in snatching fistfuls of air.

The icon flew towards the platform, passing Director Hinson at tremendous speed, burning off the side of his clipboard as it went. I heard Champ yell, 'No!' as it reached the main data monitor in the base of the trunk.

The grapes icon fragmented on impact, breaking into large then smaller glowing cubes, 3D pixels that shot through the air and penetrated the screen.

We all watched in dismay as a glowing purple energy rippled through the monitor, then phosphorescent veins snaked out along the Tree's trunk, spreading like poison.

'*Recalibration in progress*,' said the calm computerised voice.

'The egosystem is compromised!' yelled Hinson, staring at it in horror.

'Evacuate the building!' cried Thornhill.

I felt a crackle of static in the air. The fillings in my teeth were hurting. Izzy and I looked at each other in horror.

'It's too late,' said Champ, who had reached the base of the tree and was looking at the readouts in dread. 'We're being breached!'

>*flüorgp*<

>*flüorgp*<

>*flüorgp*< >*flüorgp*< >*flüorgp*<

Portals were opening all over the Control Room, ripping through the fabric of the air as they expanded in size. Horrifying figures poured through them: dozens of satyrs holding swords or spears. At the back of one of the groups, a tall figure barked orders, and my blood went cold as I recognised the cruel face of the silverback satyr, Silenus.

'Take the room,' he commanded.

His soldiers fanned out, seizing the nearest technicians and forcing them to the floor. Thornhill leaped down from the raised platform and ran as fast as his legs could carry him, diving behind a set of bookshelves to our right – the opposite side of the room from the exit. The little coward couldn't even run away properly.

Rudy took the opposite approach, letting out a huge roar and rushing towards the invading satyrs. He grabbed the end of a long wooden desk and picked it up as he ran, scattering books and instruments into the air. He swung it around like an enormous bat, swiping it into a group of satyrs and knocking them flying. Another swathe charged at him from the other side and he swung the table back at them, too, making contact with a loud crack that shattered the table, sending splinters flying.

A third group made it past Rudy, and three of them were heading right at Izzy and me; a particularly brutish creature out in front. Scott was nowhere to be seen, having legged it as soon as the portals opened. I looked at Izzy in alarm – what could we do? We had no weapons, no way of defending ourselves.

The nearest satyr was almost upon us, bloodlust in his eyes, his sword raised in the air ready to strike. Then he slammed to a halt, colliding suddenly with a golden glowing energy field; a shield in the shape of a swirling triskele symbol, which had appeared in front of him.

To my utter astonishment, the shield was emanating from a triskele lanyard clenched in the fist of Administrator Thornhill, who had stepped out in front of us defensively. He was chanting, reading from a book held open in his other hand; the shield thickening and enlarging as he spoke. The satyr staggered backwards, shaking his stunned head. Thornhill looked at us, fear etched on his face, and said one word: *'Run!'*

He slammed the shield into the satyr again, then, as the two other soldiers reached us, swung it hard to the right, then to the left, countering their attacks.

Izzy and I did as we were told and ran. The exit was on the other side of a room full of rampaging satyrs, so we scrambled to the back corner and took refuge behind one of the huge freestanding bookcases. We crouched there in terror, peering through the gap above a row of hardbacks. Should we try and help? I had barely escaped with my life from my encounter with Silenus, so what could the two of us do, unarmed, against an army of these monsters?

From our hiding place, we watched our friends and colleagues do battle. Champ had disarmed a satyr and was using its sword to combat a group of others. Thornhill was trying to protect other administrators with the triskele shield. Rudy was fighting tooth and nail in the thick of it. I saw him lift a bookcase above his head and fling it at Silenus, barely missing him.

More soldiers poured through the portals, their cloven hooves clattering against the wooden floor. Our friends fought valiantly, Champ parrying expertly, Rudy swinging sledgehammer punches and snapping spears in half with his bare hands. But the sheer number of satyrs quickly overwhelmed them.

I cried out in horror as I saw Rudy fall to the floor under a bevy of blows, then Thornhill and Champ were disarmed and forced to their knees at sword point.

Silenus' army dragged them to a group in the middle of the floor, where they had corralled Hinson and all the white-coated technicians. They forced them all to kneel, hands behind their heads, brutally striking anyone who moved too slowly for their liking.

Silenus surveyed the room with a sneer, then shouted a command. With a deafening >*FLÜORGP*<, a huge portal opened right in front of the Tree of Knowledge's trunk. Through its shimmering maw stepped a giant bearded figure, dressed magnificently in flowing robes, a laurel wreath on his head, and a powerful-looking staff grasped in his hand.

Champ was kneeling on the floor at the edge of the group of prisoners. The satyr guarding him pulled his hair back roughly, forcing him to look up at the bearded man.

'Dionysus,' said Champ, calmly.

'Hello, Champ,' Dionysus grinned, his voice deep and treacly. 'It's been a long time. I've been looking forward to seeing you again.' He pointed his staff and a bolt of energy shot out, ripping up the floor in front of Champ, knocking both him and the satyr guard flying. Champ skidded backwards towards our hiding place and crashed into a nearby bookcase, shelves breaking and books toppling down around him.

'My God!' cried Hinson.

'Not yours, old man,' grinned Dionysus, then threw back his head and roared with laughter.

Behind him, I could see the Tree of Knowledge being infected by their virus. The purple veins were slowly reaching out along its trunk, hitting one monitor after another, changing their readouts and sending corrupted data scrolling wildly across the screens.

Silenus had a quizzical look on his face. His nostrils twitched, as if detecting a familiar scent, then his eyes narrowed in suspicion. He snatched a spear from one of the other satyrs and started moving slowly in our direction, scanning the room keenly.

'He knows we're here,' I whispered to Izzy. 'We have to do something – quickly.'

Izzy looked at the MythPad in her hands, the one Champ had handed her after we materialised at HQ.

'The ley line app is still open,' she said, her eyes gleaming.

'Can you open a portal out of here?'

'I think so!'

Her fingers flew over the interface, calculating coordinates and entering instructions. Top marks in Administrator Hicc's Celtic Myths – my hero!

Izzy hit the last button and a modal appeared on the screen with Administrator Champ's name and an instruction: *Please enter password.*

We looked at each other, then over at Champ, who was lying in a pile of books and broken shelving just a dozen feet away.

Crouching in our hiding place, I peered through the crooked gap above the row of books. Silenus was moving closer to us, sniffing the air. Then he stopped and smirked, displaying his sharp yellow teeth, and started walking straight towards us.

Dionysus had stopped laughing now, and was glaring at Champ from across the room. 'Any last words before I end your pitiful life?' he taunted.

Champ pushed himself up onto one arm, turning to face his old enemy. As he did so, his eyes met ours for a brief moment. 'Darjeeling,' he said.

'What? The *tea*?' Dionysus spat, shaking his head in disgust. 'You English really are the most ridiculous of creatures. You conquer other realms, pillage them, steal their resources, then adopt them as a symbol of your "enlightened" culture. Astounding hypocrisy – even for humans. And the worst thing about this ridiculous drink of yours? *It isn't even alcoholic!*'

Dionysus lifted his staff again and pointed it at Champ. 'Goodbye, mortal,' he said, spitting the last word as though it was the lowest of insults.

Izzy flung the MythPad across the floor, spinning it towards Champ, a circle of purple lasered symbols spiralling around it as it went. It made contact with Champ's prone figure just as the app made its reassuring *ping*.

'Cheerio!' replied Champ as, with a *>flüorgp<*, the portal opened up around him. There was a flash of energy as he vanished, then a split-second later Dionysus' energy bolt hit the bookcase behind where he'd been lying, destroying it in a fiery explosion.

'Go!' screamed Izzy. I felt her hand on my back, pushing me towards the still-open portal.

We ran together, my legs like concrete, the triskele lanyard hot around my neck. The portal was glowing on the floor in the smouldering remains of the bookcase, burning books scattered around it. I could see it beginning to close already. Izzy had timed it so that nobody could follow us – clever girl!

As we stumbled towards it, half falling into the circle of glowing Celtic symbols, I had time for one last mad glance around the room. I saw Hinson and Thornhill, their hands behind their heads, staring over at us, jaws slack. Rudy, pinned to the floor by a dozen satyrs, holding down his arms. Dionysus, frowning at us, not yet quite registering what had happened.

And Silenus. Running at us, roaring in anger, teeth bared.

His arm was pulled back, tendons straining. He hurled a spear at us, sending it whistling through the air.

Then Izzy's full weight was on my back, pushing me down into the portal as it closed around us, and we were sucked down into the ley line, screams of anger echoing behind us.

SEVENTEEN

I STRUCK THE GROUND AWKWARDLY, ROLLING ARSE OVER TIT AND coming to rest sprawled out on my front with my hair in my face. Thankfully, the ground we'd landed on was soft and covered in grass.

I lifted my head up, spat dirt from my mouth, shivered and squinted. It was cold, but bright and sunny. The only sound was the tranquil chirping of birds – strangely quiet and peaceful compared to the nightmare we'd left behind. I don't think I'd ever get used to these sudden transitions when one reality suddenly screenwiped into another.

My lanyard dangled from my neck in front of me. The wood was black and scorched. What had happened to it?

My head began to clear, and I realised where we were – back on Hampstead Heath! We'd arrived on a small hill in a clearing surrounded by trees. Good old Izzy! I laughed in relief, pushed myself up on my knees, and turned to congratulate her.

'That was close! They almost...' I began, but the words stalled in my mouth.

It took a moment for me to comprehend what I was looking at. It was so unthinkable, so terrible that my mind just refused to register it at first. Then it came in small pieces: the expression on Champ's face, the limp hand in his. And the colour of the grass: slowly spreading patches of red where it should be green.

No.

Champ was kneeling on the grass, holding Izzy in his arms, her chest heaving fitfully. Her arms were limp, her body slumped. Izzy's jacket was wet and sticky. A crimson-tipped spear lay on the ground next to them.

Please. No.

I crawled over to them, trying to form words, but finding my mouth dry and empty. Izzy was breathing fast, panting sharply. I grabbed her hand, entwining our fingers, squeezing her hard. I didn't know what to do. Someone, please tell me what to do.

Izzy looked up at me, her face white, her lips pale. 'Come on… you dork,' she gasped, voice cracking. 'Day's… wasting. We don't want… to be late.'

She gazed at me—right into me—with a look of unfathomable tenderness. Then her expression changed. It was the tiniest difference really, almost imperceptible, yet signifying everything.

She wasn't there anymore.

Izzy Hirway was gone.

* * *

SOME MOMENTS ARE BURNED into your memory, but like a movie; as if it all happened to someone else and you were just there watching.

I screamed at Champ, beat his chest in anger and despair. Begged him to do something – to make it not be true, to bring her back to life.

'I'm sorry', he said, tears in his eyes. 'I can't. Some things just can't be undone.'

He let me rage at him, taking my punches, his arm gently shielding Izzy's body. All the while talking softly to me, though I could barely see or hear anything through my tears and snot.

Eventually, exhausted, I sunk into him, convulsing, sobbing, dry-heaving. He put his arms around me, kindly but firmly.

'My dear Emily,' he said, quietly. 'I'm so sorry.'

I DON'T KNOW how long we lay there, the three of us. Champ and I weeping, hugging Izzy's body and each other. Time didn't seem to exist any more – or to matter.

Eventually, my trembling subsided and feeling started to come back to my body. Everything ached. My arms felt dense, unnaturally heavy.

'Emily?' said Champ, softly. 'I'm afraid we have to move. We can't stay here any longer.' He looked over at the MythPad, which was burnt out, smouldering on the grass nearby, its glass screen spidered with cracks.

'The virus must have overloaded the network,' he said. 'Izzy saved us. She got us out of there before the whole system was compromised, but Dionysus and his people will have full control by now. I don't know what understanding they have of our systems, but it's possible they could trace us.'

I nodded. He was right, we had to go. But first, I insisted, we had to honour Izzy with a proper goodbye.

A kind of detached, quiet calm had come over me. I knew what to do now, because I'd realised where we were. Izzy had brought us to the hill with the willow tree. Our willow tree.

Doing as I instructed, Champ lifted Izzy's limp form in his arms as I held her hand clasped in mine. We walked slowly up the hill together towards the willow tree, then passed through its veil of leaves and into the domed sanctuary within.

Reluctantly, I let go of Izzy's hand, then crouched down in front of the tree's trunk, placing both my palms on the area of dirt and leaves where we had buried the box. The ground opened up, recognising that Izzy and I had returned – though in a way that neither of us could have imagined.

I felt unmoored from reality. One moment I was in a kind of dreamlike serenity, the next viscerally present, as if all my senses were on fire.

I had felt like this once before, many years ago. The shock, the denial. Having to hold the truth at a distance, only glancing at it for a moment before looking away, lest it overwhelm me. The feeling had never truly left, merely sunk deep down into me. And now it had returned; an old enemy, an old friend.

Numbly, I lifted the box from the hole in the ground, placing it to one side. Champ had removed his coat and was gently wrapping it around Izzy's body.

We held her in our arms as the tree roots pushed the ground further apart to receive her, soil cascading down the sides. Then we tenderly lowered Izzy down into the earth.

That's where we buried her. The sunlight flickering between the curtain of leaves, creating a kaleidoscope of light and shadow.

Champ said some words, eloquent I'm sure, although for the life of me I don't know what they were. I was lost in my own head, my own feelings and memories.

At the end, he looked over at me, smiled sadly, and rested a hand on my shoulder. 'She was a remarkable young woman.'

'One in a million,' I said.

* * *

SOME SHORT TIME LATER – I'm not really sure how long – we were sitting on a park bench on Parliament Hill, looking out across London. Canary Wharf shone in the distance, the London Eye, too, and the dome of St Paul's Cathedral. It had started snowing, light flurries drifting across the afternoon sky as dusk started to fall.

Families walked past; children playing, laughing and arguing, blissfully oblivious.

I wondered briefly why I wasn't cold. Why I wasn't having a panic attack or a complete mental breakdown. But I remembered how this worked; when something this big happens, this unimaginable, you can't process it all at once. Can't fit all the emotions inside your body. So, your brain puts you in crisis mode and you keep going – until some point later; hours, days or even weeks, when it suddenly brings you to your knees.

'We've been manipulated,' said Champ, solemnly. 'Like weak-minded fools. The meeting at the museum, the sirens, the Minotaur on the underground – Dionysus was behind it all. Moving us into position like chess pieces and planting the Trojan Horse on us to gain access to the control room.'

He sighed. 'It was clever, calculated. I've encountered Dionysus many times before, and this is not like him at all.'

'Perhaps he's changed. Learnt a few things since last time?'

'He's not capable of change,' said Champ. 'Like all myths, he's a constant, an embodiment of a particular set of characteristics.'

He shook his head. 'However he did it; it worked. Dionysus has taken our headquarters. He has access to our MythTec. Soon he will control the whole egosystem. He will re-forge the human world in his image, starting with London, then Britain, then the whole planet. Drunkenness, debauchery and loutish behaviour will become the norm.'

In the distance, the city's buildings started to light up, a few hundred windows at a time. A group of teenagers ambled past, not much younger than me, giggling and swigging from a plastic bottle of cider.

'Administrator Champ,' I said. 'There's things I should have told you. I tried once, in the taxi, but it was too late.'

I told him everything, about the night at Rudy's and the visit from the Oracle. There was no point holding anything back now. 'I thought maybe it was just a hallucination,' I said, in conclusion. 'From Rudy's tree-root spliff. But it must have been real.'

'Drug induced hallucination, or mythical prophecy? It's not necessarily a binary option,' said Champ. 'It can be two things.'

'We have to fix this,' I said.

'We?'

'Of course! We have to rescue Rudy, and – oh God; all the other interns! I hadn't even thought; they're still trapped back there, right?'

Champ nodded.

'And Director Hinson, and...' I paused, remembering. 'Administrator Thornhill; he saved Izzy and me, he jumped right in front of us when the attack started. I couldn't believe it.'

'Ah yes, Rupert is a rather grumpy sort. Doesn't like young people. Or women. Or me, really, for that matter. But he's a top-rate administrator – and he's no coward.'

'They're all at the mercy of Dionysus now,' I said. 'His prisoners. They might even be killed – we can't just abandon them.' I looked at him meaningfully. 'Izzy wouldn't have.'

'And neither shall we,' said Champ firmly. 'I have a plan, but it will be extremely dangerous. We have no MythTec. No weapons. No Rudy. We'll be completely on our own. This isn't training anymore, apprentice Peasbridge. This is no drill. We are at war.'

'I'm in,' I said, without hesitation.

'Very well. We will fight together; and you've shown me how. Remember the Oracle's words, *"You must open the glove box?"* Well, I know what they mean. It refers to something in my office; an extremely powerful weapon, from the old days. Getting to it, however, is another matter – I have no idea how we're going to get back into HQ.'

'Because our triskeles burnt out?' I asked.

'Yours did, yes,' he said. 'Mine is… more permanent.' He undid the top buttons on his starched white shirt and pulled it open to reveal a tattoo; a green triskele symbol in the centre of his surprisingly ripped chest. 'Had it done by an outside associate; a blind tattooist from Brighton who can graft magic onto skin.'

'There's an access point near here, as you know,' he said, buttoning his shirt back up. 'But it won't activate. The access codes will have been wiped when Dionysus recalibrated the system.'

'So, what are we going to do?'

'We will go old school; use ancient magic, from before our systems were put in place. There are mythological laws that form the underpinning of our technology. Those fundamentals will still be in place. With the right key, I can access the mainframe directly and activate the entrance portal.'

'A key?' I asked, puzzled.

'More of an avatar, really. Something that I can use as a conduit, just as Dionysius did with his Trojan Horse. It would need to have a connection to the Tree of Knowledge, but also serve as a symbol for Dionysus' realm, since he's in power there now.'

He shook his head, angry with himself. 'I'm a damn fool. I don't know what I was thinking. We'll never be able to acquire an object like that in time. It's quite impossible.'

The sun started to dip low in the sky, bathing the hill in an orange light. I looked at the box under my arm. The one Rudy had carved from the roots of the Tree of Knowledge. The one containing a bottle of wine.

'Administrator Champ?' I said.

'Yes, Emily?'

'I think this might help.'

EIGHTEEN

>*Flüorgp*<

We materialised in the foyer, dropping into crouched positions immediately, ready to defend ourselves. But the room was deserted. No alarms greeted our arrival. No sound of clattering hooves running towards us down the corridors. So far, so good.

I looked up and gasped. The ceiling fresco had changed rather radically. Dionysus now took up half the area, shown standing triumphant above all the other myths, who had retreated to the edges in fear. He was surrounded by his satyrs, who—along with various human figures—were shown engaging in a massive drunken orgy. It looked like somebody had disabled the porn filters.

'Let's get moving,' said Champ. 'My quarters are on the other side of a building swarming with Dionysus' horde – I doubt we'll get through without a fight.'

I put my hand on his arm, holding him back. He looked at me in surprise.

'We're not going *through* the building,' I said. 'We're going over it.'

* * *

WE CREPT SLOWLY into the dorm common room. There was nobody there now, although clearly there had been. The dorm's main doors hung off their hinges, and there were signs of a struggle everywhere. I hoped the other interns hadn't been hurt, that they were all just locked up in a room somewhere. Help is coming, I promised.

Moving as quietly as possible, I led the way up to our room. The door was open, but the room seemed untouched. I looked numbly across at Izzy's bed, then turned away quickly.

'Up through here,' I said, showing Champ how to climb onto a desk to get though the skylight. 'Once you're up there you can slide over to the nearest chimney stack.'

'I'll go first,' he said, leaping up and out like a cat. His face reappeared above me, a hand reaching down to haul me up.

It was cold up on the rooftop – cold enough to see our breath. The sky above was dark, and snowing gently, just like it had been on the Heath.

'Environmental controls are down,' said Champ, crouching next to me on the tiles as he surveyed the scene. 'Good. That means they haven't accessed everything yet. We still have time.'

I shivered. At least I had my uniform's jacket – Champ was still in just his shirt, though he didn't seem to notice the chill. I raised myself slowly to my feet, trying not to look down.

'Are you okay?' he asked.

'Yes,' I nodded. 'I've done this before.'

We moved across the rooftops carefully, making our way around the circular building. The snow left a thin white dusting across the tiles, making them slippier than the last time I'd been up there. At one point, I noticed a pattern of dots across a rooftop: a trail of cat paws. I was glad that Ginger was okay and not locked in Rudy's room – I hate to think of what a gang of satyrs would do to her.

There was a crash from the other side of the building. Across the atrium, through lit-up windows, we saw gangs of satyrs running rampant – laughing and shouting, knocking over filing cabinets, ripping up books and throwing furniture at each other.

We stood stock-still. Could they see our silhouettes up here on the rooftop? But none of them even looked over; they were having too much fun, swigging ransacked wine straight from the bottle as they went on their destructive spree. A chair smashed through a window, accompanied by cackling cheers. A few seconds later, I heard a splash as it landed in the atrium lake.

Champ and I exchanged a look, then kept going, moving steadily forward, manoeuvring carefully around chimney stacks, half-crawling along the thin rounded rooftops, clinging to iron railings and weathervanes for balance.

Eventually we reached the other side of the building, above Champ's office. The section of roof there was fairly flat, so we knelt down and peered over the edge at the enormous clock face. The clock's two gunmetal hands were parted below, pointing at ten past nine. I could hear the ticking of the copper second hand as it passed by on its endless circuit.

'There's a decent-sized ledge in front of the clock,' said Champ. 'Rudy goes out there on a rope to wash the glass twice a year, so it'll hold our weight, no problem. You first.'

He took me by the arms and lowered me over the edge, in front of the clock face. With my vertigo, this should have left me incapacitated with fear, yet I was merely terrified. I think my nerves had been overloaded by recent events; no longer able to process the sheer amount of danger.

I managed to balance on the six-inch ledge, clutching the

bottom of the clock's hour hand and leaning in, my face pressed against the cold glass, eyes barely open. A light breeze teased my hair, and snowflakes fluttered down onto my hands, melting immediately. I tried not to think about the six-storey drop just one step behind me.

I almost fell off in alarm when I felt something tap me impatiently on the shoulder – but it was just the clock's second-hand, rapping at me to get out of its way so it could continue its business. Sorry mate, you'll just have to wait; I'm not letting go. Time can literally stop until I'm safely inside.

I felt Champ drop down to my left, softening his impact with a crouch as he landed, then grasping the stonework for stability.

'There's a window here with a dodgy clasp,' he whispered, reaching out to his left. 'I kept putting requests in to maintenance to fix it; thank goodness for slow-moving bureaucracy.'

He grunted as he pulled at the window, then it popped and slid upwards quickly. He swung in athletically, feet first, then immediately reappeared, leaning out over the window ledge. Taking my hand, he guided me inside, then slid the window down with a click.

I slumped into a chair near the fireplace, legs shaking.

'You okay?' Champ asked.

I nodded. 'I just need a second.'

He opened a wardrobe in the corner and lifted out a long tweed coat. He held it for a moment, regarding it. 'My third one of the day,' he said quietly. Then he set his jaw and swung it on, sliding his arms quickly through the long sleeves.

'This super-weapon of yours,' I asked, breathing slowly as I rose from the seat, 'is it still here?'

'Yes, thank goodness. The room hasn't been touched.'

Champ approached his glass display cabinets, with their collection of rare antiquities and lethal-looking armaments.

He walked right past a gleaming triple-bladed sword, barely glanced at an elaborately decorated golden crossbow, and completely ignored a rune-covered Gatling gun.

He stopped in front of the glass box I'd noticed when I visited his office before; the one holding the large, battered white cricket glove that he'd called a 'family heirloom'. Champ gently touched the brass plaque on the front: *Battle the monsters. Save the world. File the paperwork.*

'Very well; we shall open the glove box,' said Champ. He put his hands down the side of the box, made a sharp movement, and the front sprang open.

He pulled out the glove and slid it on; thick around his hand, with a padded sleeve that extended most of the way to the elbow. More of a gauntlet than a glove, and bristling with MythTec, I now realised. Thick wires ran under the material, down the sleeves and along the fingers. A golden triskele symbol sat in the palm. Brass knobs and dials were embedded down one side; Champ adjusted them carefully.

'Haven't had cause to use this in a long time,' he said. He fiddled with one particular dial until it finally clicked into place. 'Always was a bit glitchy.' Then he flipped one last switch on the side, powering it up. The glove's palm started to glow, accompanied by a low vibrating hum. 'Good, good,' he said, turning it off again. 'Need to conserve power; I don't know how much charge it has without the egosystem uplink.'

Wondering if I should take a weapon, too, I examined the contents of the other glass cabinets.

'None of those can be wielded by mortal hand, I'm afraid,' said Champ. 'But I have a more powerful weapon for you.'

He slid open a desk drawer and reached underneath it, ripping off a yellowing envelope that had been stuck there with ageing Sellotape. He sliced it open with a letter opener and pulled out a bronze skeleton key with a decorative triskele-shaped handle.

'When we get to the Control Room, I'll keep the guards busy,' he said. 'Meanwhile, you'll need to use this.' He tossed me the key, which I caught clumsily. 'Get to the main control panel in the Tree. There's a keyhole underneath; slot this in and turn it all the way to the left.'

I nodded. 'That'll reboot the egosystem?'

'No, but it will power it down temporarily, halting the spread of the virus. Then, when we've regained control, our techs can go about removing it.'

I clutched the key tightly in my palm. 'I won't let you down.'

'I know you won't,' he said, smiling. 'Now, the Control Room is six floors down from here. The stairways will be crawling with satyrs, so it's my turn to show *you* a shortcut.'

He walked over to the fireplace and twisted part of the carved marble surround. A section of wall slid open. He laughed at my surprised face. 'Of *course* we have secret passages,' he said.

We entered the opening and I followed him along a dimly-lit brick passageway, then down a tiny stone spiral staircase, further and further. Surely we had reached the ground floor by now? Eventually the steps ended, and we were faced with a blank wooden wall. Champ pressed his ear against the grain and listened.

'We're directly outside the entrance to the Control Room,' he whispered. He fiddled with the glove again and it turned on, flickering at first, bathing the area in a golden glow that lit up great drapes of cobwebs.

'Remember the plan. I'll take care of the soldiers, you just get to the main control panel.'

I nodded. Champ turned a lever and another section of wall slid aside. We stepped out, Champ's arm raised and ready for battle.

The corridor was completely deserted.

The huge metal entrance doors were wide open and the room inside was dark. There was no power to any of the screens surrounding the Tree. This didn't make sense; the satyrs were rampaging through the building, but why would they leave this room unguarded?

My eyes fell on a large figure lying face-down just inside, positioned beneath the mangled remains of several filing cabinets. I recognised the brown corduroy trousers and thick orange braces immediately.

'Rudy!' I cried.

I sprinted towards him. Champ hissed at me to wait, but I couldn't stop. Was Rudy injured? Was he even alive?

I skidded up to my friend and placed my hands on him. To my immense relief, he was warm to the touch.

'Emily, get back!' cried Champ, running up behind me. 'Something's—'

But before he could finish, Rudy flipped over, whipping out an arm and striking me hard across the face.

It was a stunning blow, in more ways than one. I was sent flying backwards through the air and came crashing to the floor near Champ's feet.

At the same time, the giant doors slammed shut and all the lights came on, revealing a terrifying scene. There, sitting in a huge wooden throne that had grown right out of the Tree of Knowledge's trunk, was Dionysus, his booming laughter echoing around the room. Silenus was by his side, flanked by armed satyr guards. The monitors on the Tree were all lit up now, data rolling across their screens.

'You underestimate us, Champ,' sneered Silenus.

I was weeping, in shock as much as pain. Rudy stood up, his back to me, hunched over. I looked at him in disbelief.

'Get me more wine, slave!' ordered Dionysus.

Rudy shuffled over to a nearby table, picked up a large jug, and meekly made his way over to Dionysus' throne, pouring it into the god's tankard. Why was Rudy acting like this? He seemed defeated. Broken.

'About time you got here,' said Dionysus. 'We've been having a good look around. Silenus reckons he's got a handle on this technology of yours. We've already house-trained your little pet.'

That's when I saw it: an oversized MythTec bracelet clamped around Rudy's neck, controlling him, making him do their bidding. A single tear rolled down his hairy cheek. The bastards had put a collar on him.

Dionysus guffawed loudly and took a huge gulp of wine, spilling it down the sides of his craggy, bearded face. Champ shifted position, moving directly between the throne and where I was lying on the floor. He had his hands clasped behind his back, keeping the glove from their view. What was he waiting for?

Dionysus gestured to a tray of green apples on a table nearby. 'These are from your stockroom. They hold your data, yes?' He shook his head. 'Ridiculous. Only a human could ruin such a thing of natural beauty. You could make cider, but instead you use them to store ones and zeros.'

'You're not going to win, Dionysus,' said Champ, his voice calm and clear. 'Order will be restored; it always is in the end. Surrender now and things will be easier for you in the long run.'

They all roared with laughter. '*Going* to win?' said Dionysus. 'You pathetic creature. I've *already* won! And do you know why? Because deep down, humans *want* me to. You want to give up, to give in, to escape the manufactured burdens of your ridiculous civilisation. Why fight for something that brings you so much unhappiness when I offer you blissful escape in wine, women and song?'

Champ was standing in front of me, his hands behind his back fiddling with the cricket glove as Dionysus spoke, turning the dials and clicking the little switch back and forth.

'*That* is why I won,' continued Dionysus. 'Because, outside this ridiculous little bureaucracy, you humans don't even care for the thing you're fighting for.' He grinned as Silenus handed him the tray of apples.

'And also,' he said, picking up one of them and examining it, his eyes gleaming, 'because I fight dirty.'

He dropped the apple on the floor, lifted his huge leather boot, and stamped down, crushing it. In an explosion of light and noise, it released its contents into the room; a huge troll, twenty-feet tall at least. Arms as thick as tree trunks, head the size of a fridge, and cold black eyes recessed in a face like a weather-beaten rock. It roared, causing several of the satyrs to take a step back.

Champ's fingers moved faster at the glove controls behind his back. It wasn't working! I looked at the knobs and dials, trying to remember how he'd set them in his office. Then I saw the problem – a dial that was stuck, not quite turned all the way. I reached over, twisted it hard, and it moved into position with a satisfying *click*. The glove began to hum gently, and golden lines lit down its sides like veins.

The troll glowered around the room, enraged but disoriented. It saw Dionysus in his throne and stepped back reflexively, recognising the power of a god. Then it laid eyes on the tweed-suited figure of Champ and snarled, displaying rows of crooked teeth in a cavernous mouth.

Dionysus held up his staff and gave the troll an order: 'Take him out!'

The troll looked back at him, confused.

Silenus sighed. 'It means *kill him*,' he said.

The troll stuck its chest out and bellowed so loudly that it made my ears throb. Then it ran full-pelt towards us. It halved the distance between us in a couple of bounds, its gigantic maw wide open, saliva flinging in all directions. I scrambled backwards on my hands and knees, terrified. Champ calmly lifted up his gloved hand and pointed it palm-up at the creature. A cone of vibrating golden energy burst from it, filling the air several feet in front of him. As the creature ran into it, Champ pulled his arm back and twisted his wrist in a practiced move.

The troll's face took on a look of shock and confusion as the energy field lifted it from the floor and twirled it around in the air. It seemed to shrink, then collapse into itself; to fold up, an origami of flesh and bone, then unfold again, reformed into a different shape.

Its new form fell to the floor and skidded up to my feet: a tiny plastic doll with crazy purple up-combed hair.

'Gentlemen,' said Champ, 'let's get real.'

Roaring furiously, Dionysus leaped up from the throne and smacked the tray of apples from Silenus' hands, sending it flying through the air and crashing to the floor. The four apples smashed on impact, exploding as their contents erupted into our reality, ferocious and enraged. I staggered back further and picked up a broken chair, holding it up like a shield, for all the good it would do me.

'Eviscerate the human!' commanded Dionysus.

Three of the creatures attacked at once. A sinewy, bristle-furred werewolf sprang through the air at Champ, jaws open; a black-cloaked vampire transformed into a huge leathery bat and flew at him, screeching; and a red-skinned demon with huge spiral horns crouched then leapt forwards, belching fire.

Champ caught the lycanthrope in the glove's energy field, trapping it, then swung it around in an arc, swiping the bat out of the air and knocking the demon over like a bowling pin. The demon went skidding across the wooden floor, crashing into the wall, while the bat hit the floor face-first with a smack, transforming back into its human form, blood spewing from his broken nose. Champ twisted his wrist and pulled, collapsing the werewolf into itself and reforming it into a Blu-ray of a classic Michael J Fox movie.

The vampire and demon picked themselves up from the floor and rushed him together, the demon out in front. Champ grinned and ran towards them, moving the battle away from me.

He was magnificent to watch; a man in his element, at the height of his abilities. Racing towards the demon, he used a half-broken table as a ramp to leap up and over it, dodging its fiery breath as he blasted the creature from above. He twisted his wrist as he flew through the air, reconstructing the creature in the glove's energy field. Before Champ hit the ground, it had turned into a pile of Norwegian Death Metal albums.

Champ did a perfect forward roll as he landed, sliding flat on his back as the motion carried him beneath the vampire, which had flung itself into the air, halfway through its transformation back into a bat. He blasted it from below with the glove's energy field and twisted his wrist. A shower of plastic joke-shop fangs rained to the floor around him.

As petrified as I had been a moment ago, I swear I wanted to cheer. There was just one mythical being remaining; a golden-armoured soldier in a Corinthian helmet who had been standing back, sword in hand, watching the battle intently.

The soldier saw his opportunity and ran towards me, sword glinting. Clearly, he had identified the weak spot in his enemy's position. I held the broken chair up in front of me, not fancying its chances against sharpened steel.

But I needn't have worried; he was barely three feet away when Champ's energy blast hit him from behind. He warped in the air in front of me, shrinking and transforming completely, though keeping his golden colour. I looked down as his new form skidded to a halt between my feet: a pack of Trojan condoms.

Champ turned back towards Dionysus and his men. 'Very

well,' he said, walking towards them slowly. 'If you can't be reasoned with, we'll have to do this the hard way.'

Dionysus, his face furious, lifted his staff and pointed it at Champ. Champ raised his glove, ready to absorb the energy blast. Then Silenus whispered something in Dionysus' ear and he lowered the staff again, a smile slowly spreading across his face.

'Oh, I don't think so, Administrator,' said Dionysus. 'You see, we've been searching the records, and we know your dirty little secret – your Achilles heel, you might say.'

Champ stopped, hesitating. Silenus produced another apple—a red one this time—with the little satellite disk already implanted.

'Took us a while to find it in your ridiculous filing system.' Silenus said, 'but there it was: the record of your trip to a certain legendary fountain.' He spoke softly, watching Champ's face. 'In Africa. Sixty years ago.'

'Wait!' said Champ, panic rising in his voice.

Silenus smiled, relishing the moment, then tapped at a control panel. A beam of golden light shot out from the apple's metal funnel, enveloping Champ.

He staggered backwards and turned towards me. Energy swirled around him, pulling itself out of him, through his very skin. He looked me in the eyes. 'I'm sorry,' he said.

The golden energy flowed out of him, twisting through the air and into the apple. As it did so, Champ began ageing at a rapid rate, his skin tightening, his body slumping. He collapsed to his knees as his strength left him. The apple went *ping* in Silenus' hand and turned green.

Before me now was Champ's true form: a feeble ninety-year-old, his clothes hanging from his gaunt frame. The glove slipped from Champ's scrawny hand, hitting the floor with a thud.

Dionysus sat back in the throne, stroking his beard. 'So much for the fountain of eternal youth, old man.'

I fell to my knees in shock as two of the satyr guards took Champ by his arms, dragging his limp form away.

'The old man is yours, my lord,' said Silenus as he walked over, grinning triumphantly.

He tilted his head, regarding me. 'I have unfinished business with his bitch.'

NINETEEN

THE NEXT FEW MINUTES WERE A BIT OF A BLUR. A SATYR GRABBED me roughly, twisting my arm behind my back and hauling me away. I shouted out for Champ, I think, and for Rudy, but I couldn't hear my own voice. It was all static. I think I was in shock. I do remember the guard dragging me down the stone steps to the basement, because he wasn't gentle about it. Then he flung me into a small empty room and slammed the door shut. I heard a bolt clack into place on the other side, and that was that.

It was cold and dark in the basement room. The only light came from the horizontal slot of a tiny window high up on the wall. I thought I could hear weeping in the distance, or maybe it was all in my head. I lay in the middle of the floor in the foetal position, clutching my knees and trembling. I felt utterly alone; more so than ever before. I had absolutely no idea what to do.

The bolt clanked again and the door creaked open, light bursting in from outside. A large figure stood silhouetted in the doorway, regarding me for a moment. It was Silenus.

He walked in slowly, dragging a chair along with him, the back feet scraping along the stone floor. He stopped right in front of me then sat down, lounging back in the chair. His eyes never left me.

There was a long silence until, eventually, he spoke.

'Where's your friend, the other little girl?'

I looked up at him, my eyes red.

'Ah, I see,' he smiled. 'Well, that's mortals for you. Always dropping dead right, left and centre. Then again, she got off lightly, compared to what I'm going to do to you.'

He saw my fearful expression and grinned. 'Yes. You're a clever girl, you did your homework. You know what we satyrs are; what we do. And I'm going to take my time with you. Going to savour it.'

'You monster!' I spat.

Silenus sat back, shook his head and tutted. 'A childish label. There are no monsters. No "good" or "evil". That's the little boys' game, for Champ and Dionysus to play. We see behind it, don't we? So, let us drop such facile pretences.'

He spread his arms wide. 'We are all just animals, after all. Call us monsters if you must, but you humans made us in your own image, so what does that say about you?'

'How did you do it?' I asked quietly. 'Champ said myths don't change. How did you learn how to access the egosystem?'

'Ah, well I'm a little different you see. Unlike Dionysus, I wasn't born to power, so I never took it for granted. I had to work my way up to his side, through blood and sweat.' He leaned forward. 'I had to *evolve*.

'I saw you humans buzzing around us like flies, such short lives, but ever changing. When this ridiculous bureaucracy took control, we were all taken by surprise. But I understood how you'd done it: technology. That gave you dominion over us. I knew that only by understanding it—having mastery of it—could we take back control.

'It took me decades. I created a network of spies – those who understood, and wanted to join our struggle. Eventually, one of them managed to steal a damaged MythPad. I spent a long time studying it, trying to fix it, deconstructing the components and developing my own. I knew I needed to get into your headquarters and access your egosystem controls. But after years without success, I was almost ready to give up.'

He rose to his feet.

'Then, one glorious, happy day, a new Myth Management intern discovered her burgeoning abilities of astral projection. Her mind, flailing out wildly and undisciplined, created a hairline crack in the egosystem, a temporary pathway. To my good fortune, I was working on our MythTec device when it happened. I saw the energy spike and locked on to it, and before I knew what was happening, I found myself in your dorm room.'

He leaned forward, smiling. 'You opened a crack,' he breathed, running his tongue over his teeth, 'and I slipped right in.'

I shuddered. He sat back down, chuckling, then he went silent, eyes narrowing.

'Of course, you bested me that day. Damaged my pride and my... manhood.' He paused. 'But I had the MythPad running the whole time, gathering data. Your bosses changed all the access codes immediately, of course. Tightened security. I wasn't getting in the same way again. But the understanding I'd gained, the data I now had, was enough for me to formulate a new plan. To develop my recalibration virus. So, in truth, you see, our victory is all thanks to you,' said Silenus, throwing his head back and cackling.

I shuddered again. This was too much to bear. I wished he'd just kill me now and get it over with, but he wanted me to hear it, all of it.

'Then it was a simple case of creating enough organised chaos to distract you,' he yawned. 'All leading up to getting our little holidaymaker friend in a position to hand you our Trojan Horse.'

'He was *working* for you?' I asked.

'Oh, not knowingly. But he's a high-functioning alcoholic, you see. Very susceptible to my master's bidding. He certainly functioned very highly for us!' He laughed. 'Our little drug mule.'

He slapped his clawed hands on his knees, making me jump. 'And that's that. Job done. I'd happily slaughter the lot of you now, but Dionysus has some silly grievance with Champ and wants to make him suffer first. Watch all his friends die, and so forth.

'And as for you… well, you made it personal. So, tonight my people celebrate. But in the morning… *a fate worse than death*, I believe you call it. Maybe I'll make the old man watch,' he sneered. 'Stew on that for a while. I find anticipation enhances the flavour.'

He stood up sharply, shoving the chair backwards and crouching down, bringing his head close to mine. 'Your friend is dead,' he whispered. 'Your master is crippled, and your servant has been turned to my control. I have broken you, you pathetic, fragile creature. Did you think yourself strong? You know nothing of strength. You were but a bug that I squashed between my fingers.'

He grabbed my wrists.

'I am older, I am bigger, I am stronger, so *I WIN*.' He shouted the last part, then moved his mouth right up to my ear and whispered again, 'because that's how the world works.'

Then he flung my arms aside and slammed his hands down onto my thighs, digging his claws in. They burned like hot knives. I screamed in pain as he laughed in my face.

Then he let go and stood up, picking up the chair and knocking three times on the door.

'Don't go anywhere,' he said as the door opened. 'I'll see you in the morning, little English girl. Toodle-pip.'

He left, sliding the bolt home behind him.

* * *

I LAY there for an hour or more, sobbing harder and longer than I ever had in my life. I think I cried all the moisture out of my body. My legs were throbbing where his claws had stabbed me; they weren't bleeding too much, but I could barely move them. Any hope of escape was gone.

The Oracle's warnings had come true; when we heard the sirens, it was already too late. Then we reached the end of the line, in the tube station. And Champ's secret was indeed his undoing. But what good were the Oracle's prophecies? We did exactly what she told us: we buried the bottle, we opened the glove box, and it had done no good at all. And who was the, "Breed that turns on you", anyway? Was that the satyrs, or Rudy? I don't suppose it mattered any more.

Then there were her warnings about Rudy and Izzy: "*One will be your lifelong companion. The other will soon be gone*". That had come true in the worst possible way – Izzy was gone, and Rudy would die with me and everyone else tomorrow.

I was glad, now, that I'd insulted the Oracle at the end. As I'd thought, she had given us nothing but riddles that made no sense until it was too late.

I lifted myself up on one arm, wiping away the last of my tears. A horizontal rectangle of light shimmered on the floor in front of me; a small sliver of moonlight slicing through the tiny window high up near the ceiling. I had an overwhelming desire to see the outside world again, even if it was for the last time.

I looked around the room and saw a few empty packing crates scattered around. I moved on to my hands and knees, half-dragging my injured legs behind me as I collected them, then piled them up below the window.

I wobbled to my feet, thighs burning, and slowly climbed to the top of the pile. Lying flat against the wall, I could hold on to the bottom of the cold concrete window and peer out through the three-inch high slot.

Outside was the atrium, at ground level. I could see the edge of the grass and feel the cool breeze on my face. Up across the way were the illuminated windows of the HQ, where the satyrs had left their paths of destruction.

It all just seemed too cruel. I thought of all the times we had gazed down from our dorm skylights, the world spread out below us, as if promising a lifetime of adventures. Now I was down here, all out of options, peering up at the HQ's windows for the last time.

One particular set of windows caught my eye. They were steaming up, condensation forming on the glass as it separated the room's heat from the cold snow outside. Shapes started to appear on the glass.

It almost broke me when I realised what they were.

It was Rudy's room, and those were the doodles Izzy had made on the windows with her finger that night the three of us spent together. On the left window was the triskele symbol I'd seen her draw, with the backwards 'IH' of her initials below.

Hello to you too, Izzy.

On the right-hand window another pattern was appearing. I hadn't noticed her draw that one. It appeared slowly, a message light as vapour, from a few days and a lifetime ago.

It was a heart. No, two hearts – one with IH at the centre; the other with EP. They were overlapping, interlinked; supporting each other.

'It's always there, but you can only see it when there's a bright

light in the darkness.' My dad's words, coming to me from a time long ago.

Then Izzy's voice, joining him. *'You have two options. One: let that crap pour all over you and just drown in it. Or two: scoop it up with both hands and shovel it into your methane-powered bullshit engine.'*

And finally, the Oracle's voice, those other words she'd spoken to me at the end: *'What use is a silly girl who spends too much time in her own head?'*

It hit me like a sledgehammer. It hadn't been an insult; it was an instruction. She was telling me what I needed to do.

I reached through the window, my fingers searching around in the damp grass until I found what I was looking for. I grasped hold of the sycamore seed tightly, then carefully lowered myself back down into the room, my heart beating a million miles a minute.

The pain and horror had been drained out of me, leaving only a calm, fiery determination. Silenus was arrogant, and arrogant people always underestimate those they see as small and weak. And perhaps I was weak – on my own. Maybe we all are. But together we give each other hope; the strength to fight, and a reason to do so.

The first time I fought Silenus was to try and protect Izzy. She was gone now, and I couldn't bring her back. But I could still fight *for* her. I could fight for everyone I loved.

So that's what I was going to do. I was going to rescue Rudy. I was going to save Champ, and Thornhill and all the others – even Scott.

And I was going to do it all without leaving this room.

TWENTY

I POSITIONED MYSELF IN THE CENTRE OF THE FLOOR, PULLING MY
legs into a half-lotus position as well as I could manage,
doing my best to ignore the pain in my thighs. I rested my
hands in my lap, one on top of the other, the sycamore seed
nestled in my open palm.

Closing my eyes, I focused on my breathing, centring
myself. I thought back to the meditation ceremony in the
atrium, tried to imagine the drumbeats and chanting, and felt
a familiar feeling wash over me. I'd done this twice before; I
was getting used to it now. My palm tickled as the sycamore
seed started to move, and I reached out with my mind.

I felt my consciousness liberate itself from my physical
form and begin to slowly float upwards, a bubble rising from
the bottom of a glass. Then I was above my body, looking
down. Damn – the wounds on my legs looked really bad from
up here. I hoped my body wouldn't pass out before I could
get the job done.

There was no time to lose. Concentrating hard, I rotated
my astral form towards the thick wooden door and floated
towards it. I hit it without slowing down and popped out the

other side like a ghost. I swear I could taste the bitter flavour of the oak on my tongue.

I looked up to see a pair of satyr guards standing right next to me, and almost jumped out of my skin before remembering, with relief, that I already had.

They stood there sullenly, grasping their spears, clearly unhappy to be hanging around in a musty corridor when there was drinking and revelry happening right upstairs. I looked left and right, wondering where to go first. A soft whimpering emanated from the room opposite, so I floated forwards through its door.

Inside was a large room full of Administrators and technicians, all sitting dejectedly on the floor. Some held handkerchiefs to black eyes or bloody noses, others were nursing injured limbs. A few were crying softly to themselves, and others held their knees to their chests and rocked back and forth.

Hinson was leaning up against a wall, staring ahead with a blank look, utterly defeated. In the far corner was Administrator Burdett of Seafaring Myths, tending to a badly beaten Thornhill, whose face was etched with smears of scarlet red, and his arm held in a makeshift sling. Clearly, Dionysus' troops had shown their displeasure at his trick with the triskele shield. I whispered to them urgently, but they couldn't hear me.

I could feel my body pulling me back – the astral umbilical cord had extended as far as it would go. I floated back out of the room and into the corridor, then tried another room; the one to the left of mine. Here I found all the secretaries, huddled together and petrified. I knew the interns must also be in a room down here somewhere, but they weren't who I was looking for.

I floated through the side wall connecting back into my room, past my physical body, watching the sycamore seed rotating slowly above my palm. I carried on until I hit the wall on the other side, passing through the plaster and cracked brickwork and into the room beyond.

And there he was.

Champ's feeble, aged body lay on ripped sheets of cardboard on the floor, his clothes draped loosely around his near skeletal limbs. He was motionless. Was he even alive?

I floated up to him and, just like I had that afternoon in the atrium garden, dived straight into his head. I felt myself in his body – so weak now, compared to before.

'Champ!' I cried. 'Can you hear me? It's me, Emily. I need your help.'

I felt something move as if rising up from a deep, dark pit.

'Well, well,' said Champ's voice, all around me. 'Emily Peasbridge. You are *full* of surprises.'

'I THINK you can step outside now, my dear,' said Champ's voice. 'I'll be able to see you if I concentrate – now that I know what to look for.'

I left his body and watched as he sat up slowly from the floor and looked over at where I was floating. 'Ha!' he said, laughing – then coughing weakly. 'I'd almost say you look like an angel. But we've met those, haven't we? You're a much more refreshing sight.'

He raised himself into a sitting position against a rusty filing cabinet and looked over at me, his thin chest rising and falling with the effort. He reminded me of a baby bird I once found that had fallen out of its nest.

'I owe you an apology,' he said, his voice a cracked whisper. 'We thought we were infallible. Not just the bureau, but myself personally. Humans acting like gods. It was hubris, nothing more.'

'It was my fault too,' I said. 'I should have told you

everything sooner, but I was scared of losing my apprenticeship. It seems so ridiculous now.'

'We all make mistakes in our youth,' he replied kindly. 'There's no excuse at my age.'

'It was *you* who saved Rudy, wasn't it?' I said, with sudden realisation. 'When he was a child, I mean. That's why he looks up to you like he does. There is no "Champ Senior" – it was you all along.'

'Yes,' he nodded. 'And if I'd been quicker about it, I could have saved more of his people. But I wasn't. Rudy is my dearest, most loyal friend, and now I've failed him twice.'

He stared at me. 'There's a determined look in your eye, Emily. One I know all too well. You're planning on going after Dionysus, aren't you?'

'Dionysus was never the problem.' I said. 'It's Silenus; he's the architect of all this. But either way, I can't fight them head-on. We need to power down the egosystem, like you planned. You're in no shape to walk, even if I could get you out of here. But I can do it – I just need to know, will the key still work?'

Champ shook his head sadly. 'I'm sorry, it's too late. The virus already has complete control.' He paused. 'But there is one other way. I have no way of knowing if it will work, but it's worth a go. I mean, what the hell, eh, girl?'

'Tell me,' I said.

'Switch it off,' said Champ. 'Disconnect the Tree from the egosystem completely. There's a power source at the back of the trunk. Pull out the main cable and the Tree will shut down. It will lose all its data, I'm afraid.' He winced at the thought. 'Decades of research by generations of Administrators; things that were stored in the Tree itself and couldn't be downloaded into apples. It will be a terrible loss. But these are extreme times, and we must resort to extreme measures.'

'And this will delete the virus?' I asked.

'Yes. Dionysus will no longer have control of the

egosystem, and for a moment, neither will we.' He looked at me earnestly. 'So, you must immediately *reconnect* it. That should reset it to the very first version of the egosystem controls; the ones Myth Management initiated all those years ago. The factory settings, you might say. Quite rudimentary compared to what we have now, but enough to restore some basic order.'

'Administrator Champ,' I said, a grin spreading across my face, 'are you seriously telling me to, "*Turn it off and on again*"?' I burst out laughing. I couldn't help it; this was all too ridiculous. Champ looked at me with bemusement – probably wondering if I'd cracked under the pressure. Maybe I had.

After a moment, I pulled myself together and told him my plan. I would float up to the Control Room, right past Silenus and Dionysus, then pick the nearest guard and enter his mind, like I had with the Minotaur. Then I would convince him to unplug the cable.

'Hmm,' mulled Champ. 'It's possible you could control a weak-minded creature, but only for a minute at most. There's so much that could go wrong.'

I agreed, but it wasn't as if we had another option.

'There's something else,' I said. 'I can't seem to travel far from my body; it's like there's an invisible connection keeping me back. I was hoping you'd know how to fix that.'

'I'm afraid astral projection's not my speciality. But I believe you can anchor to another living soul. Catch a lift, as it were.'

'There are a couple of guards outside,' I suggested.

'No, the soul needs to be friendly; it has to *volunteer* to help.'

Well, that rather threw a spanner in the works. My mind raced through some options. Could I get inside a guard's head and get him to open a door? Perhaps, but the other one would raise the alarm immediately. And nobody down here would be much use, anyway. Champ could barely walk, and the other Administrators had been beaten once already.

A familiar sound caught my ear. A soft vibrating purr.

Then a meow.

Up at Champ's window, a wet black snout was peeking in, trying to get our attention. Bloody brilliant – Ginger to the rescue again! I floated up to her, her eyes following my astral form. I'd often heard that cats could see spectrums that humans couldn't, and here was the proof.

I reached out with my mind. 'Will you help me?' I asked. She meowed again – I was certain she understood. Concentrating hard, I felt around on the astral plane, found her aura, and locked on. She took a step back and I felt myself move with her.

I turned to look down at Champ, who was watching us, smiling weakly. He raised a shrivelled hand to his brow in salute. 'Battle the monsters, Emily,' he croaked, as Ginger moved away, pulling me out of the room. 'Save the world. And file the paperwork!'

* * *

GINGER DARTED ACROSS THE ATRIUM, her paws barely leaving an impression in the snow-covered grass. I held on tight, as if on an invisible leash – a pet taking me for a walk. Moonlight glistened on the still water of the lake as we bounded over the wooden bridge, then across the winding stone pathway towards the amphitheatre.

I tried asking her where we were going, but she didn't answer. I mean, of course she didn't; she's a cat. But she seemed to know where she was going, so I held on and hoped for the best.

Ginger darted through an open door in the side of the building, then down a corridor, keeping to the shadows and out of view behind tables or under chairs whenever possible.

We passed several satyrs as we went, though I only caught glimpses of them; figures in rooms as we sped past doorways, or hairy-hooved feet spied from under a table.

Then we turned a sharp corner and I crashed right into Silenus.

I passed through him, of course. Ginger had shot between his legs, pulling me through his torso before I'd had a chance to react. Even this fleeting contact with his aura gave me a jolt of nausea. Silenus stopped and looked around suspiciously as we flew past, as if he had detected a presence. Thankfully, Ginger had us around a corner and up a flight of stairs before he could react.

She slowed down as we came to the large double-doors of the second-floor kitchens, then stopped and sat down in front of them. She turned her head towards my astral form and gave me a meaningful look.

'Why have you taken me here?' I asked her. 'I need to get to the Control Room!'

She stared back at me, then looked straight ahead at the closed door. I didn't know what this was about, but she clearly wasn't going to budge.

'Okay,' I conceded. 'I'll go inside.'

I passed through the doors into the kitchens.

Inside, an enormous hairy figure hurried back and forth between a dozen huge pots of food, stirring them, tasting the spoon with the tip of his tongue, and adding ingredients. He had a chef's apron and a thick metal collar around his neck.

Ginger had taken me to her master, of course. She must have sensed his pain and was hoping that I could help him. It was sickening to see Rudy like this; neutered by the technology of his beloved bureau. But what could I do? If that collar was controlling his actions, he might raise the alarm.

There was no choice. He was my friend. I had to try.

I floated over to him and reached out with my mind, moving as gently as possible. I could feel his thoughts, but they were foggy, disrupted. I couldn't get a lock on anything, so I dug deeper into his psyche, hoping to find a level where Rudy was still himself.

I pushed through a membrane between the layers of his subconscious, and a wave of emotion rolled over me, sending me reeling. A profound sadness, deep at the core of his being; not because of what was happening now – this was the terrible loneliness of someone who was the last of his race.

I knew instinctively that this was my way to reach him. Horrible as it was, I needed to grab hold of this deep emotion and bring it up to the surface of his mind.

Cursing myself, I latched onto a memory; a vision of his sister, Lola, disappearing in front of him, and dragged it upwards into his conscious mind.

I felt Rudy's emotions exploding around me, electrifying the atmosphere like a storm after a heatwave. The interference from the MythTec collar stalled for a moment, and in that instant Rudy was himself again.

He roared, throwing his head back as I pulled away from him. Rudy grasped the collar around his neck with both hands, one at each side. In a huge effort of will, he pulled it apart, howling in pain as electricity arced between the two broken sections, sparks crackling through the air. He dashed the broken collar to the floor, shattering it into tiny pieces.

Rudy looked up at me, eyes wide, chest heaving.

'It's good to see you, Emily,' he said.

'You can see me?'

'Aye. I'm a shoggyhund. The spirit world is as real to us as the grass and the trees,' he said. I noticed his lips weren't moving – we were conversing directly on the astral plane, mind to mind.

'Right,' he said, 'what's the goddamn plan?'

* * *

RUDY HEADED towards the Control Room carrying a tray of drinks. I was locked to him now, along for the ride. After a touching reunion with Ginger, Rudy had sent the cat away, back to the roof where she would be safe – well, safer than where we were going, anyway.

The Control Room was heaving. A huge banquet was taking place, and Rudy was the catering staff. His white shirt collar was pulled up over his neck, hiding the missing MythTec collar. Hopefully the satyrs would think it was just part of a waiter's uniform – at least long enough for us to make our way to the power cables.

The satyrs sat around long tables that had been dragged in from the canteen. They were laughing, fighting, and, of course, getting drunk. Rudy made his way along the tables towards the tree, handing out tankards of wine and shouting over the colossal din to make assurances that, yes, the food was coming shortly.

At the end of one table, I was shocked to see the forlorn figure of Scott, a heavy chain around his neck. A group of satyrs had made him their pet and were taunting him, pouring wine over his head and laughing uproariously at his feeble protests.

I couldn't help him now, even if I wanted to, so we passed by, making our way towards the Tree where Dionysus was whooping it up on his wooden throne. We were close now, just one table away.

Out of nowhere, a hand reached out and grabbed Rudy's arm. It was Silenus. He yanked at the shirt around Rudy's neck.

'Where's your collar, mongrel?' he spat.

This was it. The game was up. Rudy would be captured again, and it would all be for naught. Unless I did something.

I braced myself and hurled my astral form directly into Silenus.

I felt his toxic personality surrounding me. My stomach

lurched. Is it possible to astral projectile vomit? If so, I was perilously close to doing it.

I was looking out at the world from inside Silenus' head. It was as though the contrast had been set to high, the red dial turned up to eleven. Everything was on fire. The whole world was hate and war and catastrophe.

Somehow, I was still connected to Rudy, who had pulled free and was stumbling away towards the Tree. I had a crazy split-screen experience; Silenus' view on one side and Rudy's on the other. It was like watching a conference call between Heaven and Hell.

I just needed to keep Silenus distracted for a minute. Inside the satyr's head, I used all my willpower to hold him in place and prevent him from opening his mouth. But Silenus was fighting back. He had felt me invading him and lashed out, slamming into my aura like a sledgehammer. He was so strong. I fought back frantically, wildly, but I could see I wasn't going to last long.

Meanwhile, Rudy had reached the back of the Tree of Knowledge. Just as Champ had said, there was a nest of snakelike silver power cables plugged into the base of the trunk. The big one in the middle was clearly the one to go for; Rudy grasped it in both hands and pulled with all his might.

It barely shifted.

The cable was stuck fast; the roots having grown tightly around it in the decades since it was first connected.

Silenus was beginning to regain control of his body, causing him to writhe around where he stood as if struggling against invisible ropes. The group of satyrs nearest him stopped their revelry for a moment to stare in confusion.

'What's going on?' demanded Dionysus, glaring over at Silenus from his throne seat. He gripped his staff and began to rise from his seat.

We had seconds left to act.

Behind Dionysus, on the other side of the enormous tree

trunk, Rudy exhaled deeply, wrapped one arm around the cable and put his other hand up to the bark of the tree.

'Hear me, Great Tree,' said Rudy, his voice a low whisper. 'Feel me. I, a shoggyhund, last of his kind, beseeches you. Release your roots!'

Silenus was about to break free; I could feel it. His mind was much too strong. I couldn't constrain him any longer. But perhaps… what was it Champ said, about controlling a weak-minded creature?

I leapt out of Silenus' mind. He paused for a moment in surprise, then grinned in triumph – he had made short work of the feeble young girl. He turned to Dionysus and shouted, 'Lord! We are betrayed, look beh—'

But that's as far as he got, as the next thing he knew, two hands were grasping his horns, and a glassy-eyed figure was lifting themselves up in front of him.

'Fuck the patriarchy!' screamed Scott, and kicked Silenus hard in the balls – both feet; a double-barrelled bollocking.

Silenus bent over in agony. I released my hold on Scott, who ran whimpering for the exit, the other satyrs watching him go, slack-jawed, as a sudden silence fell over the room.

Then everyone looked at the tree. Something was happening. The leaves were rustling, the branches creaking.

Silenus was limping towards the trunk, one hand between his legs, the other outstretched, pointing towards Rudy. 'Looooook!' he wheezed, his eyes red with fury. He snatched the staff from Dionysus' grasp, much to the god's astonishment.

I was in Rudy's mind again now. He had his head cocked to one side, listening. 'Yes,' he said. 'I understand. Do it.'

It was the Tree. He was talking to the Tree, and I could hear it talking back.

Everything slowed down; this was time as experienced by a giant oak. Unhurried. Deliberate. A single second stretched taut as piano wire. I saw Silenus raising the staff, inch by inch, taking aim at us.

With our minds linked, I now knew what Rudy had already learned: ripping the cable from the Tree would create a huge implosion of energy. Anyone in the immediate vicinity would be unable to escape. Their atoms would be scattered across the egosystem.

'Rudy, no!' I begged. 'There must be some other way!'

'No time, kid,' said Rudy, his voice soft and calm. 'Listen to me. Thank you. You and Izzy; your friendship was a gift. But my people are calling me. It is time for my soul to join theirs. To melt into the bark and sap.'

'Please,' I begged, crying. Not this – not Rudy, too.

'Say goodbye to my old mucker Champ,' he said, smiling. 'Now get out of here.'

With that, he pulled again at the cable and this time it started to rip away as the roots loosened their grip.

'I'm a hot dog!' Rudy laughed, digging his heels into the floor and pulling with all his might. 'Make me one with everything!'

The cable snapped free.

I don't know what it's like to be hit by a truck, but I guess it would be something like this. My astral form was flung backwards, away from the centre of the room.

As I passed Silenus, I saw the purple energy bolt leaping from Dionysus' staff in slow motion. It had barely made it a foot through the air when it was hit by a vibrating wall of green flame that was rippling outwards from the tree, disintegrating everything in its path.

I got the distinct impression that the Tree didn't like Silenus; not one bit. It began to unravel him. Slowly.

I saw his horror as he realised what was happening. His outstretched arm was unwinding, fingers and tendons coming apart and spiralling outwards. His arm splintered and his torso cracked under the unbearable pressure. I saw his veins sucked out of him, twirling like loose threads, spraying purple blood. His nervous system was being pulled from his body.

He fell apart in pieces, burning up on the edge of the expanding explosion. His head went last, sheer terror etched on his face; the final thing to go was his mouth, howling in agony.

I actually felt sorry for him. I really did.

As I moved away from Silenus, time started speeding up again. The Tree was glowing; yellow, then orange, then red.

The shockwave enveloped the whole room. The tables, the chairs, the broken bookshelves, the satyrs, and Dionysus himself, were picked up like Lego characters and sent swirling around the room, faster and faster, becoming a blur.

In my head, I heard Rudy, somehow still alive in the eye of the storm, say one last word: 'Lola?'

Then everything was sucked into the centre of the room; inhaled into the Tree like a vacuum. For a second, I hung there in a sort of green nothingness, then I heard a soft *click*; the sound of a cable snapping back into place.

I had a moment to take in the empty room, the Tree at its centre, glowing light green. Then I was snapped backwards like a fish on a line, plummeting through the wall, through the floor, back down into the basement and slamming into my real body, which collapsed backwards onto the hard, stone floor.

Now, I'm a strong, independent woman, not taken to antiquated gender stereotypes. But the physical and mental strain of the last twenty-four hours had certainly taken their toll, and I decided that, yes, now was a perfectly acceptable time to have a good old-fashioned faint.

TWENTY-ONE

I WOKE UP IN MYTH MANAGEMENT'S INFIRMARY. IT TOOK ME A while to work that out; it was all just blurry shapes and muffled voices at first. I had awoken and fallen back to sleep a few times, I think. But each time I was a little more aware of my surroundings, and now I was finally *compos mentis*.

"Infirmary" was probably overstating it, actually. It was a small office room with a couple of fold-out beds, the other one of which was unoccupied. A pile of neatly-folded towels, bandages and medicine bottles were arranged on top of a set of filing cabinets, and a potted plant sat near the window, the light from which was rather too piercing for my liking.

'Oh, you're awake then, dear?' said Administrator Hicc, her plump smiling face appearing in front of me. A cold palm touched my forehead. 'Good, good! How are you feeling?'

I tried to sit up, but my legs throbbed when I moved. Hicc advised me to take things slowly, placed an extra pillow under my head, and handed me a glass of water, which I guzzled down gratefully.

She checked my temperature, changed the bandages on my legs—which seemed to be healing nicely—and generally fussed over me like a mother hen. Only once she was satisfied with all that would she begin to answer the barrage of questions that I'd been croaking at her.

Apparently, I'd been in and out of consciousness for a day and a half. Things at HQ were mostly back to normal now – or as normal as they could be. Technicians were back in control of the egosystem and were working around the clock to restore order.

'It was Rudy, you see – he saved us all,' explained Hicc. 'We saw it all on the control room recordings; he rebooted the egosystem and sent Dionysus and his satyrs back to their realm.' She looked at me, deciding if I was up to hearing the rest of it, not knowing of course that I had been there, too, and already knew.

'I'm afraid… Rudy didn't make it, my dear. The implosion took him, sending him who knows where.' She took my hand. 'I'm sorry, I know you two were close.'

I nodded. We sat there quietly for a minute, contemplating his sacrifice.

'How did everybody get out of the basement?' I asked.

'All those dreadful satyrs disappeared when Rudy rebooted the Tree, including the ones guarding us. Administrator Burdett managed to pick one of the door locks, then they got the keys and released everybody else.'

'Including Administrator Champ?'

'Actually, that's the strangest thing,' said Hicc. 'Director Hinson said he let him out, but no one's seen him since. He's completely vanished.'

I wondered if I should reveal my part in Dionysus' defeat, but after what Rudy had done, it seemed churlish to mention it. And with Champ AWOL, I had no way of proving it, anyway.

'That's enough questions for now,' said Hicc. 'You've had a dreadful shock, and we don't want you overextending yourself.'

I tried not to laugh, and ended up suffering a small coughing fit instead.

'One more day's bed-rest and then you should be up and about again,' she reassured me. 'Meanwhile – I'm sorry, but there's also this.'

She handed me a small manila folder.

'What's this?' I asked.

'The paperwork.'

She left the room with a promise to bring me some lunch very soon. I opened the folder with a sigh. Inside were several pages of forms, including a disclaimer I had to sign, promising not to sue the bureau, *'for any injuries, physiological, psychological, or mythological'*.

There was also a small white envelope with the 'MM' logo embossed in the corner and the word 'Emily' elegantly calligraphed on the front in blue ink.

I ripped it open and unfolded the single sheet of paper inside. 'From the desk of Administrator G. S. Champ' said the letterhead. There was just one sentence, written in the centre of the page in the same delicate hand:

Discretion is the better part of valour. ~ C

* * *

THE REST of the day was a bit of a blur. I had lunch, slept a lot, woke for dinner, then slept some more. In the evening, I was able to sit up in bed without my head or legs screaming at me, so Administrator Hicc reluctantly agreed to let me have some books and newspapers to read.

I pored over the news from the last few days. *'Gas leak in Camden causes mass hallucinations'*, read one headline. *'Tube station attack may have been the work of terrorists'*, claimed another. On the opposite page was an advert for the hot new Christmas accessory, 'Your Own Personal Jesus'.

I tried meditating a couple of times and reaching out with my mind, hoping to float out and see what was happening in the rest of the building. But I became exhausted almost immediately. I'd sprained that muscle, and would need to take it slow.

I had a lot of time to think, lying there in my recovery bed. I went over the Oracle's prophecy again and again in my mind. I don't know why; it was too late to do anything now. Looking for loopholes, I suppose. *'One will be your constant companion, the other will soon be gone.'* Well, they were both gone now; first Izzy and now Rudy.

But it had been Izzy's words that had given me strength in my lowest moment in that basement. Maybe that's what the Oracle had meant; that Izzy's memory would be my *"Constant companion"*. They'd said that about my dad, too: *"He'll always be with you, in your heart'*. An empty platitude. It had made me so angry, even as a little kid. It wasn't enough. Nowhere near.

With Izzy it almost seemed worse. She was my age – just getting started. Then Silenus had snatched her life away; stolen her future. It just wasn't… Thornhill's face popped up in my head, unbidden; *'Life isn't fair'*. I shook his words away. Sure, he'd saved our lives in the Control Room, but he was still a dick.

And Izzy was still dead.

I AWOKE the next morning to a familiar sweet, musky aroma. Prying my eyes open, I saw a cup and saucer on the table next to my bed; Darjeeling tea, served in Royal Victoria bone china. I sat up quickly. Sure enough, standing over by the window, framed by the bright morning sunlight and sipping thoughtfully at his own cup, was Administrator Champ.

He turned and gave me a warm smile. 'Hello, my dear,' he said softly.

I laughed, surprised at how happy I was to see him. He walked over, away from the bright window light, and I could see that he was once more rejuvenated; strong and lean and back to his handsome thirty-ish self.

'I do apologise for my tardiness,' he said, taking a seat on the edge of the bed. 'As I'm sure you'll understand, I had to go on a little trip before I could show my face again.' He leant over to hug me briefly, before pulling back and composing himself.

'I brought you an apple,' he said, handing one over. 'It's just a normal one.'

I laughed weakly.

'You got my note?' he asked, smoothing out his jacket.

'Yes. I haven't said anything about what I did. Or about your secret.'

'Well, the latter is up to you. Director Hinson knows, so did Rudy, and a couple of others, but I'd prefer it if you kept it to yourself, all the same.'

I nodded.

'As for the former, you have a choice. You were incredibly brave and resourceful; you saved the bureau—saved the world—and you certainly deserve the credit. We can tell people what you did. But there would be… repercussions.'

'What do you mean?'

'You have a rare talent, and there are many who would want to exploit it. You'd be classified as too important to stay on the apprentice programme, for a start. I know there's still three weeks left on the internship,' he smiled, 'but I'm pretty sure you're a shoo-in for the top slot.'

Of course – the leaderboard. It had meant everything a week ago, but now it seemed so inconsequential.

'We need you here,' said Champ. 'Especially now, when there's so much to do.'

I took a deep breath. I had been happy here; happier than any other time in my life. But would it be too painful now, without Izzy and Rudy? Or maybe I owed it to them to stay and continue the good work. To keep the world safe. To make sure nothing like this ever happened again.

'Administrator Hicc says you're well enough to return today,' said Champ, looking at me carefully. 'If that's what you want?'

'Yes,' I said. 'Yes, I think it is.'

'Excellent,' said Champ, slapping his hands together. 'Then put on your uniform and meet me outside in ten minutes – there's something you need to see.'

* * *

I FOUND Champ waiting for me in the corridor, a look of quiet pride on his face. He gave me a little bow, then held out his arm. I took it, smiling, and let him lead me down the stairs. My legs still ached from Silenus' claws, and I was a little unsteady. We walked slowly out into the atrium, blinking in the morning sun.

'Here might be a good place to sit for a moment,' said Champ, gesturing to a large park bench that I'd somehow never noticed before.

The wood was curved and knobbly, but seemed newer than the others in the garden. On the seat's top bar, a sentence had been carved in a thick cursive font:

> *'In memory of Rudy Greenwood, a faithful companion*
> *who sacrificed himself to save his friends'.*

'You made him a memorial bench?' I asked. 'That's quite fitting, actually. I think he would have liked that.'

'Oh, we didn't make it,' said Champ. 'It appeared there

the morning after the... incident. Grew right out of the ground from the tree roots, inscription and all.'

Rudy had always loved the Tree of Knowledge. It seemed the appreciation went both ways.

I wiped away a tear. Champ put a hand on my arm, squeezing lightly, then let go and turned away.

'Rudy was a true and loyal friend. And one of the finest men I knew. I will miss him dreadfully. He is gone now, back to his people, I hope, wherever they are.'

I didn't say anything. What was there to say? After a moment, Champ coughed, turned back around, and stood up a little straighter, controlling his voice.

'There's a quote I've always liked from Chinese mythology: *"When he died, his breath became the wind, his voice the sound of running water, his embrace the heat of the sun".'*

We stood there for a minute, in quiet contemplation.

'What about Silenus?' I asked. 'And Dionysus? Were they destroyed too?'

'Silenus was ripped apart by the Tree's energy field. Wiped from the ecosystem. I doubt we'll be hearing from him again. As for Dionysus...' Champ breathed out slowly. 'He'll never really be gone; he's more of an idea than a man. Eventually he will reform in his realm and retake his given place in the hierarchy. Once that happens, we will resume diplomatic relations.'

'What? But... *why*?'

Champ looked at me kindly. 'Because that's how we maintain peace. It's how things work in the real world.'

There was a soft meow from near my feet. A black shape wound her way between my legs.

'Ginger!' I gasped. 'You shouldn't be out in public!'

Champ raised his hand. 'It's alright. I think we've earned the right to bend the rules a little. And anyway, with Rudy gone she needs someone to look after her. Are you up to the job?'

I nodded, picking her up in my arms. She purred softly.

'Speaking of changing the rules,' said Champ. 'I have some good news. Very good, actually.' He placed his hand on the back of the bench, rubbing his thumb across the carved letters. 'Rudy's sacrifice, along with our newly humbled bureaucracy, has enabled me to pull a few strings. I've managed to secure an exception to Myth Management's ban on,' – he looked at me meaningfully – 'non-human entities being enrolled in our academy.'

I looked back at him in confusion.

'Perhaps it's time to return to your dorm room,' he said with a broad smile.

Ginger wriggled from my arms and dropped to the grass, then looked up at me before scampering off towards the entrance.

Champ gave me a quiet smile and a little nod. My mind was racing. I turned and started walking towards the building's entrance, slowly at first, then faster. Then I began to run, ignoring the pain in my legs.

I sprinted through the corridors then up the staircase, leaping them two at a time, Ginger at my side the whole way. We ran in through the dorm entrance and across the common room, arriving at the little stairs in the corner that went up to my room. I paused there for a moment, my heart racing, then started to climb, Ginger padding softly beside me.

Could Champ mean what I thought he did? I barely dared to hope. I couldn't let myself accept the possibility in case I was wrong. But what if I was right?

Just a few steps away from the door now. Music emanated from within. Familiar music. Wonderfully familiar.

I put my hand on the door, feeling the grain of the wood beneath my hand. I was scared. Scared to know; to find out the answer.

Ginger looked up at me and meowed.

I took a deep breath, and pushed open the door.

There, dancing to the music, was the most beautiful sight I'd ever seen. Loose-limbed and blissful, hips bobbing, arms weaving.

And, of course, semi-transparent.

She looked over, grinned at me with that beautiful wide smile of hers, and flicked off the music.

'Come on, you dork', said ghost Izzy. 'Day's a-wasting – we don't want to be late.'

LEAVE A REVIEW

Reviews are gold to indie authors, so if you've enjoyed this book, please consider visiting the site you purchased it from and leaving a quick review.

BECOME AN INSIDER

Sign up and receive **FREE UNCANNY KINGDOM BOOKS**. Also, be the **FIRST** to hear about **NEW RELEASES** and **SPECIAL OFFERS** in the **UNCANNY KINGDOM** universe. Just visit:

WWW.UNCANNYKINGDOM.COM

AUTHOR NOTE

This book is a time capsule; it's based on an idea I had in my 20s, and is inspired by places and people I knew at the time. Champ owes a lot to my cousin Guy. Rudy has a lot of Alan in him. Izzy is an amalgam of my best friends; mostly Vanessa, but with dashes of Steve, Warren, Andrew and Scott. Emily and Izzy's dorm room is based on a flat I lived in for six years, a few miles from Hampstead Heath.

Myth Management first appeared as three comic strips in my self-published comedy magazine, *Mustard* (mustardweb.org), with art by Adrian Bamforth and Mike Donaldson.

For the book, Simon Cooper created character illustrations from my descriptions to help bring them to life; see them at mythmanagement.org.

* * *

This book was mostly written in the Notes app on my phone during half-hour train commutes across London. My apologies if you can tell.

THANKS

My deepest thanks to everyone who made this book possible:

David Bussell, my friend and editor, for convincing me over one of our monthly beers that those Myth Management comic strips I wrote a while back might work as a book.

Alan Moore, for advice and encouragement, and for proving that sometimes you really should meet your heroes.

My alpha-reader squad, whose detailed story feedback was invaluable: Vanessa Higham, Mary Aldenton, Savannah Christensen, Christelle Couchoux, and my wife, Pamela, who also put up with me stressing about this for two years.

And finally, to everyone else who helped with suggestions, proofreading and support: Val Stevenson, Elise Wade, Ed Musson, Stan Hutchings, Cailin Fili and Janet.

Cheers!

MORE STORIES SET IN THE UNCANNY KINGDOM

The London Coven Series
Familiar Magic
Nightmare Realm
Deadly Portent

The Branded Series
Sanctified
Turned
Bloodline

The Hexed Detective Series
Hexed Detective
Fatal Moon
Night Terrors

The Spectral Detective Series
Spectral Detective
Corpse Reviver
Twice Damned

The Dark Lakes Series
Magic Eater
Blood Stones
Past Sins

The Uncanny Ink Series
Bad Soul
Bad Blood
Bad Justice
Bad Intention
Bad Thoughts
Bad Memories

www.uncannykingdom.com

www.mythmanagement.org